Disoriented by the darkness on her side and the size of the great tank, Kit's mind began playing tricks on her, making her feel that in the dark corners of the tank the world on the other side of the glass and hers were joined.

Her eyes strained at the darkness, trying to see what was or wasn't. Deciding that she had imagined the movement, she turned back toward the tank and took a sharp breath. A huge shape was coming directly toward her. Half-believing that it might be able to reach her, she took two steps backward. At the last moment, it turned to avoid the barrier and her brain struggled with what she saw, unable to assemble the image into meaning. Then in one horrible second, the chaos cleared.

The shark had a human leg in its mouth.

— ★ —

D. J. DONALDSON

No Mardi Gras for the DEAD

WORLDWIDE.®

TORONTO • NEW YORK • LONDON
AMSTERDAM • PARIS • SYDNEY • HAMBURG
STOCKHOLM • ATHENS • TOKYO • MILAN
MADRID • WARSAW • BUDAPEST • AUCKLAND

For Doris and Don

NO MARDI GRAS FOR THE DEAD

A Worldwide Mystery/March 1995

First published by St. Martin's Press, Incorporated.

ISBN 0-373-26163-2

ACKNOWLEDGMENTS

I'm grateful to everyone who provided background information for this story. Special thanks to Drs. Hugh Berryman and Steve Symes, anthropologists in the Regional Forensic Center, Shelby County, Tennessee, for being so good at their jobs and for responding to my many phone calls and questions with cheerful good humor. A hearty thanks also to Dr. Jerry Francisco, Shelby County Medical Examiner for numerous helpful suggestions and for promptly returning my almost daily phone calls during the final stages of the writing. Thanks also to Dr. O. C. Smith, Assistant Medical Examiner for Shelby County; Dr. Allen O. Battle; Dr. Jim Mahan; Dr. John Schweitzer; Dr. Charles Wilson; Reid Withrow and Bob Paddock of the Aquarium of the Americas; Bruce Wheaton of the Crooked Creek Hunting Lodge; Doris Manning; Carol Green; and Max Grieg. The menu for the gourmet dinner was a creation of chef Jean-Louis Palladin. As usual, I would have been lost without June, my wife and in-house editor. Any errors are mine.

ONE

THE NIGHT AIR WAS WARM and humid, but her skin was pebbly with gooseflesh. Usually talkative and outgoing, tonight she lay quietly, almost pensively, her back to the stars, her face turned to the side. A fly hummed out of the darkness and landed. It briefly explored the surface of her cloudy cornea, then began to tuck its eggs into the corner of her eye. Her respiration had ceased many hours earlier, but enzymes were still functioning, acting now without direction, turning on the organs they once served. One life had ended, but millions reaped the benefits, finding passage into previously forbidden chambers where in mindless celebration they multiplied.

She was lifted from the grass and dropped into a hole in the earth, her rigidity requiring the same fit she once demanded of her clothing. Then the dirt ... filling ... covering ... hiding ...

With the sun, life spilled into the streets and the ground warmed. Though it was cool below, her red cells eventually gave up their hemoglobin, which seeped from her vessels, staining her once-blemish-free skin with reddish brown trails. A shower brought smiles to the lips of the living, but also summoned forth delicate mycelial threads from germinating mold spores that began digesting her clothing.

Days passed into weeks and the gases came, lifting the dirt, creating pressures that rearranged ... pushed ... expelled. In life, she had been desired by many. In death, she was sought by more and they came to her, embraced her and became one with her. Then as the weeks blended into months, their ardor waned and one by one they left her, until she was very much alone.

YIKES! She had forgotten Bubba.

Kit hurried down the hall and nudged the kitchen door open. Predictably, a small black nose appeared in the crack.

She slipped her hand inside and grabbed Lucky, the owner of the nose, by the collar. "Oh yes, you little varmint, you'd like to get into the new varnish, wouldn't you?"

When she was safely into the kitchen with the door shut behind her, she let the little dog go. He responded by scampering happily about the room, his claws clacking on the linoleum like a little flop-eared flamenco dancer.

Watermelon. That's why she had come inside . . . to get Bubba a piece of melon.

She washed her hands at the sink and looked out the window at Bubba Oustellette, hard at work digging the holes for the posts that would support the rose trellis in the center of her planned rose garden. Bubba was dressed as usual, in navy blue coveralls and a matching T-shirt. On his head was a dark green baseball cap bearing the logo of an ocean wave showing its teeth and carrying a football.

Poor Bubba. The posthole digger was bigger than he was and he was sweating terribly. She got the watermelon from the fridge and cut it in half. She lopped off a thick circle, put it on a dinner plate, and stuck a fork in the center, about all the culinary ability or inclination any kitchen was likely to see from her. On the way out, Lucky darted into the yard.

Bubba looked as though he'd taken a shower with his clothes on—his dark hair hanging in wet ropes from under his cap, his shirt sticking to him like a coat of blue paint. In the future, she was going to have to be more careful. She had merely asked whether he knew anyone she could hire to build a rose trellis and he had volunteered to do it for nothing. And she hadn't been able to talk him out of it. Now, here he was, giving up his Saturday and courting heatstroke, as well.

"How about a little break, Bubba?"

Bubba chunked the digger into the hole and grinned through his bushy black beard. "Ah don' need no coaxin' for dat," the little Cajun said, taking off his cap and wiping his forehead with his arm.

"Come on, sit over here in the shade and see if this melon is as good as it looks. Or, if you like, we can go inside where it's cool."

"Out here is okay."

Kit led Bubba to a pair of folding lawn chairs under a young pin oak, where Bubba didn't want to sit until she did.

"Bubba, get in that chair."

Sheepishly, he did as she ordered. "Ah think you got a little Gramma O in you," he said, taking the plate and the salt Kit held out to him.

Grandma O operated the restaurant where Kit usually ate lunch. She was Grandmother only to Bubba, but everyone called her Grandma O, mostly because that's what she called herself on the restaurant's sign and menu.

"A little of Grandma O? I'll consider that a compliment," Kit said.

"Well, Ah hope you don' let it mushroom, cause Ah got all Ah can handle with da original."

Bubba sprinkled his melon with salt and stored the shaker in the chest pocket of his coveralls. He carved a large piece from the melon's seedless center, then paused. "Ain't you havin' any?"

"Maybe in a minute," Kit said, enjoying the feeling of sitting under her own oak in her own backyard. The yard was small but was given a nice sense of privacy by the unusually tall cypress fence that a previous owner had put up.

The yard itself wasn't much to look at now: a carpet of mangy Bermuda; some scraggly privet on each side of the back door in beds lined with three different shades of brick set in the ground to resemble the teeth on a saw, and, of course, those awful clothesline poles and all that cement around them.

She looked at Bubba, intending to ask his advice on methods for their removal but realized he'd just want to help with that as well. What she needed was a...

Lord. She put her hand to her eyes in disbelief. For an instant, she had imagined she needed a *husband*. She looked warily at the house, alert now to a danger in its purchase that had not occurred to her before. She didn't need a husband. She didn't need a man at all. She stood up.

"Bubba, I want to dig the next hole. I'm going inside to change. Keep an eye on Lucky for me while I'm inside, will you? He likes to dig and I'm afraid he might try to go under the fence."

"He's good at it, too," Bubba said, pointing.

Looking behind her, Kit saw Lucky's front paws churning at the pile of dirt beside the hole Bubba had been working on. The little dog shoved his muzzle into the cavity he'd made and pulled out something white, which he dragged a few feet to the side. He lay down and began chewing on it.

Afraid that it might be something harmful, Kit hurried toward him. "No! Bad dog! Bad dog!"

She leaned down to take the object from him, but he snatched it up and darted off. Lucky ran with abandon, leaping over the lumber Bubba had brought and making a three-quarter circle around the yard. He dropped to his belly, with the object between his paws and watched to see whether Kit would come after him.

"Bubba, I'm going to need some help here."

Bubba put his plate under his chair and circled around behind the oak while Kit closed in from the front. Lucky's eyes darted back and forth between them as he triangulated their approach.

Having grown up around animals of all kinds and knowing them well, Bubba was aware that Lucky would not let him get much closer. So he flung himself into the air, covering the last few feet in a daring surprise maneuver.

When Bubba hit, driving the salt shaker into his sternum, Lucky was ten feet away, his legs a blur as he ran, the object firmly between his teeth.

It was far too hot to play this game and Kit was about ready to get the hose after the dog, when he dropped the object and went after a blue jay that had landed near the fence. Kit hurried to the object and bent down for a closer look. Despite the bright sun beating on her back, she went gray and cold inside.

"What is it?" Bubba said, getting to his feet.

"Part of a jawbone," Kit said.

"Somebody's buried pet?"

"If it is, it's been to the dentist."

TWO

"OVER HERE," KIT SAID, leading her boss, Andy Broussard, chief medical examiner for Orleans Parish to the fragment of jawbone that Lucky had found. Despite the heat and the fact that it was the weekend, Broussard was dressed for the office: slacks, short-sleeved white shirt with a bow tie, and mesh shoes, which, as he was fond of pointing out, were the only kind that kept his feet from sweating. Though they usually did not carry shoes in such a small size, the Big Man's Shop on Canal, where Broussard bought his clothes, was more than happy to special order them for him.

"That's it," Kit said, pointing to the ground.

Emitting a sound like a tire that had just run over a nail, Broussard bent down and picked up the fragment. He tilted his head so as to bring the bone into line with the part of his glasses that he used for close work and studied the fragment, turning it in his small hand. Surprisingly, he put it to his nose and sniffed it. "Which hole?" he asked.

"That one," Kit replied, pointing.

"Bubba, hold this." Broussard gave the fragment to Bubba, who took it without enthusiasm.

With Kit and Bubba close behind, Broussard walked over to the hole, removed the posthole digger, and used it as a support while he peered into the earth. The sun, now directly overhead, gave him all the light he needed.

"A few inches to the right and we might never have known anything was down there," he said.

"Then there's more?" Kit asked. Though part of her had known with certainty that there *would* be more, that this was not simply going to go away, she had been tending a small flame of hope that the dirt in her yard had been trucked in from some other place... hope that the rest of the remains that went with the fragment in Bubba's hand had already been discovered long ago... that this was old business... someone *else's* business.

"Oh, yes, there's definitely more," Broussard said.

Suddenly, Kit found the midday sun unbearable. She fanned herself with her hand, her stomach turning sour.

As uncomfortable as Kit was in the heat, she had to believe that with all the weight Broussard carried around and that beard, he had to feel worse than she did. But if he did, he didn't show it. In fact, he seemed downright cheerful.

"So what have we got?" a voice said from behind Kit.

It was Phil Gatlin, ranking detective with the violent crimes squad.

"Hello, Phillip," Broussard said. "Kit and Bubba found part of a human mandible in this hole. Show him, Bubba."

Bubba held up the bone and years evaporated from Gatlin's heavily lined face.

"Male or female?" Gatlin asked.

"Can't tell. If we had the whole jaw, I could make an educated guess. But even then there'd be..."

"The rest of it down there?"

"Looks like it."

"How old?"

"You askin' the age of the deceased?"

"No. How long's it been down there?"

"Quite a while."

"Jesus, Andy, anybody'd think you were getting paid by the question. Three months? A year?"

"Didn't have any smell, so I'd say at *least* a year."

Gatlin's shoulders dropped and the years that had left his face moments earlier returned. "Nuts," he said, punctuating his disappointment with a quick nod of his head. Hands on hips, he looked away and muttered to himself. "Nuts…nuts…nuts." He turned back to the group. "Who actually found it?"

"To be strictly accurate, I guess Lucky did," Kit said.

"Who's Lucky?"

"My dog."

"Oh no. You're not putting this off on a dog. I want human responsibility here, somebody I can get an apology from."

"For what?"

"Three months ago, a can picker found two human ears in a plastic burger box in a trash bin in Jackson Square. Male ears. Now that tells me that there's a body somewhere waiting to be discovered. And if there's a body, there's a murderer. I don't like murderers. But I can't do anything about this one until I find the body. So, when Andy called, I thought this was the break I was hoping for. Now, instead of helping me solve an existing problem, you've given me a new one." Gatlin shook his head, then looked at Broussard. "Did you call French?"

Broussard nodded.

"What'd she say? When will she be here?"

Broussard looked over Gatlin's shoulder. "There she is now."

Coming toward them was a woman wearing loose khakis, a long-sleeved white shirt with the tails tied at her waist, and heavy work shoes. Her blond hair was tied back in a bun.

"You got here quick," Broussard said.

"I was just sitting around the house wishing for a reason to get dirty," the woman said. "Hello, Phillip. How're things?"

"Not as good as they were earlier."

Broussard made the introductions. "Victoria, this is Kit Franklyn. Kit is my suicide investigator. She also does psychological profiling for the violent crimes squad. Kit, Victoria is our consulting forensic anthropologist."

Victoria French's handshake was firm and her skin was softer than Kit would have imagined for someone who did a lot of digging. She looked to be in her early forties. Despite her unglamorous getup, Kit could tell that French would be a knockout dressed up, the kind of mature beauty that would turn any man's head. The fact that she wore no rings solidified the instant bond Kit felt with her, for in Victoria French, she saw herself in ten years, or at least what she hoped she'd be: single, no family burdens, a competent professional that could still get a man's attention when she wanted it.

"And this is Bubba Oustellette," Broussard said. "Bubba runs the NOPD vehicle impoundment station and keeps all my cars runnin'."

Though Broussard had said nothing particularly complimentary, Bubba blushed as he wiped his palm on his coveralls before taking French's offered hand.

"Bubba's got the reason we called you," Broussard said.

Bubba gave her the fragment of bone. She examined it briefly, sniffed it, and said, "Been buried at least a year. From one of those holes?"

"That one," Broussard said, pointing.

"How far down?"

"'Bout three feet." For Kit and Bubba's benefit, he added, "Rare to find a body buried any deeper. Too much work."

"Any hints as to orientation?" French asked.

Broussard shook his head.

French looked at Kit. "I'm afraid we're going to have to do some digging. We'll try to take up the grass in sections so that it can be put back, but I can't promise how effective we'll be."

"This whole area is eventually going to be a rose bed," Kit said. "So it really doesn't matter."

French turned and started for the driveway. At the same time, a slightly built young man with a long, narrow face came through the gate, two cameras around his neck and a folding table in one hand.

"That's Allen, my graduate assistant," French said. "Over here, Allen."

French and Allen set up the table about fifteen feet from the hole that had produced the bone fragment. Allen put his cameras on the table and they both went back to the driveway, to reappear a few minutes later heavily laden with equipment. They put everything on the ground next to the table and began erecting an open-sided canvas tent over the area where they would be working.

While French and Allen put up the tent, Broussard went to their supplies and picked up a metal pole with a T-shaped handle. He showed it to French and said, "Mind if I go fishin'?"

"Don't hurt yourself," French said.

Broussard came back to the small group waiting. "Kit, you object to me makin' a few small holes in your yard?"

"No, why?"

"That's what *I* want to know," Gatlin said. "We're already going to have one set of remains to identify. Why do you want to go looking for more?"

"Guess I'm just irresponsible."

"It's going to be a while before French has anything to look at," Gatlin said. "So, I'm going to follow up a lead or two on some other cases. I'll be back later for an update.

And I don't want to see her starting any more excavations. Kit, Bubba... I'm not going to forget this."

When Gatlin was out of earshot, Kit said, "Surely he wasn't serious."

Broussard shook his head. "If I hadn't volunteered to fish the lawn, he'd be doin' it himself."

"What do you mean, 'fish the lawn'?"

"I'll push this rod into the ground and look for places where below the plow line the soil is relatively loose."

"And the plow line is..."

"The first six to eight inches of dirt."

"Hope you don't find anything."

"Me, too."

"Mind if Ah tag along?" Bubba asked.

"Not at all."

"But if we find anything, you gotta tell Lieutenant Gatlin dat Ah had nothin' to do with it."

Watching Broussard and Bubba work their way around the yard, Kit remembered old stories in the paper of bodies by the score being discovered in somebody's basement up north. To get her mind off what Broussard was doing, she went over to where French was watching Allen remove sod.

"Stack it over there, Allen, well out of the way," French said. "That's good."

At Kit's approach, French said, "How are you doing? I'm sure you're finding all this pretty traumatic."

"I'm coping so far. But this isn't what I had in mind when I bought the place two months ago."

"*Lagniappe,*" French said.

Kit smiled anemically. *Lagniappe*—the New Orleans term for something extra. It was sure that. "So, where are you based?" Kit asked, trying to blunt the edge on what was happening.

"Tulane. The anthropology department."

"Really. I took the graduate cultural anthro course there four years ago."

"Not my bag, I'm afraid. If you'd taken physical anthro, we might have met."

"Would you and Allen like some iced tea?"

Kit's offer was as much to give her something to do as extend a kindness. And even though French had brought a large insulated drink container with her, she said, "Yes. That would be nice."

With all that was going on outside, Kit did not want Lucky in the way. To keep him from getting out accidently while she was coming and going, she shut him in her bedroom, an act that, judging from the whining coming through the bedroom door, Lucky found wholly unacceptable.

By the time the tea was ready, Broussard had finished his search. "Looks like there's just one," he said, taking a glass from the tray Kit offered him.

"Thank God," Kit replied, holding the tray out to Bubba.

Under the tent, the dirt in a large rectangle had been removed to a depth of about five inches. Off to the side, Allen dumped a bucket of dirt onto a growing pile on the ground. French was on her knees in the excavation, scraping the soil with a mason's trowel.

"If you're ever in the market for an anthropologist, ask to see their trowel," Broussard said. "If it's a Marshalltown, hire 'em. Otherwise, send 'em on their way, 'cause they're an amateur."

"Why's that?"

"A Marshalltown is the only kind strong enough to take years of that scrapin' motion. After she's got a flat surface, the difference in texture and color of the dirt will allow us to see the outline of the pit . . . the grave."

Allen was now shoveling dirt from the pile into a box with a hardware cloth bottom.

"How about a tea break, you two?" Kit said.

Allen looked up, obviously taken with the idea, but French said, "Maybe in a few minutes." Allen went back to screening the removed dirt and Kit put the tray on the folding table.

"This is a slow business," Broussard said. "And watchin' won't hurry it. I'm gonna follow Phillip's lead and get a little work done at the office. When they get everything pretty much exposed, give me a call."

Broussard went out the gate and Kit turned to Bubba. "Doesn't look like there'll be a rose trellis going up anytime soon around here. So, if you'd like to . . ."

Bubba looked shocked. "Leave? Why would Ah wanna leave? Nothin' Ah got to do is good as dis. Fact, Ah never do *anything* good as dis." He blushed and looked at the ground. "Did'n mean to invite myself to stay . . ."

"Of course you can stay."

Bubba grinned like a happy chipmunk and took his drink to one of the chairs under the oak. With nothing to see in the excavation, Kit did the same.

For the next few minutes, Kit and Bubba sat in the shade, drinking tea and watching Allen and French work—in Kit's opinion, as though digging up bodies was some sort of surrealistic entertainment.

Soon, French stepped out of the excavation and surveyed her work. Kit and Bubba joined her.

"Can you see the pit?" she asked, standing aside and running her finger around a geometric outline in the air.

As hard as she tried, Kit could not be sure. "Maybe . . ."

"Sometimes it's easier than this one," French said. "Here, I'll show you." She stepped back into the excavation and drew an irregular rectangle in the dirt with the tip of her trowel, then stood up and said, "Allen, tea break."

French waved off Kit's offer to replace the almost-melted ice in the tea and French and Allen were soon ready to resume work.

French rummaged in her toolbox and brought out two pieces of white painted wood—one in the shape of an arrow, the other marked like a ruler. She placed the arrow in the center of the pit so that it pointed north. The measuring scale went on the grass at the pit's near end. Allen consulted a notebook and wrote FA91-51 on a small chalkboard that he propped up on the grass at the far edge of the pit. They took a Polaroid and a 35mm shot of the site and went back to what they had been doing before the break— French scraping with her Marshalltown trowel, Allen screening the dirt she produced.

All this was quite different from what Kit had imagined it was going to be like when she had first called Broussard. After all, hadn't she seen bodies being dug up with a backhoe on TV?

She watched French work for a few minutes, then walked over and watched Allen.

Then she went to her chair and watched from there.

Not content to merely watch, Bubba offered to help and was put to work with Allen. After awhile, Kit walked back to the excavation, which was now about a foot deep.

"Victoria, I'm going inside. If anybody needs anything, just come on in."

French glanced over her shoulder and waved her trowel. Allen and Bubba didn't even look up. Figuring she should stay close to the back door, Kit got a yellow legal pad and a pen and sat down at the kitchen table. At the top of the

page she wrote, "The Troubled Adolescent," which was to
be chapter eight in the still untitled book she was writing on
suicide.

A half hour later, Kit had only written three sentences,
her concentration being broken every few minutes by the
mental image of a rectangular hole in the ground. Of all the
times for Teddy to be on a business trip.

Teddy, was Teddy LaBiche, *La* capital *B* to distinguish
him from the small *b* Labiches who did not have Teddy's
aristocratic ancestry. Though they had never discussed his
finances, Kit had always assumed that something had gone
wrong somewhere, because Teddy made his living operating an alligator farm 125 miles west in Bayou Coteau. Every
Saturday, he drove to New Orleans and he and Kit would
spend the day and usually the night together. Beyond an
unspoken understanding that they were not seeing anyone
else, there were no strings and no promises on either side,
which was just fine with Kit. Teddy had not come over today because he was out on the West Coast until Friday lining up buyers.

There was a knock on the back door and Victoria French
put her head inside. "May I use your telephone?"

"Of course. I'll show you where it is."

French pulled off her dirty shoes on the back steps and
followed Kit through the kitchen into the wide hall that had
made Kit want the house the moment she had seen its tall
oak columns and Victorian beadwork.

"Great house," French said. She gestured at the temporarily displaced furniture. "I *thought* I smelled varnish."

"I just had the living room floor done. There's the
phone."

French entered a number and waited for an answer. "Oh
hi, it's me. Look, I'm going to be here the rest of the after-

noon. Can you take Johnny to his trumpet lesson? And
pick Jessica up at Barbara's? Good. Thanks. I thought we'd
have spaghetti for dinner, okay? Great. See you soon." She
made a kissing sound into the receiver. "Kids," she said,
hanging up. "They've got a busier schedule than I do."

Kids. Victoria French had kids...and a husband. Of
course she wasn't wearing any rings. Who would with her
job? Already off balance from the events outside, Kit now
felt confused, for Victoria French had kids...and a husband. And she seemed to be doing just fine with everything.

"Maybe while I've got my shoes off, I should visit the
powder room," French said.

"Sure, it's down there," Kit said in a daze. "Across from
the kitchen."

Still thinking about French and her family, Kit took some
ice and the tea pitcher outside and checked the excavation.
Two bony protuberances now visible in the center of the pit
got her mind back on the more pressing issue. Shivering
despite the heat, she refilled everyone's glasses and went
back inside.

"The rest of the afternoon," French had said. It was
pretty clear that there was no point in continuing to work
on her manuscript. Instead, Kit went to the bookshelves in
her study and got the Pat Conroy novel she had bought a
few weeks ago but hadn't had the time to start.

Having seen those two pieces of bone in the pit, Kit
found that she did not feel much like looking into it again.
So she mostly stayed inside and read, avoiding the pit when
she went out every thirty minutes to refill the tea glasses.
Her reading was interrupted once by Allen looking for the
same room that French had needed, and by Bubba seeking

it, as well. In Bubba's case, though, she had to guess what he wanted because he was too embarrassed to ask.

Finally, around five o'clock, French stuck her head inside and said, "This would be a good time to call Andy."

THREE

"FOUR FEET, THREE and a quarter," Allen said.

The two anthropologists had driven a gutter spike into the ground at one end of the pit and had hooked the end of a tape measure over it. Allen was in the pit with the other end of the tape. While French scribbled the measurement Allen had given her onto a graph-paper sketch, Kit tentatively approached the pit and looked in. Broussard had been right. There was indeed more. What appeared to be an entire skeleton lay sprawled in the bottom of the hole. Above the bones, a good-sized tree root passed from one side of the pit to the other. Despite the presence of the root, French had skillfully removed the soil between the bones and around the circumference of the skeleton so that it rested on a pedestal of dirt that varied from one to six inches in height. Surprisingly, the ribs did not form the barrel she had expected to see but were collapsed.

The skull basically lay facedown, but turned slightly to the right, an angle that had allowed the posthole digger to shear off a part of the jaw without doing any other damage. Kit knew enough anatomy to recognize that she was also looking at the backs of vertebrae rather than the front. Obviously, the body had been pitched into the pit facedown. Allen and French continued to make measurements until Broussard and Gatlin arrived together.

"We ready to learn something?" Gatlin said.

Broussard looked into the pit, a lemon drop bulging one cheek. "Gonna be a cold trail behind this one."

Gatlin peered into the pit and smirked. "Gatlin's law."

"Thought you'd like to be here for the ribbon cutting," Broussard said. "Allen, would you do it, please?"

Allen got a bow saw from the supplies, stepped into the pit, and began to saw the root at its narrow end. When he finished, he crossed to the opposite side and cut it there. Broussard helped Allen out of the pit and Allen gave him the root.

Broussard examined the cut surface on the thick end and glanced at the back of the house. "That faucet work?"

Kit said it did, and Broussard walked over to it and twisted the handle. He held the root under the hose nozzle and waited for water. After washing the root, he looked at it again, nodded with satisfaction, and turned off the tap.

"Body's been down there at *least* ten years," he said, coming back to the group.

"Growth rings?" Gatlin said.

"Ten of 'em, clear as can be." Broussard gave the root to Gatlin.

He looked at it too quickly to have counted the rings and put it on the folding table. "So let's do it."

French stepped into the pit and picked up the skull. She studied it face-on, looked at it from the side and the top, turned it over, and looked at the base.

"Caucasian female," she said, handing it to Broussard. "At least twenty years old." She bent to pick up something else.

"How does she know those things?" Kit asked.

Broussard held the skull up in profile. "Notice how the upper and lower parts of the face are vertically aligned? In blacks the lower jaw protrudes." He turned the skull so that it was facing them and ran his finger along the lower border of the nasal openings. "These sharp sills also show it's a Caucasian. In blacks, this area is slightly guttered." He turned the skull to the side and pointed to the tooth farthest back. "Third molars are up...that usually doesn't occur before age eighteen." He looked at the base of the skull and pointed to a region in front of the large opening that in life transmitted the spinal cord. "See how smooth this is right here?"

Kit nodded.

"Well, it's not one bone as it appears, but two. Before about twenty years of age, the suture line is obvious... like this." He turned the skull over and pointed at a sharp wiggly line that crossed the crown of the skull from side to side. "The female part is sort of a guess at this point. In males, the sites of muscle attachment to the skull are more pronounced than what we see here...and here. As for her occupation..."

"You're not telling me you know her occupation?" Gatlin said.

Broussard shifted his lemon ball to the other cheek. "Wouldn't surprise me to find out she was a prostitute livin' pretty close to the edge."

"Where do you get that?" Gatlin said in a challenging tone.

Broussard turned the skull over and held it out toward Gatlin. "What dental work she had was mostly in front, even though she needed some in the back."

"Kinda like when you get a quart of strawberries home from da market and find dat da only ripe ones are on top," Bubba said.

"Much the same," Broussard said.

"Not dat Ah got any personal experience here understan'."

"So you're saying if she was a high-priced hooker, she'd have had the money to fix all her teeth," Gatlin said.

Broussard nodded.

Gatlin shook his head. "Pretty flimsy, Andy. Poor, I'll give you that. But a hooker... I dunno..."

"Bein' a workin' girl'll get you a shallow grave a lot faster than just bein' poor."

This last point seemed to score.

"Pelvis looks female, too," French said, holding up the two hipbones and the tailbone as a unit.

Allen took the skull from Broussard and put it on the table. French handed the pelvis to Broussard, who looked at it briefly and said, "Nulliparous."

"Remember us ordinary folks?" Gatlin said.

Broussard smiled inwardly. Often Gatlin would see things before Broussard got a chance to point them out. But today, he had Gatlin just where he wanted him. "It's likely she never had kids," Broussard said. "No parturition pits."

"How about I go over to Tulane," Gatlin said, "and learn to speak say... Russian. Then when we get together like this, you speak pathology and I'll speak Russian and we'll see how far we get."

"I'd like that," Broussard said.

"Parturition pits?" Gatlin said, reminding Broussard of the point that had led to their digression.

Broussard handed one hipbone and the tailbone to Allen. He held the other hipbone out to Gatlin. "Parturition pits are small depressions in the bone along here." He ran his finger over the upper margin of a deep notch. "And here. They're produced by damage to ligament attachments during birth. No pits... likely no kids."

"Sternal end of the clavicle is incompletely fused," French said, passing the two bones to Broussard.

He looked at the end of one of them and said, "Complete fusion of the shaft with the sternal end in this bone is usually complete by age thirty."

"So she was in her twenties when she died," Gatlin said.

"Looks that way."

Kit noticed a hint of sadness in Broussard's voice.

"Take a look at this," French said, passing up three small objects.

Kit leaned over to see into Broussard's hand as he studied the bones French had given him. One of the bones was oval, the other two, elongated.

Nodding knowingly, Broussard offered the bones to Gatlin, who kept his hands at his side. "Just show me."

"These three bones are all part of the hyoid, which sits right here." Broussard made a U with his thumb and index finger and put it on his neck, just below where his short beard ended. He held the bones up in the palm of his hand. "In older folks the three parts are fused, oval body in the center, a wing on each side." He pointed at one of the elongated bones. "See the fracture?"

Gatlin leaned closer. "Damaged during the digging?" Sensing the dirty look French was giving him, he glanced her way and threw up a hand in apology. "No offense, Doc."

"No way," Broussard said. "The fracture site is as stained as the rest of the bone."

"So she was—"

Not wanting Gatlin to say it first, Broussard interrupted, "Most likely strangled. Ordinarily pressure on someone's neck won't fracture a hyoid wing unless the parts are fused, but it happens."

"Allen, get the cameras and the markers," French said, setting aside the white bucket she had been filling with vertebrae.

"Somethin' important?" Broussard asked, edging to the pit. The others followed.

"Could be," French replied. Allen handed her the arrow and the scale and she arranged them on the ribs, which she had yet to pick up. She took a 35mm shot standing up, then changed the focus, bent down, and took another. Bubba was leaning over so far to see what she had found that he lost his footing and would have fallen into the pit had Kit not grabbed him by his coveralls. French swapped the 35mm camera for the Polaroid and took another couple of shots with that, passing the pictures to Broussard as they whirred from the camera.

"Looks like a toothpaste tube," Broussard said, inspecting one of the pictures.

"Any chance it was superficial debris that got shifted down when the hole was dug?" Gatlin asked.

"Highly unlikely," French said. "It was under a thoracic vertebra, which means that it went into the hole at the same time as the body."

Gatlin wiggled his finger at the pit. "Let's have a look at the real thing."

French picked up the object and brushed the dirt from it with a paintbrush. She looked the object over and handed it to Broussard. "Nothing left of the lettering, I'm afraid, but a D and an A on a flaked red background."

Broussard examined it on both sides, then unscrewed the cap and gently squeezed. A dark cylinder of material began to ooze from the tip. "Contents have expired," he remarked, putting the cap back on.

"Suppose it *is* toothpaste," Kit said. "Why would somebody be carrying around a tube of toothpaste?"

"If Andy's right about her being a hooker, I could come up with a reason or two why she might have to have had some toothpaste handy," Gatlin said.

Kit saw what he meant and she felt her cheeks flush. "Any sign of a purse?" It was a question asked as much to get everyone's attention off her as to inquire after a salient point.

"Can't say for sure what we might find under the rest of the bones," French said. "But I don't think they could cover the remains of a purse."

When the entire skeleton was out of the pit and onto the table, French said to Broussard, "Andy, we've been at this for five hours and I've had enough. I think Allen has, too. Plus, it's getting late and we have to take the remains back to the university. We still need to screen the pedestal for artifacts, but Allen can do that in the morning." She looked at Kit. "Sorry to drag this out for another day. Is it all right for Allen to let himself in tomorrow?"

"Certainly."

"Allen, we'll leave the tent, but take everything else with us. Whatever you need in the morning, you can bring back."

Dogged by their lengthening shadows, French and Allen spread a piece of black plastic over the pit and secured it with dirt. Then they wrapped the bones in virgin newsprint and packed them in long cardboard boxes.

COMPARED TO MOST of the houses in the heart of the city, Kit's tiny driveway, which was two cars wide and barely two deep, was spacious. Having found it filled when she arrived, French had parked in the narrow one-way street out front. When she and Allen had everything loaded into her van, she signed a chain-of-evidence form indicating that she had taken possession of the remains. Broussard kept the original and gave her the carbon.

Kit saw this as another surrealistic touch in a Salvador Dali day. Thank you very much, ma'am. Appreciate your business. If you're ever again in the market for the remains of a murdered young girl, hope you'll remember us.

"What happens now?" Kit said to French.

"Monday, I'll make some measurements on the skull and plug them into a computer program I've been developing for facial reconstruction. Should have a face by Tuesday."

French went around to the driver's side of the van and got in. As they pulled away from the curb, Allen waved limply out the open window. Feeling that it was a little inappropriate to respond in kind, Kit did not acknowledge their departure but turned instead to Gatlin. "So what's *your* next step?"

"I'll go back to the office, write up a report, and start a file."

"And then?"

"Then I'll continue working on murders I've got some chance of solving. Generally, if you can't cough up a suspect within forty-eight hours of the crime, your chances of ever solving it go *way* down. After ten years...well, it's the kind of thing you work on when you've got nothing else to do."

"But there'll always be something else to do."

"Tell me about it."

Kit's large eyes narrowed and she looked at Gatlin suspiciously. "This cavalier attitude wouldn't have anything to do with the fact that she might have been nothing but a prostitute, would it?"

Gatlin's naturally unhappy expression darkened. "No," he said sharply. "It's because the case is at least ten years old, like I said. Social class is something you have when you're alive. Murder is a great equalizer. A dead hooker and a dead senator are equally dead and their killers are guilty of the same crime. So you'll forgive me if I find your remark offensive."

Kit melted under Gatlin's hot response. "I'm sorry, Lieutenant, I had no right to say that. Guess I'm just feeling a little involved in this case."

The sparks in Gatlin's eyes went out and his face softened. "No apologies necessary, Doc. I understand. Now, I better go and write that report."

As Gatlin's Pontiac pulled out of the drive, Broussard said, "You gonna be okay?"

"Sure, you go on."

"All right, see you Monday. Bubba, you still comin' over tomorrow to clean that carburetor?"

"Be dere about ten," Bubba said. "Which one is it?"

"The yellow one." In addition to the white '57 T-bird now sitting in Kit's driveway, Broussard had five more at home, all with the original paint. "If I'm not there, just go on into the garage."

Broussard slid behind the wheel of the little car, an impossible act that usually reminded Kit of the Ferragammos in her closet that were too tight to wear and too expensive to throw out. But today, her mind dwelt on other things.

Broussard angled the T-bird into the street and headed for St. Charles Avenue, which he would have to reach by circling the block.

"If you want and Allen is finished," Bubba said, "...Ah could work on your trellis some tomorrow afternoon."

"Appreciate the offer," Kit said. "But why don't we let it ride for a while."

She watched Bubba back his old truck into the street, where the sincerity in his wave good-bye coaxed the same from her. Turning to go inside, she saw the drapes in nosy old Mrs. Bergeron's side window drop shut.

FOUR

LISTENING CAREFULLY at Broussard's door, Kit thought she heard him tell her to come in, but the hall air-handler unit overhead was making so much noise, she couldn't be sure. All day Monday and for a few hours today, she had been working an apparent suicide that had occurred the previous Friday. Upon hearing a gunshot, a woman had gone to her husband's study and found him dead on the floor beside the household .38. The physical circumstances pointed to suicide, but he had left no note and, by his wife's account, had no motive for such an act. Broussard had therefore been quite eager to see what Kit would come up with as she probed the man's background.

Kit peeked around the door and saw Broussard at his desk. He waved her inside.

Before she could mention her report, he picked up an X ray, shoved it into the clips of a view box on the table behind his desk, and flicked on the light.

"What do you see?" he asked.

She leaned across the desk. There was a white blur at the top of the X ray and what looked like collarbones at the bottom.

"An X ray of somebody's head and shoulders," she said.

"And...?"

"You're lucky I see that."

"Here...right here," he said, running a chubby finger along a line just below the skull.

"I'm going to need a *much* bigger hint."

"You do see this curved structure?"

"I do."

"It's a set of dentures, caught in the larynx. Poor old fellow got lost while he and his wife were goin' to visit their daughter. He got upset at bein' lost and somehow his teeth slipped into his throat. When the ambulance arrived, they tried to intubate him but couldn't get the tube in because of the dentures and they couldn't see the dentures because the tooth side was down and the side facin' up was flesh-colored."

"Thanks for sharing that with me," Kit said.

"So take care of your teeth," Broussard replied. "What can I do for you?"

She handed him a manila folder. "That's my report on the Paxton case. I've gone as far as I can. From talking to people at the bank where he worked, I get the feeling there's money missing and that the deceased was involved. But no one will talk openly about it. To get more, somebody with a badge is going to have to go over there."

"Sounds like you did all right."

"Time will tell, I guess. Since I'm pretty well caught up, I thought I'd go over to Tulane. I checked with French and she said she's got a face to go with the bones we found in my yard."

"You handlin' that all right?"

"If you call thinking about it five or six times a day, handling it."

"Maybe it'd be better to let it go."

"I can't. I've got to know what she looked like."

Kit left Charity Hospital and proceeded to an All Right parking lot where they knew better than to put her car up on one of those forklifts they used to increase the lot's capacity. Many of the cars she passed had cardboard sun screens propped on the dash—one with a pair of giant sunglasses painted on it, one that looked like white shutters, another that read HELP, CALL THE POLICE.

The small crack she had left in the driver's window had done little good and her car was like the inside of a dishwasher in midcycle. She started the engine and flicked on the air conditioner, closing the door only after the fan had pushed all the superheated air to the outside.

When French had said that she was in Dinwiddie Hall, Kit had made a mental note of the fact and thought no more about it. Now, as she turned onto Tulane Avenue, that seemed odd, for Dinwiddie was where the geology department was located. Anthropology was way across campus. At Lee Circle, she looped to the right, stayed in the right lane, and turned onto St. Charles.

Even if French's office had been on the other side of the Tulane campus, Kit would probably have come this way, for she loved the street's graceful old oaks and Victorian homes. Two streetcars going in opposite directions passed in what the natives called the "neutral ground." Inside, the passengers on the aisle seats fanned themselves with folded newspapers, while those beside them hugged the open windows.

Kit reflected once again on how fortunate she had been to find an affordable house within walking distance of the untouchably valuable real estate along this street. For the next ten minutes, she concentrated on the scenery, forgetting for a while the thoughts that had been tumbling in her head since a talented married woman with kids had dug a murdered girl from her future rose garden.

Dinwiddie and the other towering gray stone buildings at the Audubon Park end of the campus was where Tulane first began. "This," a visitor approaching from St. Charles would say, "is what a university *should* look like." But it was a case of architectural bait and switch. Behind this auspicious start, succeeding architects had done pretty much what they pleased. The result was, to Kit's mind, an eclecticism that marred an otherwise-fine institution. Though if anyone else had made this observation, Kit would not have let it go unchallenged. After all, this *was* her doctoral alma mater.

Dinwiddie was cool and slightly musty and the slightest sound echoed through its empty halls. Momentarily puzzled at the lack of students, Kit remembered that it was summer. High on the wall to the left, the fossilized remains of a long-tailed creature embedded in rock too uniform to be real hung in a dark oak frame. Straight ahead was the darkened door to the physical geology lab; beside it, a glass case containing a rock display to whet the budding geologist's appetite. A young female voice coming from the floor above spilled down the stairs to Kit's right. "Did you hear what happened to the Cro-Magnon that had unprotected sex?"

"No, what?" another female asked.

"He got plesiosaurs."

One of the women screamed, then both laughed hysterically. A door slammed and they were heard no more.

The first thing Kit saw when she opened French's door was a glass case on the far wall containing a very stocky-looking skeleton, which, except for a peculiar outward flaring of the back part of the jaw, looked human. But what did she know about it? Probably, it was either some other primate or an archaeological specimen. Next to the glass case was a long table with a computer and printer on it. Beside the computer keyboard was a skull, perhaps the one from her yard.

"Over here," a voice said from behind the bookcases on the near wall that blocked her view to the right.

She stepped into the room and saw Victoria French at her desk. Her hair was freshly done and she was wearing a tan safari outfit with lots of buttons and buckles. Searching for a word to describe her, Kit decided on *tawny*...like a plains lioness. On the wall behind French's desk was a framed piece of shale with several glistening black trilobites embedded in it. Kit didn't know much about paleontology but she knew a trilobite when she saw one, because when she was a kid, her father would always take her with him on those Saturdays when he got a haircut. The barber's hobby had been trilobites and he had had a big case of them for kids like her to look at.

On each side of the shale was a picture of an archaeological dig in progress, everyone in the picture looking sunburned and wind-tousled. Under the shale, stuck to the wall with tape, was a piece of construction paper with a crude crayon sketch of a house with smoke coming out of the chimney, trees that looked like green cotton balls on sticks, and a flat father and mother with hair that resembled the foliage on the trees.

"Did you have to walk far?" French asked.

"I got lucky and found a parking place right out front." Kit pointed at the skeleton. "Is that human?"

"Yes. I inherited it from my predecessor. It was found bricked up in an old house that burned in the French Quarter."

"Murdered?"

"Quite likely. Have a seat. Just push those boxes out of your way."

French was referring to a short stack of long cardboard boxes on each side of the wooden chair in front of her desk. "Are there bones in them?" Kit asked.

"If you see a cardboard box anywhere around me, it'll probably have bones in it. Just move them aside."

Kit cleared a path to the chair and sat down.

"Sorry we didn't have a chance to talk Saturday," French said, "but a forensic dig is always pretty intensive."

"Why is your office here rather than in the anthro department?"

"They're short of space over there and since I have a secondary appointment in geology, everybody involved thought it was a good idea. I earn my keep over here by helping out in the basic geology course."

On French's desk was a small sculpture of a tree with a distinctly nonhuman primate clinging to the top like a Christmas angel. Increasingly human-looking figures were arranged in descending order on the side branches. A man in a derby hat and smoking a cigar stood at the base, with his fingers proudly in his suspenders.

"That's cute," Kit said, pointing to the sculpture. "Does it come with a woman at the bottom?"

"Oh, there aren't any more," French said. "I only made one. It's not *a* man. It's *man* in the generic sense."

"You made it? I'm impressed."

"Don't be. It took forever and I probably started over fifty times before I got it right."

Anthropologist, geologist, sculptor, wife, mother—was there *anything* this woman couldn't do? If you had asked, Kit would have said that her only reason for coming here was to see the facial reconstruction French had been working on. But there was another reason, one that lay just at the interface of the conscious and the subconscious. She had dimly hoped to find that French wasn't all that *good* an anthropologist. It was, of course, a hope born dead, because Kit had already seen her in action. The confusion that had spawned this illogical hope now made Kit say, "How do you do it?"

"Do what?" French said kindly.

"Take care of a family and still have a professional life?"

French considered the question. She smiled more to herself than at Kit and, for a moment, reminded Kit of Broussard and how he would sometimes mentally leave a room when he had thinking to do.

Something clicked in French's eyes and she said, "Do you know the name, Aleš Hrdlička?"

What French had said didn't sound like a name at all but just a bunch of random syllables.

"No, of course you don't," French said, answering her own question. "Aleš Hrdlička is the father of physical anthropology. The entire discipline goes back to the work of this one man . . . and you've never heard of him."

"I'm sorry. . . . I . . ."

"Don't be," French said, "I wasn't implying that you *should* have heard of him. My point was that even a man that great is known only to a handful of people."

"So, you're saying that no matter what you accomplish professionally . . ."

"In the big picture, it isn't going to matter much. If Hrdlička hadn't come along, it would have been someone else. Don't misunderstand me—I love what I do and I think I'm respected for my ability. I have a decent list of publications and I do my share of committee work, but I set limits. I don't let my work consume me. There's more to life than anthropology."

Kit took this news hard, for she had come to believe that "you can have it all" articles belonged in supermarket tabloids, right next to the "impregnated by alien" stories. Now, sitting across from her was a clear challenge to that belief.

French was blushing slightly. "It wasn't my intention to get on a soapbox, especially with thoughts that I wouldn't want my male colleagues to hear. Anyway, I'm diverting you from the purpose of your visit."

French got up and came around the desk. "Can't imagine what's wrong with my printer," she said, going to her computer. "But I can still show you the facial reconstruction."

Kit left her chair and joined French at the computer, where with a single keystroke, French called up the color image of a skull on her monitor. Her fingers clacked over the keyboard and a scan line dropped from the top of the screen and migrated downward, putting hair and flesh on the skull.

I REALLY NEED TO TALK....

"You understand," French said, "that there's some guesswork involved in all this, in the length of the nose, for instance, the thickness of the lips, and the color and style of the hair. But with this program, we can pick any hairstyle and color we..." Glancing at Kit, French paused in midsentence, for Kit looked quite ill.

French pulled the computer chair over and gently guided Kit into it. "I'll get you some water," she said, hastening from the room. But it was not water that Kit wanted. She wanted only to go home.

Without waiting for French to return, Kit made her way back to her car, seeing nothing, hearing nothing but the face and voice in her brain.

I REALLY NEED TO TALK....

Guided by instinct, she started the car and got it moving. A few minutes later, she missed her street and had to make a U-turn at the next one, nearly getting clipped by a streetcar whose looming shape and clanging bell went unnoticed.

Lucky met her at the door, but no matter what he did, he couldn't get his head scratched. With Lucky darting and panting at her feet, Kit went to the bookshelves in her study and took down the *Jambalaya* that had been issued her second year in graduate school. She thumbed through the pages until she got to the School of Social Work.

I REALLY NEED TO TALK....

Her reddened eyes went to the middle of the right page, to a girl with the high cheekbones of a model but with eyes too widely set and a nose too broad for her to be truly beautiful.

Leslie Music: a happy name for a tormented girl.

It had been nearly five years, but Kit could still remember the phone call word for word.

"Kit, this is Leslie.... Could you... Could you come over for a while? I'm feeling kind of low."

Why hadn't she gone? God. She had known how unstable Leslie was. It wasn't as though it was a stranger calling.

"Gee, Leslie, this is such a bad time. I've got a date and he'll be here any minute."

"I *really* need to talk."

Looking back on it, the desperation in her voice had been so *obvious*.

"Look, tell you what. I'll give you a call when I get home and if you still feel like talking, I'll come over. How's that?"

"Okay, fine...that's...fine. Sorry to have bothered you. Have a good time. Bye."

Sure, she had thought about Leslie a couple of times during her date. Big deal. But she hadn't *done* anything. Then much later that night, the phone call to Leslie's apartment that rang and rang and rang...a life preserver thrown into an empty sea.

She laid the annual aside and got out the manuscript box that held the first seven chapters of her book on suicide. She removed the lid. As yet untitled and barely a quarter finished, it already had a dedication. Oh yes, it had that. In fact, there had been a dedication before there was anything else.

Kit's finger lightly touched the two words that had marked a beginning she hoped would somehow give meaning to the ending she had been too selfish to prevent.

FOR LESLIE

The face that French had reconstructed was not Leslie, of course, but bore such a resemblance that it had brought back the most painful memories in Kit's life. And suddenly, Kit knew what she must do. It was as if she had been given a way to atone for not having being there when Leslie needed her. Now someone else needed her, and this time she would not turn her back. If Gatlin wouldn't look for the killer of the girl whose bones they had found, she would do it herself . . . for the victim and for Leslie.

FIVE

THE NEXT MORNING, Broussard said that if Gatlin gave her permission to work on the case, it would be all right with him as well. Gatlin put up a short, unspirited defense against the idea, then gave in, warning her that he was to be kept apprised of any significant developments.

Since she was already in the building and had seen French's facial reconstruction, Gatlin suggested that Kit look over the old unsolved missing persons files. She agreed and spent an hour going through a two-foot stack of manila folders in a sparsely furnished, windowless room that smelled of stale cigarette smoke.

Nearly all the files contained photographs of the missing individual and those that didn't had vivid verbal descriptions of the subject. The net result of this activity was nothing more than a slightly stiff neck and a sore rear end from the hard chair she had been given.

Next, she made a quick trip out to the Tulane campus, where she apologized to French for leaving so abruptly on her last visit and obtained from French's repaired printer a hard copy of the facial reconstruction. Though she didn't know what she was going to do with it, Kit also requested and got the toothpaste tube that had come out of the pit that first day, as well as the artifacts that French's assistant had found when he screened the pedestal the following morning. As collateral, she left her signature on a chain-of-evidence form.

By 10:30, she was back in her office, wondering what to do next. She studied the facial reconstruction for a minute, then opened the Baggie containing the artifacts and spread them out on her desk. There wasn't much: six opalescent buttons probably from a blouse, a black button and zipper from a skirt, some chrome hooks and eyes that most likely were part of a bra, and two small pieces of metal that she thought were once high-heel tips—ordinary items that had been witness to an extraordinary event. But how to get them to talk? She dumped the toothpaste tube from its Baggie and examined the two remaining letters on it: *DA*.

Where to begin?

There was a knock at her door and a familiar shadow on the glass. Broussard stuck his head inside.

"So what happened?" he asked, a lemon ball clacking against his teeth. "You on the case?"

"Already at work," she replied, gesturing to the items in front of her.

He came into the room, took a quick look at the artifacts, then sat in her visitor's chair and folded his hands over his belly. "What are you gonna do first?"

Before he had showed up, Kit had been mentally circling the problem. Now, ready or not, she had to make a move, for she did not want him to think she was slow-witted.

"Gatlin suggested that I start by checking the old missing persons files, but they were no help."

"I guess that picture there is French's reconstruction?"

"Yeah." She picked up the picture and handed it across the desk, using the few seconds this bought to order her thoughts.

"Pretty girl," Broussard said, returning the picture. "Why do you figure she wasn't in the files?"

Kit shrugged. "Maybe she was new in town and didn't have any friends or relatives here to miss her." Kit's eyes rolled to the side. "I wonder..."

"Wonder what?"

"I was thinking she might have been killed in another city and brought here, but that's pretty unlikely."

"So, what's next?"

"I think this can be approached from two different angles." A part of her was talking and another part was waiting to see what she would say. "One way is to come at it from the direction of the victim . . . try to identify her."

Working with Broussard was both a privilege and a giant pain in the backside. What he didn't know about pathology wasn't worth knowing and behind those glasses tied to the lanyard around his neck were eyes that missed nothing. At a scene, he was like a large vacuum cleaner sucking up facts and storing them for later. And as far as synthesis, she'd match him against the best detective minds in the country. That was the privilege part. But this . . . this patient paternalism where he let you talk until you put your foot in it was the pain. Still, she wouldn't have traded places with anybody.

"I thought I'd call the *Picayune,*" Kit said, "and see if they'd like to follow up that small article they did Sunday with a bigger one, including this picture, under the heading 'Do You Know This Girl?' And give my name and phone number as a contact. Maybe somebody will come forward with some information."

Broussard shifted his lemon ball to the other cheek. "Oh, you'll get phone calls. Might even get a confession or two, if the moon is right."

"Then this is a bad idea?"

"No, it's a good one, just be sure and hold back some important detail so you can screen the real from the real strange. You said there were two different angles to approach this. What's the other one?"

"To find out who was living in my house when it happened."

"But we don't know when it happened."

Kit hesitated, sensing a trap. She mentally checked her facts and found them correct—unless, of course, the old vacuum cleaner had sucked up something he hadn't yet disgorged.

"That's right, we don't," Kit said. "There's no way of knowing *when* that root grew across the pit. So all the root does is establish the *minimum* amount of time that's passed. Somehow I've got to come up with a more reliable number... maybe from these artifacts." She picked up the toothpaste tube. "So far, though, no progress."

Broussard slapped his thighs and stood up. "Sounds like you've got it under control. I was on my way downstairs to get a diet soda. Want anything?"

"No thanks."

"Then I'll just tend to a number of things I've got to do in the morgue before I come back up."

Broussard left Kit's office, went to the elevator, and took it to the hospital basement. Before going through the scarred double doors to the morgue complex, he paused in the vending area and looked at the soft-drink machine. *Diet soda?* Why, he'd never had a diet anything in his life. And soda? A soda had ice cream in it. A *number* of things to do. He chuckled softly. Maybe she'd get it, maybe she wouldn't. If not, he'd try again.

Back upstairs, Kit was trying to figure out what the writing had been on the toothpaste tube. *DA.* Those were clearly the last letters. *DA.*

She took out a legal pad and began writing down all the words she could think of that ended in *DA.* It wasn't as easy as it appeared and for a while she couldn't think of any.

Freda.

Yeah right, toothpaste Freda.

Elbows on her desk, she closed her eyes, put a hand over them, and tried to concentrate. *DA*.

DA.

God, this was hard.

Colada, as in pina colada, an unlikely choice, but she wrote it down just to have something on the paper.

DA.

Ramada. That went down under *colada*, though it seemed equally useless.

Armada. She was rolling now. Four stupid words in a row.

DA.

Soda. Baking soda. Toothpaste could have baking soda in it. She looked to the left of the *DA* and mentally measured off the space needed to complete the phrase. There was definitely room for *baking soda*.

Soda. I was on my way downstairs to get a diet soda. Had that old rascal...? To do a number of things... A *number*...

She turned the tube over and inspected it carefully but found no numbers. The end had been crimped and rolled up several times. She unrolled it and there it was, pressed into the soft material of the tube: EX720Y8932, a lot number.

She lugged out the phone book and looked up the number of the information service of the public library. A pleasant librarian's voice answered on the first ring.

"I've got a tough one for you," Kit said. "Can you tell me what companies made a baking soda toothpaste between ten and twenty years ago?" Her estimate of twenty years as the maximum period of interest was purely a guess.

The librarian took Kit's number and promised to get back to her. Ten minutes later, she did, with the news that

Procter & Gamble was a likely candidate, and she even provided a corporate phone number.

At Procter & Gamble, she talked to six people before finding someone who had knowledge of what the company had been making during the period in question. "What color's the tube?" he asked.

Kit looked at it again. "I think the tube was white. The logo—at least what's left—was mint green lettering in an oval with a red background."

"Doesn't sound like us. What's the lot number?"

When she read it to him, he said, "Sounds like a Hoch-Matthis number, hold on—"

Hoch-Matthis? That was a new one, but Kit supposed it was one of those corporations that owned a lot of subsidiaries—diversified, so that when folks got afraid to eat hot dogs, the lawn furniture division could take up the slack.

Her contact came back on the line with the Hoch-Matthis phone number and a name to ask for. But when she called, she got a busy signal. Since the phone was already in her hand and she needed to kill a minute or so, she called her answering machine and signaled it to give up her messages. There was only one.

"This is John Tully. Please give me a call when you can. Seven-eight-three, five-four-three-two."

Kit jotted down the number on her list of words ending in *DA*. John Tully was one of the charter members of the Greater New Orleans Rose Society, a group Kit had recently joined. What could he want?

She tried Hoch-Matthis again, but the line was still busy.

John Tully was a retired setup man for the Upton Corporation. When Kit had asked him what a setup man did, he had told her that he did setups for the night shift. Kit had nodded knowingly. Since he was retired, he might be home now. She tried his number and got him on the fourth ring.

"John, this is Kit Franklyn."

"Kit. Yeah. Kit Franklyn. How are you?"

"Fine, John. You called?"

"I called? Yeah. Yeah. I called. Wonder if you'd do me a favor?"

"If I can."

"Louisiana Rose Society is havin' a contest to find the new rose with the best fragrance. I've got some contenders I've developed, but they allow only one entry per person. So I'd like your opinion on which one *you* think is best."

"Be glad to help. How about I drop by around...four o'clock?"

"Yeah. Four o'clock. That'd be good. You know where it is?"

"No."

Tully gave her the address and directions, thanked her, and hung up.

This time, her call to Hoch-Matthis went through. The contact Procter & Gamble had suggested was a good one. "Could be one of ours," he said. "Gimme the lot number."

She read him the number and he put her on hold. About the time she had begun to think he had forgotten her, he came back on the line. "I sure wouldn't use that toothpaste," he said. "Our records indicate a production date for that tube of August 8, 1962. With a shelf life of three years, you're about what...twenty-seven years too late for that tube."

Twenty-seven years...long enough for the killer to be long gone, maybe even dead himself.

Armed with a pretty good fix on the time of the murder, Kit decided to use that to screen anyone who might contact her in response to the picture she was going to give to the paper. She'd say the body had been there at least ten years. That would both eliminate some calls and get people to thinking beyond the recent past.

ON THE WAY to John Tully's, Kit remembered that she was out of heartworm pills for Lucky. She made a small detour past the vet's to pick some up.

Tully lived in a 1920s brown brick bungalow with a front porch enclosed with old black screening that would have made Kit think the occupant was retired even if she hadn't known him. When she tried the porch screen door, she found it locked. Fortunately, the door fit so poorly that her knuckles made quite a rattle, bringing Tully without much delay.

Under six feet tall and reasonably trim, Tully was dressed in a plaid short-sleeved shirt, baggy Levis, and blue deck shoes. Kit didn't know his exact age, but he couldn't have been having any trouble getting the senior citizen's discount at restaurants, for he had thin white hair and pale lips that were almost the same color and texture as his face, giving him the appearance of a fading photograph. His most distinctive feature was a vine-shaped pattern of congested blood vessels on each cheek.

He unlocked the screen door and pushed it open. "Hello, young lady."

In one hand, Tully carried a narrow wooden tray. The other, he offered to Kit.

She hesitated, his rippled white skin, as usual, calling to mind the time Broussard had shown her how the skin on the hands of a corpse sometimes sloughs off like a glove with fingernails. Toughening, she took his hand, their previous handshakes at the three Rose Society meetings she had attended making the strength of his grip no surprise.

"Good of you to come over and do this," Tully said.

"I'm flattered to be asked."

She followed him into the house, which was a shade too warm for her taste and smelled a bit like an old book. They were in a living room with furniture that looked as soft and lived-in as its owner. Apart from three or four days' worth of newspapers scattered on the floor beside an easy chair, the room was neat, though Kit suspected that a good shake of the drapes would be something to regret.

"Back here."

Tully led her to an interior hallway. On the way, she glanced into the kitchen and saw more newspapers, this time spread out on the kitchen table. On the papers was a mound of soil, some clay pots, and other potting paraphernalia.

Tully took her to a room that most people would have used for a bedroom, but he had it filled with crudely made three-tiered planters with Gro-Lites at each level. Each tier was filled with trays of rose seedlings.

"I figure I got about sixteen thousand plants goin' right now," Tully said proudly. "Ten in here and six in another bedroom in back. I was about to collect the ones we want when you knocked. Won't take but a minute."

The seedlings were far too small to have flowers on them, but one planter contained much larger plants that were either in bud or already blooming. Tully moved around this planter like an aging bee, making his selections and putting them in the tray he was carrying. When he had chosen six plants, he came back to her. "Let's go into the kitchen, where there's more room."

"It must take a lot of time to care for so many plants," Kit said, following him.

"Time? Yeah. It does that. But since I'm retired, I got the time."

In the kitchen, he put the tray on the table and looked at her with rheumy eyes. "And you know, it's like havin' sixteen thousand friends...friends that don't ever want to borrow money or want you to take 'em somewhere...or want to talk when you want to watch the news."

As Kit listened to the old man rattle off the advantages of roses over people, she had the feeling that he would have traded all his roses for one friend who would want to borrow money, was always begging rides, and would talk during the news.

Tully took the six plants out of the tray and arranged them around the edge of the kitchen table. "Time to choose," he said.

"What am I looking for?"

"Fullness of fragrance, agreeability, and staying power...how long the fragrance lasts after you come away from the flower."

"That's a lot to think about."

"Just do your best."

Kit made the rounds of the six flowers, considered for a moment, then went back and sniffed numbers two and four again. "It's close," she said, "but I'd pick number four."

Tully grinned. "Yeah. Number four. That's what I thought. Guess my sniffer ain't gone yet. Say...I got a few more crosses ain't bloomed yet. You mind comin' back when they do and we'll pit 'em against number four and see what happens."

"I can do that."

ON THE WAY HOME, Kit could not help but be struck by the way that events had thrust the contrasting lives of John Tully and Victoria French under her nose: the ghost of Kit that would be or the ghost of Kit that might be....

She dismissed the melodramatic analogy with a blink and a shake of her head. Still . . . there *was* her membership in the Rose Society. Could a bedroom full of rose seedlings be far behind?

SIX

THE NEXT MORNING, Kit anxiously unfolded the morning paper.

There it was. *DO YOU KNOW THIS GIRL?* The quality of the reproduction was excellent and Kit was optimistic that it would jog someone's memory. They even spelled Franklyn with a *y* instead of an *i*.

After feeding Lucky, she got the new bottle of heartworm pills from the top of the fridge, unscrewed the top, and shook a pill into her hand. Instead of the red pill she was accustomed to, these were white.

Ordinarily, Lucky liked his heartworm pill and would eat it from her hand as though it was dessert. But when she offered him this new pill, he sniffed it and backed away.

"Come on, you little varmint, don't give me a hard time over this." She grabbed him and pulled him closer, his claws trying in vain to get a grip on the shiny linoleum. With one knee on the floor, she turned him around, pried open his muzzle, and popped the pill into his throat.

"There now," she said, releasing him. "That wasn't so bad, was it?"

Lucky blinked and looked at her in bewilderment. She scratched his neck and got to her feet. "You be good now."

Lucky followed her to the front door and watched sadly as she left for work. When she was gone, he trotted into the kitchen and went over to the fridge, where he made a little noise like a door latch catching. The pill clacked onto the linoleum and rolled against the counter baseboard. Before leaving to get his morning nap, he batted the pill around the floor, soon losing it in the space between the fridge and the counter.

Kit heard her phone ringing even before she could get her office door open. She dashed inside and snatched up the receiver.

"Kit Franklyn."

"You the one that's lookin' for information on that picture in the paper?" a male voice said.

"Yes, do you know something?"

"She sat next to me for six months in the shorthand class at the Eason Business School."

Kit's heart was beating fast. "When was this?"

"Back in 19...80."

Kit wilted. "I'm sorry, but that couldn't have been her."

"Why not?" The voice had a hint of anger in it.

"I can't say, but it's definitely not her."

"Yeah, well see if I ever do you a favor again," the caller said, banging down the receiver.

The phone went off again as soon as she cut the connection.

"Kit Franklyn."

"Saw your name in the paper this morning," a husky male voice said. "Kit. What's that short for, Katherine?"

"I don't think that's—"

"Kit... It makes me think of kittens and that makes me think of pussy.... I'll bet you've got—"

Kit slammed the receiver into its cradle, shuddering at the way the pervert on the line had blindly guessed that Kit was indeed short for kitten, a fact she kept from even her closest friends.

After another half dozen useless calls, there was a lull that gave her time to consider how she might go about finding out who lived in her house at the time the murder had been committed.

The old city directories seemed like a good place to start. She thought they were in the library but called to find out for sure, discovering that they were in the Louisiana section on the third floor.

She dialed the forensic office and asked Margaret, the senior secretary, to screen any calls that might come in regarding the picture in the paper. She told her how to do it and punched in the code that would route all incoming calls to the other phone.

The library was only a few doors from the hospital, but even with so short a distance, the hot sidewalks made her toes tingle and she arrived wearing a thin film of perspiration that turned to ice as she entered the well-cooled library lobby.

The city directories were in the back, past the microfilm readers. She stood in front of them and scanned the dates.... The toothpaste had been made in 1962. She pulled out the directory for that year, sat down, and turned the pages until she found her street.

Beside most of the addresses was a name and a bell in a circle, the latter indicating that the address had a telephone. There were also some letters and numbers she didn't bother deciphering, for beside her address, there was only the notation. "No return," apparently meaning that the occupant had not returned the form the city had mailed out.

Suddenly getting a distinct feeling that she was being watched, she looked to the right, where at a table six feet away, a swarthy weight-lifting type in a fishnet shirt was pretending to be deeply absorbed in the book in front of him. This was not an unusual occurrence. Throughout her life, men had been stealing glances at her and then looking away when she tried to catch them at it.

She pulled down the directory for 1963 and flipped through it. No luck there either—still that useless entry. "No return."

The feeling of being watched came again. She looked quickly at the guy in the fishnet shirt, but he was too quick for her.

Going back to work, she checked the directories for 1964 and 1965 but could find only "No return" beside her address. Whoever had lived there in the early sixties had not been very civic-minded. But had they also been a murderer?

What to do now?

She drummed her fingers on the directory in thought. Old tax records. Maybe she could get the owner's name from those. But where were they? Obviously, it was back to her office and the telephone.

After she had gone and the elevator doors had shut behind her, a figure approached the directories and pulled down the one for 1964. Pages were turned until the desired street was found. A finger ran down the addresses and stopped.

"No return."

The sigh of relief was almost a moan. At the next table, the man in the fishnet shirt pulled his book closer, the better to concentrate.

BACK AT THE OFFICE, Kit learned that in her absence there had been one call about the murder, but the caller had been way off on the timing. She got out the phone book again and turned to the blue pages of government listings. She ran down the entries until she found a number for the Bureau of the Treasury-Tax Records, which was answered by someone who didn't have a clue as to where the old tax records were but thought the assessor's office would know.

The assessor's office believed that the Louisiana section of the library might know. This was getting ridiculous. She had just come from the library.

The librarian at the Louisiana desk also had no idea where the old tax records were but suggested that she could track the previous owner of her house at the conveyance department in City Hall, where all the property-transfer information was kept. Too cautious to plunge into the heat outside without knowing with absolute certainty that she wasn't going on a wild-goose chase, she dialed the number the librarian had given her for the conveyance department and got a very helpful woman who verified what the librarian had said.

City Hall was on Perdido, two blocks from the library. Despite this modest distance, she arrived in the lobby breathing hard, her underwear clinging wetly to her skin. Ahead of her, a long-haired young man pulled at his sweat-soaked T-shirt and looked up at the older man walking beside him. "Summer sucks, man."

Kit had to agree.

Checking the directory on the wall, she found no listing for the conveyance department. She looked around for help. There was an information booth in the lobby but it was unmanned. Though edgy from the heat and miffed at not having thought to verify the location of the convey-ance department when she'd had them on the phone, she found the silver foil-covered suggestion box on the counter of the empty information booth an amusing touch.

She could have sworn when she entered the building that the lobby had been full of knowledgeable-looking men in suits. Now when she needed one, they had all disap-peared. Presently, the only sign of life was a long line of glazed-eyed citizens snaking through a door down the hall.

She walked to that doorway and looked inside, but the clerk at the counter appeared too harried to bother.

In desperation, she opened the next door she came to and barged in. The room contained a lot of empty desks and one of those suits that had gone into hiding.

"Conveyance department?" he said. "It's in the basement of the civil court building."

Before she could get too upset at having to plunge back into the heat and walk God knows how far to get to the civil court building, the suit said, "Just go down this hall, across the little drive, and up the first set of steps you see. Ask the guard inside how to get to the basement."

Three minutes later, she was standing in the doorway of a large room filled with huge books in individual cubicles that ended chest-high in tilted work surfaces where the books could be examined. Here and there, people sat in uncomfortable-looking chairs at long wooden tables, writing reports. Off to the right was a small cluster of computer stations that appeared to be available for use by anyone who felt so moved.

Inside, at the desk to the left, was a heavyset woman with beautiful olive skin. Dressed in an expensive green silk dress with lots of gold jewelry at her throat and wrists, she looked as if she didn't need this or any other job. Kit explained what she needed and the woman patiently showed her how to use the big books, calling her "hon" at least four times and frequently touching her arm. The clerk spoke with the accent of a native New Orleanian where words with an *or* sound are pronounced *aw*.

"Nawmally, hon, you'd start over there, but in yaw case..."

In her case, since she had purchased her house so recently, Kit was instructed to start at the computer by entering her name. A succession of screens showed a variety of information regarding her purchase of the property: the sale price, legal description of the property, the seller's name, and, finally, what she was actually looking for, a pair of three-digit numbers separated by a slash mark—what the woman had called the COB number, which was simply the book and page number where she would find information about the previous sale of the property.

She left the computer and roamed the rows of books until she found the one she was looking for. She pulled it from its cubicle and plopped it onto the tiled reading surface, where she turned to the page the computer had given her. There she discovered that the person who had sold her the house had bought it eight years earlier from someone named Hataway at a fraction of what she had paid for it. Once pleased with the purchase price, she now felt she should have dickered harder. Noting the COB number of that transaction, she went looking for the next book.

Hataway had held the property only six years, having bought it from someone named Marzoni. Another COB number.

Marzoni had kept it for nine years, buying it from a woman named Guillot in 1968. That COB number led her to the discovery that Guillot had bought the property in the fifties, well before there had been any body under the grass in the backyard. Now, all she had to do was find…Shirley Elizabeth Guillot.

On the way back to the hospital, she imagined Shirley Elizabeth Guillot, her hair hanging in greasy tangles, her eyes wide and round, shining with a demented light as she choked the life from . . . a prostitute?

The image vanished. It was a song with all the wrong notes, like a child banging on the piano. Still, there was no one she wanted to talk to more than Shirley Elizabeth Guillot…no one, that is, until Margaret told her upon her return that she had taken a call from a Lily Lacaze, who said the picture in the paper was a friend of hers that had disappeared in the early sixties.

So nervous that she misdialed on the first try, Kit called the number Lacaze had left. The phone was answered by a hoarse female voice with a death rattle in it that made Kit glad bacteria and viruses could not travel through telephone wires.

"Ms. Lacaze?"

"Who wants to know?"

"Kit Franklyn.... You called me about the picture in the paper."

"Then why weren't you there? Person puts their name in the paper and wants help, they should be there when a person calls."

"I am sorry, but I had to do something important."

"And this ain't important? 'Cause if it ain't, I got other things I could be doin'."

"No, please. The errand I had to run involved this case. I assure you, right now, this is my top priority."

"There a reward for information? 'Cause I'm used to gettin' paid for my time."

"Well ... I suppose if your information is good, I could manage something, say"—Kit grabbed a number out of the air—"twenty dollars?"

Lacaze snorted. "Oh yeah, I can see this means a helluva lot to you. Make it fifty and we got a deal, and even then I wouldn't be doin' it if it wasn't for Francie."

"Francie?"

"That's her name ... the girl in the paper. Christ, don't you pay attention?"

"How will I know that ... Francie is really whom we found?"

"I got a picture of her. You can judge for yourself."

"When can we meet? My office is in Charity Hospital."

"Two o'clock. Only I ain't goin' in Charity Hospital. I've known too many that have gone in there with a little case of the clap and come out feetfirst."

"How about Grandma O's restaurant? Do you know where that is?"

"I know where everything is. Two o'clock. If you're late, you can forget it. How will I know you?"

"I have long auburn hair and I wear it pulled back from my face with combs. By two o'clock, there probably won't be many people there. How will I recognize you?"

"I'll be the one says, 'I'm Lacaze.' "

Lacaze hung up without saying good-bye, and Kit turned her attention back to Shirley Elizabeth Guillot. Tired of getting out the phone book and putting it away, she had left it on her desk. Now, she flipped to the G's: Guerro... Guidry... Guillard... Guillot.

Lord.

There were three columns of Guillots. She ran her finger down the list of names... no Shirley. But there was an S. Guillot, meaning that it was most likely a woman. She dialed the number and let it ring a long time. Just as she was about to hang up, a shaky little old lady's voice answered, hardly the voice of a murderer.

Kit told the old lady that she was trying to find Shirley Elizabeth Guillot so that she could be given her share of an inheritance a distant relative had left her. Kit felt ashamed at being such a liar, but she couldn't tell the old lady the real reason she was calling. It all fell apart, though, when the woman said her name was Sarah.

Faced with an awful alternative, Kit called in a favor she was owed by someone in the utilities offices, who verified that the old lady's account was indeed in the name of Sarah Guillot. Thinking that the Guillot she was looking for might not even *have* a phone, she got her contact to check for *any* billing to a Shirley Guillot. That, too, proved fruitless.

She drummed her fingers on the desk. Her hand went to her hair and she began to twirl it with her fingers, a habit she had tried to break, as it tended to make her hair curl up on one side.

An idea.

She hadn't checked *all* the Guillots in the phone book. She turned to the back, to the listings for the small towns surrounding New Orleans. Delacroix, Jesuit Bend, and Lafitte had no Guillots at all. Lake Catherine had two, but no Shirley. Nor did she pick up anything in the listings for St. Bernard and the misplaced suburb of Detroit, Yscloskey.

There was only one thing to do—call every blessed Guillot in the book, most of whom wouldn't even be home during the day. She flipped back to the front of the phone book, sighed at how many there were, and began: Aaron Guillot, 728....

There was a knock at the door and Broussard stuck his head in. "I just got a call about a hangin', a teenager. You interested?"

Faced with the formidable task before her, which likely was going to be a huge waste of time, Kit would have accepted any offer to do something else. But this was actually important, a case that might illustrate some of the points she was planning to make in chapter eight of her book.

Today, Broussard had driven his red T-bird. As they drove, Kit was once again struck by how odd it was that such a big man would have a passion for such small cars. He was so tightly wedged against the steering wheel, she imagined that his shirts wore out in a narrow band across the belly long before the collars frayed.

"How you doin' on that skeleton?" he asked, glancing at her.

"Oh yeah, thanks for the tip."

"What tip is that?"

"You think I don't catch you at those little games you like to play? Diet *soda* . . . a *number* of things to do. . . ."

Broussard chuckled, a sound like a timpani drumroll. "So, I need to work on subtlety?"

"I'd prefer that you simply tell me if you have an idea that'd help."

Broussard chuckled again and unbuttoned the pocket on his shirt. He fished out a lemon ball and popped it into his mouth. "I didn't forget you," he said, pointing to the glove compartment. "In there."

The glove compartment held a cache of lemon balls individually wrapped in cellophane, his response to her unwillingness to accept naked ones from his pocket, which often came mixed with lint and other debris and which he'd touched with hands that had been God knows where. Though she already had a large collection of them in her handbag, and was just as unlikely to eat these, she took two and put them with the others.

Broussard changed lanes without looking. "You were about to tell me what you'd accomplished."

Kit brought him up-to-date and said, "And now I've got to go Guillot by Guillot through the phone book."

Broussard fell silent and his finger went to the bristly hairs on the end of his nose, a sure sign that he was working on her problem. Eventually, he glanced at her and said, "Want a suggestion?"

"I'd love one."

"I once had occasion to look through the conveyance books for some property I was thinkin' of buyin' and it seems to me that every entry included either the initials or the name of the notary involved in the sale."

"So?"

"If it was just a notary, I'd say, 'so nothin,' but the notary in a real estate deal is usually also the lawyer who drew up the papers. Wasn't that true at your closin'?"

"Who knows. Isn't that why you hire lawyers in the first place . . . so you don't have to worry about that stuff?"

Broussard clucked his tongue and shook his head as though she was a real sad case. But she was too excited by his suggestion to fight back. "So you're saying that the lawyer who handled the paperwork when Guillot bought my house might know where she is."

"And he might not. Real estate law is such a specialty that they could have met for the first time over that one deal and he never saw or heard of her again."

"Hey, this was your idea. How come now you're arguing against it?"

"I don't want you blamin' me if it doesn't pan out."

"No deal. That's the risk that comes with butting in."

They rode in comradely silence until Broussard turned into a subdivision that had been around long enough for the one tree in each yard to look like more than a stick. They followed the winding street to a modest little brick house that had been built many millions of times in this country and that she had seen at least six times since leaving the highway.

There was a motorcycle and a silver car in the carport. The vinyl roof of the car was coming off in strips, like one she had seen peeled by monkeys in a drive-through game preserve in Florida. Behind the silver car was an NOPD cruiser and, behind that, Gatlin's Pontiac. A car she recognized as belonging to Jamison, the police photographer, was parked next to the curb. Across the street, a woman with twins in a double-seated baby carriage and another woman carrying an umbrella to keep the sun off the baby strapped to her back exchanged views on what was happening.

Somehow, Broussard got out of the car and went around to the trunk for his forensic kit. They went up the driveway and down the short sidewalk to the front door, which was manned by a perspiring cop fanning himself with his hat. "Bedroom to the right," the cop said without being asked. "An' it ain't pretty."

They stepped into the living room, where a gray-haired woman sitting on a sofa against the wall to their left had her arm around a woman who was sobbing quietly into her hands. Broussard identified himself and Kit followed him hesitantly into a hallway to the right, mentally preparing herself for what she was about to see.

Her book was to be the most comprehensive ever written on suicide, and would even include the forensic details at suicide scenes. To write such details with authority, she had decided that she must see them, not just rely on Broussard's descriptions. This decision was complicated by Broussard's unwillingness to let anyone give him more than the most rudimentary details over the telephone when he was called out. Consequently, unlike this case, where suicide seemed a distinct possibility, there was usually no way to tell in advance whether she should accompany him. She just had to go along and take the useless along with the useful.

In these many trips, she had seen things that most people experience only through nightmares or Hollywood special effects. Despite her burgeoning experience with the dreadful, she had emotionally remained a novice, unable to adapt or accept these things as everyday events. It was therefore not surprising that when she got her first look at the body, she froze.

Dressed only in cutoff denims, he was almost kneeling, his body suspended from a rope tied to a chinning bar resting on crudely notched two-by-four supports. His swollen face was the color of a nearly ripe grape and his eyes were turgid and amphibious. For an instant, she was puzzled by the dark object between his lips, then realized it was his tongue. Pale over most of his body, his limp arms were also grape-colored from his elbows to the tips of his fingers, as were his legs from the knees down. It was the first hanging she had ever seen, but even if she had seen others, there was a twist to this one, for his fly was unzipped and there were pictures of nude women spread out on the carpet in front of him.

The room disappeared in the light from a camera flash, snapping Kit out of her hypnotic fixation on the body and making her aware that the buzzing in her ears was Phil Gatlin talking to Broussard. "Ambulance team took one look at him and left. Didn't even bother cutting him down."

Jamison, the police photographer, circled the pictures on the floor and got off another shot before Kit thought to look away. When her vision returned, she saw Phil Gatlin put on a pair of white gloves and gather up the pictures on the floor. With his path cleared, Broussard stepped up to the body and tried to lift its right arm, which resisted his efforts.

"I'm through, so I'm gone," Jamison said, grabbing up his equipment bag from a chest of drawers.

Kit stepped inside the small room. As Jamison passed, he winked at her and said, "Y'all have fun."

Gatlin acknowledged her presence with a faint nod.

"He's been here awhile," Broussard said. "When was he last seen alive?"

"Yesterday morning," Gatlin replied. "His mother's a rep for a local dress manufacturer. After they had breakfast together yesterday around eight, she left on an overnight sales trip. When she got back an hour ago, this is what she found. She said that thirty miles before hitting the city limits, she got the distinct feeling her son was in trouble. What do you make of that?"

"Good instincts," Broussard said. "Just bad timin'. I take it there was no note."

"Were you expecting one?"

"Doesn't hurt to ask. It's an accident, of course."

"That's what I thought," Gatlin said. "But I figured you ought to have a look."

Broussard motioned Kit over. "This is a classic case of sexual asphyxia, not a suicide. In some circles, it's thought that partial asphyxiation heightens the pleasure of orgasm. This washcloth"—he pointed to something Kit had not noticed, a folded washcloth between the rope and the deep groove in the victim's neck—"shows that he never intended to harm himself. The pictures were for stimulation.

"The hidden hook here is that even though it's relatively loose, the ligature obstructs venous return from the brain, which is mediated by vessels that lie so near the surface of the neck they can be compressed by even slight pressure. So, even though the arteries lie deeper and are not affected by the ligature, circulation to the brain is still impeded. The victim loses consciousness, the noose takes his full weight, and he dies. Been more than one fooled into thinkin' somethin' like this was a suicide. Might be good to have a section on these cases in your book." He looked at Gatlin. "Let's get him down."

Gatlin's lined face twisted into a scowl. "Let the boys in the wagon do it."

Broussard looked at Gatlin over the rims of his glasses. "If it was *your* son, would you let him hang till then?"

"Turn the screw, why don't you?" Gatlin said. "Just a minute."

He got a towel from the bathroom, went behind the chinning bar, and wrapped his arms and the towel around the body. He lifted and Broussard cut the noose free at the front of the victim's neck with a pair of chrome surgical scissors from his bag. Broussard then moved the bar out of the way and picked the body up by the ankles. "Let's put him on the bed."

When the body was on the bed, Broussard went back to the bar and tied the cut ends of the noose together with a piece of wire from his bag and slipped the rope off the bar. Gatlin put the rope in a large Baggie while Broussard went into the bathroom and washed his hands.

"Why keep the rope if it's an accident?" Kit asked.

"Because you can look stupid if you throw it away and something fishy crops up in the autopsy," Gatlin said.

"Phillip, you gonna stick around till the wagon comes?" Broussard asked from the doorway.

"No. I've got an appointment back in town. The uniform outside can handle it."

On the way out, Kit glanced at the victim's mother, who was now clinging to the other woman in such despair that Kit wished she had paid more attention to those lectures on grief therapy. Outside, the hot sun had shrunk the grass into thin spines, but Kit was so glad to be out of that house, she didn't mind the heat. The cop who had been at the front door was sitting in his cool cruiser with the motor running.

On their way out of the subdivision, Broussard said, "Would you do somethin' for me?"

"Sure, what?"

"Just so our records'll be complete, I'd like you to draw up a short report on that kid's mental state the last couple a days. Nothin' extensive ... whenever you have the time. Right now, I'm gonna show you where to get the best quiche in New Orleans."

At a pleasant little restaurant with pink tablecloths and a small bouquet of fresh flowers on each table, Broussard attacked his quiche with gusto. Still haunted by the awful image and tawdry circumstances of the hanging she'd seen less than a half hour ago, Kit could do no more than pick at her food.

Aware that their absence would be questioned by the proprietor where they usually ate lunch, Broussard paused between bites and said, "I'm gonna let you tell Grandma O why we weren't there today."

Grandma O. Yikes. Kit looked at her watch.

"What's the matter?" Broussard asked, his fork poised at his lips.

"I've got to meet someone at Grandma O's at two and it's already quarter past one."

Broussard signaled for the check and Kit was off to meet Lily Lacaze.

SEVEN

A QUICK STOP at an ATM to get the fifty dollars she had
promised Lacaze and Kit walked through the door of
Grandma O's with three minutes to spare. Always packed
from 11:10 to 1:45, the place was now nearly empty, the
only customers a touristy-looking couple in Rockport
walking shoes who were poring over a map. Never one to
relax, Grandma O was up on a stepladder behind the bar,
using a Dustbuster to vacuum the stuffed armadillos and
nutrias on the ledge above the mirror. When she saw Kit,
she turned off the Dustbuster and came down, her flared
black taffeta dress catching on the ladder, the bar, and her
stock of liquor. She patted and pushed her dress back where
it belonged and came from behind the bar, her huge hips
and the dress claiming a considerable proportion of the
restaurant's floor space.

"You takin' lunch kinda late today," she said. "An'
where's city boy?" "City boy" was what she called Broussard.

"We sort of had lunch already," Kit said. Grandma O's
black eyes flashed. "We were out on a case and it got so
late..."

"An' how was it?" Grandma O said, her thinly penciled
brows raised in warning.

Well aware that she wasn't asking about the case, Kit
said, "Compared with your cooking...no contest."

Grandma O's lips spread in a wide grin, the light flashing off the gold star inlay in her front tooth. She laughed,
a cackle that made the tourists look up from their map.

"So Ah guess now you want some *real* food?"

"Actually, I've arranged to meet someone here...if that's all right."

"Course it is. You welcome here anytime. Ah'm surprised you didn' know dat. Go on back to your table and Ah'll get you a glass of iced tea. You boun' to have a need for some tea, hot as it is out dere."

While Grandma O rustled off to get the tea, Kit threaded her way through the restaurant's round marble-topped tables to one that was larger than the rest. She took the seat next to the wall so that she could keep her eye on the door. Seconds later, a skinny woman wearing white clamdiggers, a wrinkled white blouse, and Dr. Scholl's clogs came in. She took a quick look around and headed for the big table.

"I'm Lacaze," she said in a rattly voice Kit recognized from their phone conversation.

She had peculiar coppery blotches on her neck and wore a reddish purple lipstick that looked as though it would glow in the dark. Hair curlers poked at the dirty pink scarf on her head. What at first appeared to be a birthmark on her right cheek Kit now saw was a small tattoo of a daisy.

"One of those things that don't seem like such a good idea the next mornin'," Lacaze said, reading Kit's mind. She pulled out a chair, sat down, and plopped a black clutch bag on the table. "You got the fifty?" she said, reaching into her bag.

"Yes."

Lacaze brought out a box of thin little cigars and put one in her mouth. She lit it with a plastic lighter, blew some smoke at the ceiling, then took the cigar out of her mouth and picked some tobacco off her tongue. "I ain't seein' any green."

"You show me yours and I'll show you mine," Kit said.

Lacaze studied Kit for a few seconds through shallow, vacant eyes that looked as though their fuse had blown. She produced a narrow strip of photographs from her bag and flipped them onto the table. Kit picked them up.

They were bus station snapshots of two women mugging for the camera—one of them a startlingly young Lily Lacaze sans tattoo and the other clearly the face in French's reconstruction. Kit looked for a date on the back but found none.

"Ain't that her?" Lacaze said self-importantly, blowing smoke at the ceiling.

Grandma O rustled out of the kitchen and put Kit's iced tea in front of her. She looked at Lacaze. "Anything Ah can get for you?"

"That bar there just for looks?"

Grandma O did not believe that the customer was always right but, rather, judged the correctness of a customer's position on an issue by how closely it reflected her own. Nor was she partial to wiseacres. Kit was therefore not surprised when Grandma O puffed up like a toad and said, "Ain't nothin' in here jus' for looks."

"A Bloody Mary, then," Lacaze said. "You know how to make one?"

Grandma O seemed to grow even larger. "Ah'll jus' muddle through an' if Ah get it wrong, you be sure an' tell me."

Lacaze watched Grandma O rustle over to the bar. She blew more smoke at the ceiling and looked at Kit. "What's with her, she can't act civil toward somebody? You satisfied with the picture?"

"Yes. What can you tell me about her?"

Lacaze put out her hand. Kit got two twenties and a ten out of her purse and put them in Lacaze's palm. "Francie O'Connor was what she called herself," Lacaze said, tucking the bills into her bag. "But I never saw no proof that was her real name. Wouldn't say where she was from, but sometimes she'd buy a Dallas newspaper, so you figure it out."

"Was she on the street . . . a hooker?"

Lacaze's eyes narrowed. "You probably think there's somethin' wrong with that. Only difference between girls on the street and you starchy little suburbanites is that workin' girls know what it's worth. They don't give it away." She wrinkled her nose. "Damn, I'm gettin' blocked up again."

She fished a tube of Preparation H out of her bag, squeezed some onto her little finger, and thrust it up one nostril, a trick Kit recognized as one druggies use to heal the damage cocaine does to their nasal lining. Lacaze repeated the procedure on the other nostril and put the tube back in her bag. "Only thing that works," she said. "All that spray and shit just makes it worse."

Grandma O brought the Bloody Mary and left it without comment.

"Here's to suburbia," Lacaze said, raising her glass. She took a long pull at her drink and another drag on her cigar.

"Francie O'Connor . . ." Kit said, nudging Lacaze back to the subject.

"Yeah, Francie worked the streets, but she didn't let it harden her. You take a lot of girls, they hit the bricks, they get—what's the word?—cyn—"

"Cynical?"

"What's the matter, you couldn't wait for a person to get it themselves? Yeah, cynical. But Francie didn't. She was always real upbeat, like she thought she had a future or somethin'. Then one night, she just up and vanished. I seen her about eleven o'clock at Royal and St. Anne. We shot the shit for a while and then split up. I never saw her again.

Her landlady said she never even came back for her clothes.''

"If you were her friend, why didn't you go to the police?''

"Me and the cops never exactly been on speakin' terms. An' it wasn't like this was anything real unusual. I knew lotsa girls who were there one day and gone the next. Some bum sweet-talks 'em into goin' off to New York or L.A., they split. Thing is, on the street, somewhere else always sounds better'n where you are.''

"But how many others left their clothes behind?''

"Mor'n you'd think.''

"But Francie didn't leave town..."

"No she didn't... poor kid. You know what she liked mor'n anything? Mardi Gras. Girl was nuts for parades or a band. If there wasn't nothin' but a horse left in a parade, she'd stand there till it passed. Had a dream that someday she'd ride on one of those floats. Instead, she got killed. I don't guess there's any Mardi Gras where she's been.''

"Did Francie have any enemies?''

"Who doesn't? But none that ever threatened her, if that's what you mean.''

"How about a pimp, mad at her for something... wanting to teach her a lesson?''

Lacaze shook her head. "Back then, it was all right to free-lance. There was so much business, nobody worried about new talent cuttin' them out.''

"Did she have any regular customers?''

Lacaze downed half of her remaining Bloody Mary and blotted her mouth with a napkin. "She didn't want regulars... preferred to do it all anonymously.''

"So whoever killed her likely just pulled up at the curb, she got in, and that was it?''

"Like I said, anonymously. Whoever killed her, she probably had never seen 'em before." Lacaze finished her drink and took another drag on her cigar.

"When did Francie disappear?"

"Early sixties, like I said on the phone."

"Could you be more specific?"

"Not about somethin' happened that long ago."

"Can you give me the name of anyone else that I might talk to about her?"

Lacaze shook her head again. "Look, I gotta go. I'd like to help more, but I'm dry. Thanks for the fifty. Hope you catch the shit that did it. See you." Lacaze got up and started to leave, then paused. "What will they do with her...what's left of her? Will there be a funeral or anything?"

The question caught Kit by surprise. It was something that had not crossed her mind. "I don't really know."

Lacaze nodded. "I probably wouldn't go, anyway."

Kit watched Lacaze clomp out the door, then picked up the strip of pictures and studied them. She had hoped that Lacaze would give her a few leads, point her toward some other contacts. That hadn't happened, but she had gotten a little insight into the victim, some photographs of her, and her name. That was worth fifty bucks. Francie was now not only more real to Kit but would no longer have to face eternity as anonymously as she had lived.

"Somethin' wrong with your tea?" Grandma O said ominously.

If you didn't finish what Grandma O served, you had to have a good reason. Rather than try to explain, Kit simply picked up the glass and drained it.

"Hope Ah wasn' too tough on your friend," Grandma O said. "Ah tried to hold back."

"She wasn't a friend, just somebody I wanted information from."

"Sure wish Ah'da known dat," Grandma O said, staring wistfully at the door.

Upon her return to the hospital, Kit called the conveyance office and coaxed the woman she'd met there to look up the name of the notary involved in the sale of her house to Shirley Guillot. The woman returned with the name Harry Isom. Kit gushed her thanks, hung up, and flipped to the attorneys in the Yellow Pages, hoping that Harry Isom was still alive.

She found a listing for the firm of Isom and Loscovitz and learned from their secretary that the senior partner was indeed named Harry and that he specialized in real estate law. But unfortunately, he was out of town for a few days. Kit left her name and number with a request for Isom to call her when he returned.

KIT SAW THE HANGED teenager again as he was the moment she had first laid eyes on him. In his bed, Francie O'Connor and Leslie Music lay with the covers tucked under their chins, their lifeless eyes staring at the ceiling. Lily Lacaze was there as well, taking pictures with a camera that spit out strips of bus station photos.

Kit moaned and rolled over. Beside the bed, Lucky's ears lifted and his eyes opened in alarm. Kit moaned again and Lucky jumped onto the bed. With his paw, he nudged her shoulder until she woke and put her arm around him.

"It's okay, varmint," she said sleepily. "I was just having a dream. Everything is fine."

Outside, a car slowed in front of Kit's house, its driver staring at her front door, the third time he had been past in the last half hour. It was a fruitless activity, stupid even, but he was so empty and cold inside, and so afraid, that he could not help himself.

THE NEXT MORNING, while Kit was opening a can of Alpo beef chunks for Lucky, she knocked a fork off the counter into the space between the counter and fridge. Bending down to get it, she saw the pill that Lucky had failed to swallow.

"Why you sneaky little monster." She turned and saw Lucky hauling his little brown behind through the crack in the kitchen door as fast as he could go.

Since the direct approach had failed, Kit decided this time to be sneaky herself. With a steak knife she cut a small slot in a beef chunk and slipped Lucky's pill inside. She hid the doctored morsel under some others and went to get him.

He attacked his food without hesitation, proving that humans are far smarter than even the cleverest little dog. While Lucky ate, Kit went into the bathroom and made a few adjustments to the combs in her hair and put on some lip gloss, thinking how glad she was that it was Friday. Just one more day until she would see . . .

Her thoughts were interrupted by the sound of the telephone. She hurried into the hall and picked up the receiver.

"Just read the article in yesterday's paper," a familiar voice said. "And I thought you might need some moral support."

"Teddy. I was just thinking about you."

"I'm surprised you can think of anything but that skeleton."

"It was a shock at first, but I'm handling it okay now," Kit said, seeing no point in telling him how rocky she still felt.

"Get any leads from the story?"

"A small one, but it didn't go far."

"We still on for tomorrow?"

"Of course. How was your trip?"

"I think I accomplished something. I'm just sorry I wasn't with you Saturday."

"You can make it up to me tomorrow."

"I'll certainly try. See you then. Take care."

WITH HARRY ISOM out of town and several hundred Guillots waiting for her in the phone book, Kit decided to work on the hanging case from the day before. From the victim's mother, she got the names of some of his friends and spent the morning tracking them down. By noon, she felt she had all she needed. By 2:30, her report was finished and she went to Broussard's office to deliver it.

When she opened Broussard's door, she found Charlie Franks, the lanky deputy medical examiner, sitting on the edge of the table that held Broussard's microscope, his long arms folded over his chest. Ordinarily a man who seemed never to have a bad day, Franks looked as though the odds had finally caught up with him.

"So if it could happen to Babe Ruth," Broussard said to Franks, "it could happen to anyone."

A Babe Ruth story.

Incredibly, Franks was getting a Babe Ruth story, something Broussard dispensed only when someone had really screwed up and he was trying to make them feel better. Having been Ruthed on two occasions herself, she knew exactly how Franks felt.

"Sorry to interrupt," she said.

"It's okay," Broussard replied. "Charlie was just leavin'."

On his way out, Franks waved a couple of fingers limply at Kit and mumbled something she couldn't understand.

Broussard shifted the lemon ball in his mouth from one cheek to the other and rocked back in his chair, his hands folded over his belly. "What's up?"

"Here's the report on that sexual asphyxia case." She dropped the folder on the desk. "There's no evidence that he was suicidal."

"How'd your meeting go yesterday?"

"My meeting yesterday...not too bad. I found someone that knew the victim. Her name was Francie O'Connor and you were right, she was a prostitute. I also got some pictures of her." Kit dug in her handbag and handed the photos to Broussard.

"French came pretty close, didn't she?" he said, looking at them.

"Very close."

"Who's the other girl?"

"The one who gave me the pictures. She's changed some since they were taken."

"Haven't we all."

"Unfortunately, she couldn't or wouldn't steer me to anyone else who knew Francie."

"You check on the real estate notary?"

"Got a name, but he's out of town for a few days. I was wondering...what will happen to Francie's remains... after this is all over?"

"Anthropologists love to dig things up, but they hate to bury 'em. If no relative comes forward to arrange burial, Victoria'll just keep 'em."

"Why?"

Broussard shrugged. "It's evidence. Even when a case appears to be closed, sometimes later, questions pop up...."

"That seems sad...to keep her on a shelf."

"Believe me, Victoria'll take good care of her...better than the parish would if she was sent to potter's field. To change the subject, you think your appetite'll be better Monday night than it was yesterday at lunch?''

"Why?''

"Before Charlie came in, I had a conference call with the other five members of my gourmet club and they wanted me to invite you to our annual dinner this Monday at my place. We always invite someone who's been in the news recently, to liven up the conversation.''

"Was inviting me your idea?''

"Actually, no. Someone else mentioned your name and the others, includin' me, agreed.''

"How nice.''

"The short notice doesn't tell you anything?''

"What do you mean?''

"Nothin'. Forget it.''

"Fat chance. Give.''

"Our first choice canceled this mornin'.''

"So I'm a substitute?''

Broussard nodded. "Sad but true. Does it matter?''

Kit considered the question briefly and said, "When I was a kid, we used to have a minister back home that liked to say he wanted to be the last one through those pearly gates. And when people would ask, 'Why would you want to be the last one, reverend?' He'd say, 'Because then I'd be *in*.' I didn't agree with everything he said, but that always made sense to me. I'll be there.''

BACK IN HER OFFICE, Kit turned to the Guillots in the phone book, stared at all the listings for a minute, then began at the top: Aaron Guillot, 728 . . . Thirty Guillots later, she put the receiver back in its cradle and let her ear cool off. Thirty calls—only five people home, an expected yet discouraging result.

While she reflected on whether there was any point in continuing, the phone rang.

"Kit Franklyn."

There was no answer.

"Hello. This is Kit Franklyn. Anyone there?"

"Yes...I'm here," a male voice said hesitantly. Another pause.

"What can I do for you?" Kit said.

"I...know something...and I think..." Another pause.

"Yes. You think..."

"I think...we need...we should talk."

"Is this about the picture in the paper?"

"Yes."

"You know something about the case?"

"Yes."

"You knew the girl?"

"Not exactly. I was..." Another long pause.

"You were...?"

"I was there...when she...died."

"When was this?" Kit said.

"I'd rather...I don't want to get into any details like that yet...."

"But I have to know if your information is accurate."

There was a long pause, then he said, "It was...more than twenty years ago, and...she liked Mardi Gras."

Mardi Gras. Kit's heart climbed into her throat. Lacaze had said that about Francie O'Connor. This was definitely the genuine article. But he was nervous and not sure that making this call was the right decision. She felt that she had to be careful, bring him along slowly, or she'd lose him.

"So this has been on your mind for a long time..." Kit said.

"Yes. A very long time."

"And you would like to tell someone about what happened."

"I want to... but I'm not sure... it's..."

Kit felt as if she was trying to edge up on a wild deer with a bunch of grass in her hand. One wrong move... "I can help you. We can talk and afterward you'll feel better."

"I want to... but maybe it's not... wise."

"No. It *is* wise. You're doing the right thing."

"No. I'm sure I can't... shouldn't. I've got to go."

"Wait. Wait. We don't—"

Click. Mocking silence filled the receiver.

She had blown it. Disgusted at her ineptitude, she slammed the receiver down. "Damn."

He had been practically in her hands and she'd let him get away. Franks couldn't have deserved a Babe Ruth story any more than she did right now.

EIGHT

KIT PICKED UP Lucky's bowl to wash it and groaned at what she saw. In it was the pill she had hidden in his food the previous morning. She looked at Lucky and wagged her finger. "Why won't you *cooperate?*" He sat down on his haunches and hung his head, looking so guilty, she had to laugh. Reflecting on it, she realized that it had been two weeks to the day since she had felt this cheerful, and there was no doubt about the reason. It was the expectation of seeing Teddy.

In the newspaper story accompanying French's reconstruction of Francie O'Connor's face, Kit had indicated that the phone number listed for her could be called even on weekends. Before leaving the hospital on Friday, she initiated call forwarding on her office phone so all calls that came in over the weekend would be automatically transferred to her home. Now, with Teddy's arrival imminent, her mood was so upbeat that she believed the mystery caller from the previous day might try again. So rosy was her outlook that she half-believed he might even leave his number on her answering machine if she was out when he called.

She dried Lucky's bowl with a paper towel and shifted her thoughts to the dog's unwillingness to take his pill. This could not be allowed to continue. But what was the answer?

Ahhh.

She put some beef in the bowl, then folded one of the pills in a kitchen towel. With the heavy handle of a case knife, she pounded the pill almost into a powder and mixed it with the food.

"Breakfast, you little twerp," she sang, putting the bowl on the floor. Lucky ran to the bowl and sniffed it suspiciously. He circled it and sniffed some more. Then he dropped to his belly, his chin resting sadly on the linoleum.

The doorbell. Teddy.

She hurried to the door and opened it. A strong arm went around her waist and she was enveloped in a delicious cologne. Lips pressed against her. She returned the kiss.

Releasing her, Teddy said, "Does this mean you *will* buy an upholstery steamer from me?"

"I don't do upholstery," Kit said, pulling Teddy inside by the front of his shirt. "But upholstery steamer *salesmen* . . . that's a different matter."

Teddy had two major trademarks: a great cologne and his stylish straw hat with a black band. Though he belonged to a sex that thinks nothing of blowing their nose at the table and believes a belch is a creative achievement, Teddy wouldn't even wear his hat inside. His features were fine and delicate, like expensive porcelain, and he always looked as though he had just come from the barber. Kit often thought of him as appearing newly minted . . . uncirculated. He was dressed casually—short-sleeved pale blue shirt of brushed oxford cloth, jeans that showed his slim hips, alligator skin belt and boots. In the hand opposite the one he'd hugged her with, he was carrying a suit, shirt, and tie on a hanger.

"Why's all the furniture in the hall?" Teddy asked.

"Had the living room floor refinished last week. Could we put it all back before we go out?"

"How about right now?"

Kit took his suit to her bedroom closet and came back to the hall. As they carried the carpet into the living room, Teddy said, "I've been thinking about this case you're working on...the skeleton...I hope you're being careful."

"Careful? How do you mean?"

They set the carpet down. "Like keeping in mind that whoever did it is probably getting very nervous."

"That's what I'm counting on."

"Nervous may not be a problem, but nervous could lead to desperate. And when animals get desperate, even the meekest will turn and fight."

"I'll keep that in mind."

"I hope so."

When the furniture was all in place, Teddy looked at Kit with a puzzled expression. "Where's Lucky?"

"In the kitchen. He's not very happy, I'm afraid."

Teddy followed Kit to the kitchen, where Lucky was still sprawled forlornly in front of his bowl.

"He won't take his new heartworm pills, so I ground one up and put it in his food. He liked the other pills, but not these new ones."

"Bet I can get one down him. Where are they?"

Kit gave Teddy the pills and he tapped one into his hand.

"It won't work," she warned.

"I've been around dogs all my life," Teddy said. "If I can't pill him, I'll take the pill myself."

Teddy pulled Lucky into his lap, forced the dog's mouth open, and chucked the pill into his throat.

Lucky blinked and swallowed.

Teddy let him go and capped the pills. "All in the wrist," he gloated, handing them to Kit.

Lucky made a faint metallic sound. His head bobbed and he opened his mouth. The pill plinked onto the floor.

Teddy looked at Kit and shrugged. "A deal's a deal." He got a glass from the cupboard, filled it with water, and picked the pill off the floor. The hand with the pill flew to his mouth. He followed it with a long drink, then rolled his eyes. "Not bad. What did you say was in them?"

"Estrogen," Kit said, going to him and prying his hand open. In it was the pill. "Guess I'll have to grind it up and put it in *your* food," she said, kissing him.

"How about letting both of us off the hook and just get Lucky his old pills."

"Agreed," Kit said, wondering why *she* hadn't thought of that.

While Kit got Lucky some fresh food, Teddy looked out the window over the sink. "That hole where they found her... it's still out there?"

"Yeah."

"Want me to fill it in?"

Kit had not set foot in the backyard since the day the skeleton had been found. But she had looked out the window many times at the pile of dirt that French and Allen had left behind. She had expected that Allen would fill in the pit when he came back to screen the dirt from the pedestal, but he hadn't. Surprised, she had mentioned this to Broussard and learned that anthropologists always leave the filling in to others. He had not been very clear on who the "others" might be. At first, she had wanted the pit filled, wanted to forget that it had ever existed. But that was before she had seen how much the victim had resembled Leslie. Now, it was more than a pile of dirt. It had become a symbol of something unfinished, a dept unpaid. "No thanks," she said. "I'd like to leave it as it is for a while. What are we doing today?"

"How about the zoo?"

"Great. I haven't been there in years." Kit gave Lucky his food, then went to the closet and got the large-brimmed straw hat she had bought in anticipation of doing some gardening in her new backyard. "If you're ready, I am."

Teddy drove a shiny red pickup with a cartoon picture of a baby alligator emerging from an egg on each door. Under the pictures were the words BAYOU COTEAU ALLIGATOR FARM. Having long ago wrestled with and reconciled her self-image and the truck, Kit climbed in with no misgivings.

Teddy took St. Charles to Jefferson and crossed over to Magazine. The zoo was not more than a mile and a half away, sitting between Magazine Street and the Mississippi River, at one end of Audubon Park. Once an embarrassment to the city and a liability to the upscale neighborhood surrounding it, the zoo was now a respected equal to the best the city had to offer.

Teddy turned into the drive leading to the zoo's parking lot. On the grassy plot next to the drive, they saw a group of old folks standing on the grass, their arms out in front of them, heads thrown back, mouths open, eyes closed. Leading them was a much younger male Oriental.

"What are *they* doing?" Kit asked.

"Extremely low-impact aerobics," Teddy replied, entering the parking lot.

It was still early and the heat and the crowd were still well below the day's predicted maxima. As in other cities, the Audubon Park zoo had replaced the cramped cages of less enlightened times with natural habitats enclosed by moats and simulated rock walls. Teddy paid the entrance fee and they began at the Asian Domain, following an elevated walkway made of logs and planking to the first exhibit—the bears, all of whom appeared to be asleep. The crowd was not only relatively small in number but was also very small in stature, with noisy children careening from rail to rail and occasionally off Kit's legs.

Children, Kit thought. Something Leslie Music and Francie O'Connor never got a chance to experience. Something that maybe Kit Franklyn should be thinking harder about.

A mother put her son on the step in front of the plaque for the bear exhibit and pulled his hand to the brass bear claws projecting from the plane of the plaque.

"That's how they dig for honey," the mother said.

Expecting now that the plaques for every exhibit would have a touchie-feelie associated with them, the boy ran to the cranes and climbed onto the step in front of that plaque. He proceeded to rub his fingers in a big dollop of bird droppings left by a mockingbird a few minutes earlier.

"A story his mother can tell at his presidential inauguration," Teddy whispered.

Watching his mother search vainly in her purse for something to wipe the boy's hands, Kit pulled a tissue from her own bag, went to the boy, and cleaned his fingers. Apparently offended for some reason at Kit's kindness, the mother grabbed the child by his clean hand and pulled him to the next exhibit.

"I didn't know you liked kids," Teddy said.

"Neither did I."

It was too lovely a day to dwell on anything negative, so Kit put a cap on the pit where those gremlins dwell and let herself enjoy the animals.

After finishing the Asian Domain, they wandered over to the Mombasa Depot Café, a concession stand that made no attempt to look Mombasa, where they each had a DoveBar.

Wondering where to go next, they were drawn to the World of Primates by a series of shrill hoots that sounded like something worth seeing. The dozen or so excited animals they expected to find turned out to be a pair of siamangs, large black primates perched in the top of a dead tree that the keepers had provided. Up close, their cries were unbelievably loud and clear, the power apparently coming from the volleyball-sized sacs under their chins.

According to their plaque, the vocalizations were meant to drive away intruders. In this case, the main intruder was a potbellied guy in a sleeveless undershirt, yellow Bermuda shorts, sandals, and black socks. The guy was egging the animals on by hooting back to them and waving his fist.

In response, the siamangs shook their tree and hooted madly in return. With each exchange, their war escalated. When the animals couldn't shake their tree any harder or hoot any louder, one of them left his perch and scurried to the ground.

Kit jumped at the feel of a hand on her arm.

"You two had better come over here," a voice said. "Hurry."

It was someone Kit knew. "Adrian. What..."

"Hurry now."

Teddy and Kit joined the man behind a stand of bamboo that shielded them from the siamangs' view. Kit tried to speak, but the man pointed behind them.

They turned and saw a projectile of monkey feces fly through the air and splatter against the hooting man's undershirt, some of the scatter hitting people around him. Women screamed and the crowd ran for safety, all except the hooting man, who was so dazed, he took another hit before wandering out of range.

"Thanks for the warning," Teddy said.

"Teddy, this is Adrian Iverson, president of our local Rose Society. Adrian, Teddy LaBiche, a friend from Bayou Coteau."

Teddy and Iverson exchanged a handshake.

"How did you know that was going to happen?" Kit asked.

"I'm on the zoo's board, so I come here a lot to see how things are going," Iverson said. "And I've seen those rascals do the same thing before. I've mentioned it to the director, but apparently he hasn't gotten a warning sign made yet."

Iverson was in his late fifties. He was tall, with thinning brown hair that formed a prominent widow's peak on his modestly freckled scalp. Punctuated by a nose already beginning to cauliflower, his long face was bracketed by a pair of large ears. There was a chevron of three deep lines on his forehead and a dark crease under each puffy eye. Dressed in a tan linen suit, pale blue shirt, and a cream tie with large blue dots, he was proof that style and manner more than compensate for physical imperfection. Though he never did, Kit always expected him to speak with an English accent.

"Fortuitous running into you this way," Iverson said to Kit, "because I was going to give you a call later."

"What about?"

"The Louisiana Rose Society is sponsoring a contest to find the most fragrant new rose and I was wondering whether you would be willing to come over and give me your opinion on some hybrids I've developed."

"Of course. Be glad to help."

"Would tomorrow be convenient . . . say around two o'clock? Mr. LaBiche, of course you're welcome, as well."

"Thanks," Teddy said, "but I have to leave in the morning."

"Two would be fine, Adrian," Kit said. "Where do you live?"

"Off Sabine Road, about a mile from its intersection with highway ninety. It'll be easy to find. There's not much else around."

"Two it is, then."

At the exit to the primates, Iverson excused himself and went off in the direction of the birdhouse. Kit and Teddy went in the opposite direction.

"Nice fellow," Teddy said.

"He sort of put me on the spot."

"How?"

"I've been advising one of his competitors on *his* hybrids for the same contest."

"Doesn't matter, as long as you don't tell either one how you think the other's doing."

"Sounds right."

"Look at this," Teddy said, walking up to the rail of an exhibit of black humpbacked creatures with yellow tusks that curved upward from their lower jaw to rest alongside an ugly snout. "Russian boars. One of the meanest, most fearless animals on earth. If you've got a death wish, you hunt old *Sus scrofa* with a bow and arrow."

"What makes him so dangerous, those tusks?"

"That's a big part of it. They get you down, they can rip you open with them. But their hooves are sharp, too, and they like to stamp on your face. And they die hard. In Europe, when they used to hunt them with lances from horseback, they had to put a stop on the lance to keep the boar from running up the lance and gutting the horse. But more than his physical equipment, he has a dangerous mind. Experienced boar hunters all know that a boar will come for you."

"Come for you?"

"Stalk you while you stalk him. Want to go boar hunting sometime?"

"Sure, but I have to bungee-jump off the World Trade Center first."

Instead of bypassing the Louisiana swamp exhibit, as Kit thought Teddy would, he pulled her through the entrance, saying, "There's something in here I want to show you."

Deep in the exhibit, which consisted of a raised wood walkway wandering through a re-created swamp, they stopped at a glass tank containing what appeared to be two white rubber alligators about four feet long, floating motionless, with only the upper half of their heads out of the water. Kit leaned closer and looked at their eyes.

"They're not real, are they?"

"Sure they are."

She looked again. "I don't think so."

Teddy made an odd clunking sound in his throat and the two alligators began swimming hard, pressing against the glass with their noses.

"Another fellow and I are the ones that found them," Teddy said. "We actually found four. I think the other two are in the aquarium on Canal. At least I hope so. Hate to think anything happened to them. Possession of a white alligator is considered good luck."

"Then why did you give them away?"

Teddy shrugged. "We found them a short while after we first met and I figured that I already had all the good luck anybody deserved."

AN OLD GRAY-BEARDED black man weighted down with most of what he owned and accompanied by a black Labrador stepped into the recessed frontage of a dress shop. He put down his load and spread out a blanket for the dog to lie on. When the dog was stretched out and comfortable, the old man unfolded the chair he'd brought and settled in himself, a keyboard in his lap, a trumpet close at hand. In the shop behind him, a blond woman straightened the necklace on a mannequin in the window and came outside, locking the door behind her. She spoke a word to the old man and stroked the dog's head before hurrying off down the street. A few feet away at a table for two in the window of the Royal Orleans Rib Room, Kit's eyes were on Teddy.

"Today was nice," she said.

"For me, too," Teddy replied.

"I liked your alligator story."

"One of the few you haven't heard before."

"But the best."

"Really? I kind of like the one where the alligator bites down on a metal rod so hard, he drives two teeth through the top of his skull."

"That's good, but it's not in the same league with the white alligators."

"Well, what I said was true and it makes me worry about this case you're working on. You should think about carrying a gun. It wouldn't have to be a Dirty Harry model. There are nice little discreet bangers powerful enough to stop an alligator. Get one of those. I could teach you how to use it or you could go to the police firing range. I'm sure they could provide some instruction."

Kit wrinkled her nose. "I'm not a gun person. Besides, I'm not serving warrants or making arrests. I'm just turning over stones."

"Sometimes stones have snakes under them."

"Considering how long ago this murder happened, this snake probably hasn't got any teeth left."

"I don't even want one gumming you."

Kit's attention was taken by a couple being seated across the room, a distinguished-looking man with streaks of gray in his hair and an elegant blonde in a pink silk jacket over a sequinned ivory shell and an ivory skirt with a tulip hem. Kit probably wouldn't have given them more than passing notice if the blonde hadn't been Victoria French.

As French sat down, she saw Kit and waved. Kit waved back. The sight of French gave the cap on Kit's gremlin pit a hefty shove and the creatures inside worked at the resulting opening all through dinner.

Hours later, with Lucky shut in the kitchen and Teddy's heart beating against Kit's naked breasts, the gremlins made their escape. Sex with Teddy was always a storm of white pleasure whose furious winds blew away all thought and worry, a tempest that turned flesh and sinew to quicksilver. But tonight, the winds blew weakly and there was no magic.

Realizing that something was wrong, Teddy raised his head and looked at her. Seeing that her eyes were open, he lifted off her and dropped onto his back, breathing hard. "Have I done something wrong?"

Kit turned on her side and bunched her pillow under her head so she could see Teddy's face. She put her hand on his chest and lightly stroked the soft hairs there.

"Where is this going?" she said. "Where are *we* going?"

Teddy turned his head to look at her. "Does every ship have to have a destination?"

"I used to think it didn't, but now I'm not so sure."

"Why the concern all of a sudden?"

"I don't know exactly... things I've seen, things I think about... the future... what it will be like."

"What I said when you asked me why I gave the white alligators away... I meant that."

"Then it seems that there should be more to our relationship."

"Maybe there will be . . . eventually."

"I'm not sure that's enough."

Teddy rose up and sat for a moment on the edge of the bed, his back to her. Kit sat up and pulled the covers to her chest. Teddy turned to her. "Didn't you once tell me you broke off with what's his name—David . . . somebody— because he was pressuring you into commitments you weren't ready to make?"

"That was then and this is now."

"Now you're ready?"

"I'm not sure."

"Kit, how can I respond to that? You're asking me to make a decision you haven't made yourself."

"I know."

Teddy turned and sat quietly on the edge of the bed, his hand rubbing the back of his head. Then he stood up. "I think I should go."

"That's not necessary," Kit said. "It's so late."

He reached for his shirt. "I kind of like to drive at night. And you need some time to think without me around."

Silently, Kit watched him as he finished dressing and picked his hat off the dresser. He got his suit out of the closet and draped it over his arm. "If it's okay, I'll leave my other things in the bathroom . . . just in case. When you get this worked out in your mind, call me. I guess . . ."

"What?"

"I guess I should have kept at least one of those white alligators."

Then he was gone.

As the front door shut behind him, Kit put Teddy's pillow on her knees. She pressed her face into it and muttered, "Damn."

NINE

K<small>IT</small> <small>HURRIED TO THE PHONE</small>, hoping to hear Teddy. She didn't. But the voice *was* familiar.

"Sorry to call on a Sunday... but the paper... the article said it would be all right."

The mystery caller from before, the one who said he'd been there when Francie O'Connor died. Kit pressed the phone tightly against her ear as though that might somehow make it harder for him to bolt. Her mouth was dry and her tongue was a wooden block. "I'm glad you called," she said. Rather than risk pushing too hard too fast, she decided to let him take the lead.

"When we last spoke," the mystery man said, "you thought we should talk. I think so, too... But... I can't come to... I don't want to be seen with you."

"You pick the spot, then."

There was no answer and Kit felt that she was about to lose him like last time.

"Would you be willing to... come alone and not tell anyone about this until... afterward?" the caller asked.

"Agreed."

"How do I know you're not lying?"

A reasonable question, Kit thought. And one that she had better answer convincingly. What to do? How to sound trustworthy? Staying with her earlier decision not to press, she said, "You *don't* know if I'm lying. But if this is eating at you like I think it is, the only way you're going to get relief is to take the chance."

Silence—but he was still there, obviously chewing on what she had said. Her pulse was racing and she realized that she was breathing unusually fast. She shifted the receiver so that he couldn't hear.

Click!

Her heart seemed to stop. In her mind, she saw the white flanks of a deer disappear into a dense thicket. Gone. She had lost him...*again*.

She replaced the receiver, took a deep breath, and looked at the ceiling. *Call origin*. After his first call, why hadn't she contacted the phone company and ordered call origin for her office and home phone? Then she would have had him. It wasn't a mistake she would make again. First thing Monday...

She was sitting so close to it that the sound of the phone ringing again startled her.

"You're right," the mystery caller said when she picked up and identified herself. "I'll have to take a chance. I'm tied up today until late tonight. So I guess it'll have to be tomorrow sometime."

"Why not tonight?" Kit said. She knew that she was pressing now but didn't want to give him time to change his mind. Besides, his speech pattern was not as hesitant as before, so a little aggressiveness seemed safe.

"I suppose we could," he said. Then after a short pause, he added, "Yes. That would actually be good for me ... quieter ... no one to ... yes, tonight. Come to the main entrance of the Aquarium of the Americas at twelve-thirty tonight."

"How will I know—"

He hung up.

With her mind still grappling over what to do about Teddy and now this new development, Kit was in no mood to go to Adrian Iverson's to smell roses. But she *had* promised.

Sabine Road was across the river near Waggaman, which created a distinct dilemma for Kit. The shortest route was out Jefferson highway and over the Huey P. Long Bridge. But that old bridge was so high and its two lanes in each direction so narrow that it scared the pants off her to go over it. So she never did.

The only other choice was to go downtown, use that bridge, and loop all the way around the bend in the Mississippi. It was a horribly long way to go and there would be all that construction traffic associated with the new West Bank Expressway.

Deciding that it was foolish to be so frightened of a bridge that thousands of cars used every day, she turned right on St. Charles, took another right on Louisiana, and headed for South Claiborne, which, eventually, becomes Jefferson Highway.

As she drove, she thought about her appointment at the aquarium. Had that been smart? Suppose Teddy was right. This could be one of those rocks with a snake under it. But if this *was* a setup, would the caller have acted so hesitant to meet at all? Not likely. Then, too, *she* had been the one to suggest meeting tonight. He had wanted to wait. No, everything was fine.

Ahead, a car with a bumper sticker that read YOU GET HIS FAZER, SCOTTY, I'LL GET HIS WALLET signaled for a right turn. She slowed and the Trekkie angled into the parking lot of a K & B. Fine? Sure, everything was fine—except for her love life, which was not only not fine but bordered on abysmal. Maybe she should have kept quiet last night. But Teddy had noticed that *something* was wrong. How would she have explained? A headache? He certainly would have spotted that for what it was.

And so it went until she turned onto the Huey P. entrance ramp. For the time it took to cross, there would be no extraneous thoughts, only utter concentration and a peculiar fluttering in her stomach, which was already beginning. The ground below dropped away and the road climbed toward the sky. She could see on the fringes of her concentration, toy barges plying the café au lait waters of the Mississippi far below. Thankfully, the railroad track separating inbound and outbound traffic was empty. Too cautious to speed across the bridge, Kit stayed in the slow lane, which put her on the outside, where all that separated her from empty space was a thin concrete curb and a flimsy railing.

She was nearing the highest point now and each turn of the car's wheels tightened the spring in her belly. Soon it would be all downhill and the river would be getting closer instead of farther away. Damn, but these lanes were narrow. She saw a black smear of rubber on the curb, three bars in the railing missing. Subconsciously fearing that the spot might reach for another victim as she passed, she let the car drift to the left.

The blare of a horn.

Startled, she overcompensated to the right, barely avoiding the dreaded curb but scaring the living hell out of herself. Where had *that* car come from?

She reached the West Bank drained and angry at how she had let the bridge control her.

Sabine Road ran south, into a sparsely populated, soggy forest of skinny trees with Spanish moss hanging languidly from their skeletal branches. A mile from Sabine's origin with highway 90, a driveway appeared on her right. Flanked on each side by a curved iron fence set into lush green grass, it was a welcome human sign in a landscape more suited to things with tails and fur.

She turned in and paused at the mailbox, which was set into a brick pier supporting the fence. Under the mailbox was a brass plaque that said IVERSON. Satisfied that this was the right place, she nudged the gas.

Inside, the drive was bordered by full-flowered crepe myrtles large enough to shade the azaleas planted at their bases. On each side, the gloomy forest pressed against the bright swatch that had been cut through it, patiently waiting, it seemed, for Iverson's lawn mower to throw a rod and his weed eater to cough up its bearings.

The drive made a gentle turn to the left, then resumed its former course, coming eventually to a duckweed-covered bayou nearly fifty yards across. She stopped at the foot of the bridge spanning the bayou, unable to proceed because a section of the bridge about five yards long was pointing up and down the bayou instead of across it. Beside the road was a small metal box on a pole. Under the box was a sign: CALL FOR ADMITTANCE.

She got out of the car and opened the door on the metal box, which contained a telephone. She lifted the receiver and punched in the number displayed on another sign inside. On the first ring, Adrian Iverson answered.

"Adrian, this is Kit."

"Right," Iverson said. "I'll let you in."

She heard a groan of gears and the misaligned section of road slowly began to move. By the time she got back behind the wheel, it was only another minute or so before she was able to proceed.

The crepe myrtles continued on the other side of the bridge, but instead of forest beyond them, there was a welltended lawn. The limits of the estate were marked by more brick piers and iron fencing that did not stop at the bayou but extended all the way across it. Thirty yards from the bridge, a service road went off to the left, toward four large greenhouses.

The main house lay directly ahead, a delightful sprawling white two-story with green shutters that looked as though it had been lifted from The Battery in Charleston by a hurricane and deposited here. The front of the house was dominated by four huge square columns that served as piers for the green wrought iron enclosing the upper and lower porches. Atop the metal mansard roof, which was painted dark green, was a widow's walk surrounded by more green iron fencing and containing a whimsical windowed cupola topped with a copper dome. Iverson was waiting on the front steps.

"Awfully good of you to come," he said as she got out of the car.

He was dressed in brown slacks and a yellow knit golf shirt with a brown collar.

"I didn't have the bridge open for you because I get a lot of folks driving into the property just to see what's back here. Please come in."

He stood aside and Kit stepped into the entry foyer. Despite having once read that it was considered cheeky among the rich to compliment them on anything they owned, Kit could not help saying, "Adrian, this is wonderful." The huge foyer was lined by dark wood gleaming as though oiled. On one wall, the wood was intricately worked over a large fireplace. At the rear, a glistening staircase began between two imposing fluted columns and rose to a landing bathed in the light from a massive stained-glass window whose brilliant colors were woven into a theme of morning glories and dragonflies.

"Come on back to my study," Iverson said, "where we can talk."

Foyer...study, these words were too ordinary to describe Iverson's home. On the far wall of his "study," between two huge oval-topped windows magnificently draped and swagged, was a fireplace with a white marble mantel and a Chinese-red plaster overmantel. A recess in the overmantel contained an English landscape painting depicting a hunting dog on point. In front of the fireplace, the veined marble floor was covered by a needlepoint area rug with black and white stripes reminiscent of the pattern on a zebra. Facing each other across the zebra rug were a pair of brocaded wingback chairs. On the left wall, tall bookcases made of teak or some other black wood were decorated with six green marble columns with gilded acanthus capitals. To the right was a gun cabinet and half a dozen rifles. From somewhere, Kit heard Westminster chimes strike the hour.

Iverson waved her to one of the brocaded chairs. "What can I get you? I've got about anything you could name."

"I'm fine, Adrian. Are you a hunter?"

"Not at all. I like guns. I guess most men do. But I believe they should be used only on paper targets. Since you won't let me get you anything, perhaps you'd like a tour instead."

"I would."

"The best place to start is on the roof."

Kit followed Iverson back into the foyer and up the great staircase to the second floor, where a narrower version of the stairs continued to the cupola Kit had seen coming in. Surprisingly, even though it sat fully exposed to the sun, the cupola was as cool as the rest of the house, a feat accomplished by a large air-conditioning duct in its ceiling. Iverson opened the door and Kit stepped onto the deck, into air superheated by the sun and the reflection of its energy from the metal roof underneath.

"Obviously, it's much nicer up here around dusk, when the sun isn't blazing so," Iverson said.

Kit walked over to the waist-high fence. "Watch your hands," Iverson warned. "That metal is probably hot.'

He came up beside her. "As you can see, we're actually on an island. The bayou you came over leads in both directions to a large cypress swamp that surrounds us on three sides."

Hand shading her eyes, Kit followed the sweep of Iverson's hand. A roar echoed from the swamp.

"Bull alligator," Iverson explained.

Kit shuddered.

"Are you all right?" Iverson asked.

"I'm fine. I once had a bad experience with an alligator, is all."

"What happened?"

"It's something I'm trying to forget."

"I understand. Before I had the fence put up, the alligators used to wander all over the place at night, destroying the flower beds...not on purpose, you understand, just didn't know any better."

For a brief moment, Kit thought she saw two dark shapes in the forest on the other side of the iron fence, but they quickly disappeared into some palmetto. Whatever they were, they weren't alligators.

"And those are my greenhouses," Iverson said. "Still don't know how I ended up with so many. Why don't we go down and have a look at them?"

Kit found that a welcome suggestion, as the heat was becoming quite uncomfortable. The cool air of the cupola was a distinct relief.

They went downstairs and returned to the study, where Iverson parted the sheers over one of the windows beside the fireplace and Kit saw that it was not a window at all but a pair of French doors. They stepped into a large rose garden enclosed by seven-foot brick walls covered with espaliered climbing roses with huge yellow blooms. Other beds full of bushes with glistening leaves, canes as thick as a broom handle, and luscious blooms that looked as though they would last for months radiated from a cast-iron fountain, sending an umbrella of water high in the air.

"I'm sorry you weren't here in the spring," Iverson said. "It was glorious."

"It's not bad now," Kit replied, enjoying the pizzicato notes of falling water plinking into the reflecting pool. "A house like this must require a large staff."

"Five gardeners, two maids, and a cook."

"I haven't seen anybody else around."

"They all live offsite and none of them are here on weekends. The gardeners take care of the greenhouses and the lawn, as well as my lily and perennial gardens. But no one tends my roses but me. I don't even allow them *in* here. It's for their own good, really. When one of my other plants dies, it's a sad thing. When one of my roses dies, it's a catastrophe. So it's better if I haven't anyone to blame but myself."

In places where the mulch was disturbed, Kit could see that each rosebush appeared to be in a plastic container that had been sunk into the ground. She made a mental note to ask the purpose of this trick later. Right now, there was something else she wanted to know. "Adrian, I don't believe I've ever heard anyone say what your occupation is."

"I used to be a surgeon. But I'm retired."

"You look too young to be retired."

Iverson tapped his head. "Guess I'm older in here than I appear. They say if a man stays in a police uniform for twenty years and retires, his life expectancy is significantly reduced compared to the general population. All that stress takes an invisible toll. Same thing for surgery—at least for me...too much stress. Much better all around for me to be here. Fortunately, I made some lucky investments. Now let me show you my perennials."

They went through a wooden door into an adjacent courtyard so skillfully planted and so filled with butterflies that she found it every bit as appealing as the roses.

"This is false indigo," Iverson said, "and Jupiter's beard, Chinese lantern, Japanese anemone...and here"—he went to a plant with shiny leathery leaves—"is a plant that shouldn't be growing at all this far south."

"What is it?"

"A gas plant. If you damage the roots, they release a flammable gas that will make a little explosion if you put a flame near them. Come see my lilies."

Eventually, they reached the first greenhouse. "This is my tropical forest," Iverson said.

The greenhouse had a knee-high cement table on each side and one down the middle. All were filled with lush green foliage as dense as any unexplored rain forest. It even sounded like the jungle.

"Are those birds?" Kit asked.

"Keep going."

A few feet from where they had been standing, Kit came upon a long aviary filled with twittering finches sitting on the middle table. Something tapped at Kit's shoe. She looked down and saw a fluffy white chicken pecking at her shoelace. Another chicken came out from under the table, then another.

"Keep going," Iverson urged.

A little farther down, she came upon another cage with two huge parrots in it, a tabby cat asleep on the top. Toward the end of the greenhouse, the foliage again gave way to a cage, this one containing three flop-eared rabbits and two yellow tortoises.

"Be careful of that fan and all the others, as well," Iverson said, pointing to one of two large exhaust fans that flanked the door at the end of the greenhouse. "They're new and the covers haven't arrived yet."

Coming back on the opposite side, Kit's way was suddenly blocked by a black pig that seemed to be grunting a warning. She took a step backward.

"He won't hurt you," Iverson said. "He's hungry. His food is under the table in that box with the hinged lid. Feed him if you like."

Kit reached down to open the lid and the pig put his wet snout on her hand and snorted against her skin.

"He likes you," Iverson said.

"I'm glad," Kit replied, filling the metal scoop in the box with brown pellets. She emptied the scoop beside the box and the pig stopped grunting and began to eat. "I thought pigs were pink," Kit said.

"I used to have a pink one, but he got so big, he couldn't get under the tables or navigate the aisles. This is a Vietnamese potbellied pig. He's as big as he's going to get. Watch this."

Iverson clapped his hands together. Without lifting his snout from the food, the pig raised his left leg. Iverson snapped his fingers and the pig's leg went down. Two more claps. Still snuffling at the brown pellets, the pig raised his right leg. Another snap of the fingers and he dropped it.

Hardly the Moscow circus, Kit thought, but interesting.

"Pigs are very trainable if you spend the time with them," Iverson said. "Take the connecting passageway to the next greenhouse and I'll show you my orchids."

Over the next fifteen minutes, Kit saw many kinds of flowers, as well as fish tanks and ferrets, lizards and guinea hens. Near the end of the tour, she pointed at Adrian's shirt. "You've picked up a passenger."

Adrian looked down and brought his finger to the small insect near his pocket, nudging it until it climbed on. "One of my little aphid exterminators," he said, holding it aloft. "You probably know it as a praying mantis, but it's also known as devil's horse or mule killer. The original of *devil's horse* escapes me, but *mule killer* refers to the belief that if a mule eats one, both will die."

The mantis swiveled its head as though listening to Iverson's discourse. "Fascinating little insect, but very ill mannered," Iverson said. "The females have been known to begin consuming the male at the head while still copulating."

He gently put the mantis on some nearby foliage. "Now, maybe you're ready for some refreshment."

"What about the roses you wanted my opinion on?"

"They're inside."

They went back to the study, where Iverson brought Kit a lemonade and went to get the hybrids he had developed. Instead of the entire plants, he returned with a silvery tray bearing four blooms in clear plastic containers with hinged lids. He handed her the first container. "Now, tell me what you think."

He watched with great interest as she opened it, brought it to her nose, and inhaled deeply.

"That's nice," she said, closing the container and handing it back.

Before giving her another, he picked up a gold hand fan with a pink rose painted on it and fanned the air around her chair to dissipate any fragrance remaining from the first flower. She sampled the next three and found herself sure of only one thing: Number four was totally without distinction.

She looked at Iverson. "Could I try the first three again?"

After sampling them one more time, she said, "Number two. Definitely number two."

AT THE DOOR, Iverson shook her hand warmly. "Can't tell you how much I appreciate your coming. Not only for your help with my hybrids but for the company. It's odd, but sometimes, even when all the staff is here, the place seems too quiet. Promise you'll come back."

"I promise."

While crossing the bridge over the bayou, Kit considered Iverson's remark about how the place seemed too quiet even when the staff was all there. What he meant was *lonely*. The lesson was clear. Despite the great discrepancy in their financial status, John Tully and Adrian Iverson were pathetically similar, both alone, both sublimating the need for companionship into a passion for roses, and in Iverson's case, animals.

This realization should have set to rest her ambivalence regarding what had transpired with Teddy. Why continue a relationship with someone you can't count on for the long haul? Still, by forcing the issue and worrying about *eventually* being in the same boat as Tully and Iverson, hadn't she already climbed aboard?

Needing to get her mind off Teddy and her impending visit to the aquarium, she decided to go to the office and put chapter seven of her book, which she had written longhand, into the computer. With the office as a destination, it would be about as quick to take the West Bank Expressway to the downtown bridge as go over Huey P.

Huey P. God how she hated that bridge. Even thinking about it made her pulse race.

Two minutes later, at the cloverleaf where those who wanted to take the West Bank loop to downtown went straight, Kit firmly gripped the wheel and turned left, toward Huey P.

In the next fifteen minutes, she crossed Huey P. twice, coming off it the second time with one less thing in her life to worry about.

TEN

THE DOORS TO THE ELEVATOR opened and there was Broussard in a white lab coat.

"Dr. Franklyn...here on a Sunday," he said. "We may have to give you more money."

The door closed behind her and the elevator began to move. "Thought I'd work on my book a while. What are you up to?"

"Minin' for lead...readin' some slides."

"Mining for lead" was what he called digging for bullets. The elevator shuddered to a stop and the doors clattered open. Broussard let Kit get off first, then from behind, he said, "Hold still."

Kit felt a touch on her shoulder and turned to see what was going on. Raising his hand to eye level, Broussard said, "Where'd you get him?" On his extended finger was a small praying mantis.

"Probably at Adrian Iverson's," Kit said. "He's the president of the Rose Society I belong to and his greenhouses are full of them."

"How is Adrian? Before he retired, I used to see him every month at the meeting of the hospital board. Rarely run into him now."

"He seems reasonably content."

"Great place he has out there. Wouldn't mind ownin' it myself. What are you doin' for dinner?"

"No plans."

"How about we go to Gramma O's around five?"

"Sure, what are you going to do with *him?*" She pointed at the mantis.

"Margaret's been complainin' about aphids in her terrarium. I'll put it in there."

"She might prefer the aphids."

Around four, Kit felt the birth of a headache in the back of her skull, but two aspirin from Broussard sent it on its way. At dinner, when he asked whether she had picked up any new leads in the O'Connor case, she nearly told him about the mystery caller and her appointment at the aquarium. But since she had promised not to talk about it, she didn't.

She got home a little after seven and took Lucky for a walk. Then, with five hours before her appointment staring her in the face, she returned to the Pat Conroy novel she had started while French dug up Francie O'Connor.

Since there wouldn't be much traffic and there was plenty of parking about the Hilton at the foot of Poydras, just a short walk from the aquarium, she didn't leave the house until 12:10. Though the sun had been down for hours, the ground and the pavement had stored its energy, releasing it now so that the grip of summer never loosened.

She slid behind the wheel and started the engine. She put it in reverse, pulled on the lights, and nudged the gas. The car went nowhere. A little more gas and the car lurched backward. She realized now that it was also listing to the right.

Going around to the passenger's side, she saw in the dim glow of the neighbor's porch light . . . a flat. Great. Having allowed so little time to get downtown, there was no question of trying to change it.

She hurried inside and looked up the taxi listings in the phone book. As it turned out, she probably could have changed the tire in the time it took for the cab to get there.

At least she wouldn't have to hoof it from the Hilton. She ducked her head and got in. "The aquarium on Canal, please."

The overweight black woman behind the wheel looked at her in the mirror. "It ain't open."

"I know. And could you hurry? I'm late for an appointment."

The cab pulled away from the curb, went to the corner, and turned right. There was a crucifix dangling from the rearview mirror and a lot of religious porcelains stuck all over the dash.

"Tha's the trouble with the world," the driver said. "Everybody's in a hurry. Got no time for the Lord. Too busy chasin' money or sex. Which is it with you?"

"Money *and* sex," Kit said. "Could we go a little faster?"

They drove in silence for a while, then the driver said, "You seen how funny the moon's been lookin' lately?"

"No, I hadn't really noticed."

"Now why you suppose that is? You obviously a well-educated person. How come somebody that never finished high school notices somethin' you don't?"

The insolent tone in the woman's voice was beginning to get under Kit's skin. She looked for the driver's ID on the back of the front seat but found none.

Wishing to avoid an unpleasantness, she did not respond in kind. "People are different," she said. "You see changes in the moon, I might see things you don't."

"Now tha's an ignorant answer." The woman looked at Kit in the mirror. "And don't you be givin' me that look like you think I'm crazy."

"Stop the cab."

"We ain't there yet."

"I don't care. I want out."

The meter said $8.20. Kit flipped a ten into the front seat and scooted out of the cab. As Kit shut the door, the cabbie said pleasantly, "Now you have a nice night."

The cab went off down the street and Kit looked at her watch: 12:40. Already ten minutes late. Where the hell *was* she, anyway? She set off in the direction the cab had been going and got her bearings at the next corner. In the French Quarter, the streets would be jammed, but here on this side of Canal, the city was dead—no cars, no people. Only empty streets with cold, quiet buildings looming on each side.

As nearly as she could figure it, Poydras was a couple of blocks straight ahead. It was a major street, where she might find a cab. And even if she didn't at least there would be people.

She began to walk briskly, trying not to give in to the knowledge that this was something a woman does not want to be doing in any city, let alone one where the degenerates have their national headquarters.

A car with a noisy water pump approached from behind her and slowed. Aware that any display of nervousness could provoke an undecided psychopath into attacking, she resisted the impulse to look back. She had been blessed—or, as she felt now, cursed—with a provocative little fanny that was hard to camouflage in slacks, even though she always chose them carefully. She found herself wishing she was built more like Grandma O.

The car eased slowly past, its driver so faintly visible inside that he must have turned off his dash lights. His features were obscured, but she could tell that he was leaning in her direction, looking her over. Then, abruptly, he increased his speed, proceeded to the corner, and turned right.

Kit sighed and came back to earth, feeling as though she had been walking on her toes. Despite being greatly relieved at the disappearance of the car, the experience left her with a heightened sense of vulnerability, as though a dog with a reputation for biting was sniffing at her heels.

She began to walk faster. At the corner, she looked in both directions, hoping to see some sign of life. By now, even a bum would have made her feel better. But there were only mocking shadows.

She hurried across the street, forcing her mind to happier circumstances—to the Rib Room, to the murmur of conversation, the gentle ring of her wineglass touching Teddy's. Then the sweat creeping down her back turned cold. The car with the noisy water pump was back.

Its engine slowed and she could feel red eyes burning into her. She tried to put more purpose into her walk, at the same time searching the empty streets for help. But there was none. With all the people in this city, why couldn't there be just one when she needed them?

The car was pacing her now—from the sound, very close. Her heart was hammering in her ears, making it hard to hear what was happening behind her. Through the heart noise, she heard the car stop. At the same time, one of its doors opened and footsteps came quickly toward her.

She broke into a run and heard the car begin to move. But there were still footsteps coming. Her brain howled in misery. *There were two of them.*

A hand grabbed her by the arm and she pivoted on the ball of her left foot, bringing her fist around in an arc that she hoped would hit *something*. But another hand grabbed her wrist. In the confusion, she saw a blue shirt and the flash of silver.

"Miss. Miss. It's all right. I'm a cop."

The words slowly filtered through her flaming fear. *I'm a cop. COP.*

She stopped fighting and the cop let her go.

"Sorry, I shouldn't have come up on you like that without identifying myself," the cop said. "Hope I didn't hurt you."

He was young and clean-cut, but she'd have felt the same gratitude if he had looked like Quasimodo.

"You really shouldn't be out alone around here."

"Point taken," Kit said, breathing hard.

"Where are you going?"

She almost said the aquarium but saw what was coming. Imagining what her mystery caller would think if he saw her arrive in a police car, she said, "The Hilton on Poydras."

"Come on, we'll take you. And another word of advice . . . get some training in self-defense."

At the Hilton entrance, she thanked the cops and went inside, staying just long enough for them to get out of sight. When she had come in, the doorman had managed to keep any sign of curiosity off his face. On her way out, he didn't.

"None of your business," she said, stepping into the street.

She checked her watch: 12:55. She felt moist and clammy from all the walking and the air-conditioning in the patrol car and the hotel, but she ignored it and moved faster, past the World Trade Building and beyond, past the entrance to the Algiers ferry, down the sidewalk to the green glass aquarium, which sat on the bank of the Mississippi like a huge lipstick.

The aquarium entrance faced the river, across a brick promenade. She reached it hot and sweaty, only to find no one waiting. Her eyes swept the promenade, searching each of the benches that surrounded the small trees spaced over the brickwork. A quarter of a mile away, she could see the illuminated spire of the St. Louis Cathedral. Out of the corner of her right eye, she detected movement behind the largest of three metal sculptures that projected from the bricks like shark fins. She moved closer and saw that it was only a couple kissing.

Too late. He had not waited for her. She had let him get away again.

Her gaze drifted across the river, to the lights on the cranes at the Algiers iron works. Then she had a thought. He had said to come to the main entrance of the aquarium, which didn't necessarily mean that he was planning to arrive as she did, from some other location. He might have been there already. She walked to the doors of the darkened aquarium and gave one a pull. It wasn't locked.

Inside, it was cool and the overhead lights were turned way down, so that she could barely see. At the rear of the huge entry, the interior of the building was divided by a square column that rose from the floor almost to touch the ceiling far overhead. As her eyes adapted to the dark, she could see that the column was actually a metal sculpture, worked to look like fish scales. At its base was a pool. Probably during the day, water cascaded over the scales and was recirculated from the pool.

"Is anyone here?" she said meekly.

For an answer, there was only the faint whoosh of the air-conditioning and the intermittent sound of water gurgling down pipes. Ignoring the wide stairs with yellow railings to her right, she cautiously moved deeper into the building. "Hello...anyone here?"

Her course took her to the right of the fish-scale sculpture, where she paused and stared into the yawning black space beyond. "Helloooo."

Slowly, she moved forward, entering a less expansive passage, fancifully imagining herself descending into the bowels of some creature that had been lying in the dark with its mouth open—the sound of moving air its lungs, the gurgle of water its kidneys.

A huge porthole appeared in the wall to her right. Through it, she saw dim shapes slipping by, seemingly suspended in air. She moved along the wall, finding comfort in the touch of her fingers against the cool cement. The passage curved to the right and within a few steps she could no longer see the front entrance when she looked back. Abruptly, the wall opened onto a vast space bounded by a transparent barrier that hardly seemed there at all. She paused in awe, then moved forward until she stood in front of an extraordinary view eerily illuminated by scattered red night-lights affixed to manmade shapes that rose from the floor to crisscross in the gloom and pass out of sight far above her. A massive torpedo shape glided between her and one of the lights, its sleek outline topped by a triangular dorsal fin. Higher up, another light winked out as a second, larger shark slipped by.

Disoriented by the darkness on her side and the size of the great tank, Kit's mind began playing tricks on her, making her feel that in the dark corners of the tank, the world on the other side of the glass and hers were joined. Shivering at the illogical but all too real sensation that one of the fearful fish might be circling her, she glanced over her shoulder, into her own watery gloom, whose tidal currents nudged the prickling hairs on the back of her neck.

In the direction she had come, something moved—or was it merely an illusion? Her eyes strained at the darkness, trying to see what was or wasn't. Deciding that she had imagined the movement, she turned back toward the tank and took a sharp breath. A huge shape was coming directly toward her. Half-believing that it might be able to reach her, she took two steps backward. At the last moment, it turned to avoid the barrier and her brain struggled with what she saw, unable to assemble the image into meaning. Then in one horrible second, the chaos cleared.

The shark had a human leg in its mouth.

ELEVEN

"THE DIVERS GOT HIM OUT . . . at least what's left of him," Broussard said to Gatlin. "You want to have a look before they take him away?"

Gatlin shook his head. "You tell me what I need to know."

"His left arm from the shoulder down and everything below the sternum are missin'."

Kit was sitting on the brick wall around the pond at the base of the fish-scale sculpture, beginning to recover from the shock of what she had seen. Broussard's description of the body set her progress back.

"You need the rest of him?" Gatlin asked.

"Not really. No reasonable way to get it, anyway. We don't even know which fish took part."

Took part. *Took parts,* Kit thought, her mind's uncontrolled wordplay making her stomach even sicker.

"Who was he?" Gatlin asked.

"Aquarium director said his name's Paul Jarrell. He was the senior saltwater aquarist, but he'd been doublin' as freshwater aquarist 'cause they're shorthanded. You ready to see the layout above the tank?"

"Yeah. Be there in a minute. Let's get him loaded."

Broussard walked back to the spot where Kit's emotions had been thoroughly scrambled less than an hour earlier. The two men who had come to transport the remains to the morgue were standing in front of the big Gulf of Mexico display, whose lights were now on. Inside the tank, remorseless sharks patrolled the underpinnings of a mock oil rig as if expecting another treat. "You can take him now."

"After this, I ain't ever goin' swimmin' again," one of the transporters said as they all went back to the entrance.

"I may not even take a bath," the other one added.

They went up the stairs and walked past the upper reaches of the fish-scale sculpture to where the remains of Paul Jarrell lay on a stretcher, a sheet clinging wetly to his abbreviated shape. Off to one side, their backs to the stretcher, the aquarium director, the night engineer, and a uniformed security guard were talking quietly. A few feet away, Jamison, the police photographer, was fiddling with his camera.

Back at the entrance, one of the cops who had been the first to arrive came in and called Gatlin aside. "Lieutenant, my partner and I gave that woman a ride to the Hilton about fifteen minutes before we found her over here. Obviously, she lied to us about where she was going."

"I'll be sure and point that out to her. Thanks."

Gatlin and the cop watched the stretcher bearers bring the remains down the stairs, both of them noticing how there didn't appear to be much under the sheet. Kit did not look at all. The cop went back outside and Gatlin said, "Doc, you interested in the tour?"

Had the entire body been out of the building, she might have felt a little better, but most of it was still back there—in the belly of animals that little kids would be looking at happily the next day. She didn't want to see that, but she definitely wanted to know how Paul Jarrell had gotten into the tank. She rose and followed Gatlin up the stairs.

They encountered Jamison coming the other way.

"Where *you* going?" Gatlin asked.

"To get a few shots of the front of the tank."

"What have you taken so far?"

"Just the body. The divers are getting dressed, so I'm gonna have to wait a few minutes before I can get into the room over the tank."

"Okay, but come right back up."

Gatlin and Kit had already met Lester Thomas, the aquarium director, and the two men with him, so no introductions were necessary. Thomas was probably in his late thirties. He had a high forehead, soft brown hair, and an ill-advised beard and mustache that reminded Kit of Bermuda not getting enough sun. His white shirt was misbuttoned.

"I want to see where he went into the water," Gatlin said to Thomas. Gatlin gestured to an open door. "This it?"

Thomas nodded.

"Lester, I'm going back to my station," the engineer said. "Anybody needs me, that's where I'll be."

Thomas led the group into a long gray room whose floor was little more than a narrow path around the perimeter of the shark tank, which lay beyond a shallow connecting pool straight ahead. As Thomas took them around to the main tank, he explained that agitation of water in the shallow pool created ripples on the surface of the big tank so that viewers on the first floor couldn't see above the waterline.

When they reached the main tank, Gatlin expressed the thought that had also occurred to Kit. "There's no guard-rail around this thing."

"No," Thomas said. "We'd discussed installing one, and probably now we will."

Broussard stepped to the edge of the shark tank and looked in. Kit hugged the wall. While Gatlin wrote in his little black book, Thomas continued walking, toward the superstructure of the shark tank's mock oil rig, a maze of gray pipes that extended from the water to the ceiling. He paused just shy of the rig and Kit thought he might go up onto a yellow metal catwalk that ran from the edge of the tank to its center. Instead, he looked to his left, into an alcove whose contents were hidden from the group, and said, "We got a lady here. So make sure you're zipped up." He turned to Kit and the others. "The divers," he explained.

Two lanky young men in jeans and blue polo shirts with aquarium logos on them came out of the alcove. Both wore grim expressions and looked pale and shaken. "Hope I don't ever have to do anything like *that* again," one said.

"If you don't need us for anything more, we're gonna go get drunk," the other one added.

Thomas looked at Gatlin, who motioned to the men with his black book and said, "You can leave."

Everyone let them by and Gatlin walked back to where they had been dressing.

"What would Jarrell have been doin' up here?" Broussard asked.

"Any of a dozen things," Thomas replied. "I'm surprised, though, that he wasn't wearing his life jacket."

"Life jacket?" Gatlin said, rejoining the group.

"Paul couldn't swim. Crazy, isn't it, for a man who spent his life working with fish?"

"Yeah," Gatlin said, "downright loony. He always work at night?"

"Not always, but often. Some things can be done from the back of the displays, but he was reworking a couple of the Amazon rain forest exhibits. No way to get at them from behind. So they can be worked on only at night while we're closed. When it comes to underwater landscaping, Paul is a . . . was a real artist. I don't know what we're going to do without him. Damn."

"What's wrong?" Gatlin asked.

"I just remembered, we've got five hundred school kids coming in tomorrow from Thibodaux."

"So?"

"How's it going to look if, when they're all standing in front of this tank, a shark passes one of Paul's sneakers?"

"You surprised the sharks went for him?" Broussard asked. "I imagined they'd be so well fed, they wouldn't do somethin' like that."

"A shark is always hungry, or at least interested enough to take a bite. When we clean the tank, it takes three divers, two to do the actual cleaning and one to keep the sharks away. And night is our worst time for losing the tarpon in the tank to the sharks. You can't imagine the headaches involved in running an operation like this."

"Was Jarrell working alone tonight?" Gatlin asked.

"He shouldn't have been," Thomas said. "Bobby Poag, one of our junior people, was scheduled to help."

"He did," the security guard said. "At least for most of the evenin'."

"Well where is he?" Gatlin asked.

"That's what I asked Jarrell when I didn't see Poag on my eleven-fifteen pass by," the guard said. "Jarrell told me he'd sent him home. Said they were so close to bein' done, he could finish by himself."

Gatlin made more notes in his book and said to the guard, "When did you last see Jarrell alive?"

"Twelve-fifteen. I get around the whole aquarium 'bout once an hour."

"Where exactly was he then?"

"Right where he was an hour earlier... at the piranha exhibit."

"You notice anything about him tonight that was out of the ordinary?"

"Well..."

"What?"

"I ain't one to speak ill of the dead, but he had alcohol on his breath. Never knew him to be a boozer, but he'd sure been at the grape tonight."

"You sayin' he was drunk?" Broussard asked.

The guard shook his head. "Didn't seem to be. I mean the displays he was workin' on don't look like they been put together by a drunk. Then, too, he was workin' with the piranhas and still had all his fingers...."

Gatlin looked at Thomas. "Did Jarrell have an office in the building?"

"First floor—do you want to see it?"

"Yeah." Gatlin turned to the police photographer, who had returned from downstairs. "Ray, get all this, will you?"

They cleared the room and waited while Jamison blanketed it with snapshots. When Jamison emerged, Thomas locked the door and set off through the exhibits, motioning for the others to follow.

In the wastebasket in Jarrell's tiny office, Gatlin found two small airline-type liquor bottles that had once held scotch. On the wall behind his desk was a full year's calendar from Carolina Biological with cryptic notations scrawled in the squares for various dates. Kit checked the current date but found it blank. Next to the calendar was Jarrell's bachelor's and master's degrees in zoology from Tulane. Under the degrees were two simply framed eight-by-ten aerial color photographs of a tropical island fringed by pale green water that deepened to cobalt blue farther out. Looking at them from a picture on his desk was a woman in her early forties.

"How old was Paul Jarrell?" Kit asked Thomas.

He looked at the ceiling as though Jarrell's resume was written on it. "Forty-seven—no, forty-eight. He had a birthday last month. Why?"

"Just curious."

"Which reminds me—" Thomas said, "why were you in the building and how did you get in?"

"It's a long story."

Thomas looked at Gatlin. "Am I—whose... whose job is it in situations like this to tell his wife?"

"I can do it," Gatlin said, "unless you'd prefer to."

"No... no. I'd much rather you did it."

"I'll need his address and phone number and the same for Bobby Poag."

"I'll get them for you."

"I also want to talk to that engineer for a few minutes. Where is he?"

"In the west wing. I'll show you the way."

"And the displays Jarrell worked tonight. I want to see them." Gatlin looked at Jamison, who was standing just outside the door. "Ray, you can go. Thanks." Then to Kit and Broussard, he said, "I won't be long. Can you two stick around? We have things to discuss."

"OKAY," GATLIN SAID, over the sound of his Pontiac's air conditioning. "What have we got here?"

From the backseat, Kit said, "Isn't it obvious? We've got a murder. Jarrell calls me earlier, admits to witnessing the murder of Francie O'Connor..."

"Who?" Gatlin asked.

"Francie O'Connor. That's the name of the woman we found in my backyard."

"How'd you get her name?"

"A friend of hers saw the picture in the paper and identified her for me."

"I thought you were going to keep me informed."

"I was waiting until I had a little more to tell you."

Gatlin leveled a finger at her. "Written report, on my desk by five o'clock tomorrow. Everything you've learned to date. You were saying?"

"Jarrell agreed to meet me at twelve-thirty, except that when I went to my car to come here, I had a flat, clearly arranged by someone who wanted me to be late, which I was, partly because of a cabdriver from hell who was acting so strange, I had to bail out before getting here. That's when the cops found me."

"And when you lied to them," Gatlin said.

"Of course. What was I going to do, pull up at my meeting in a cop car after promising that I wouldn't say anything? How much would I have learned if he saw me do that? So I had the cops let me out at the Hilton, then I came over here, and you know the rest. Obviously, Jarrell was murdered by someone who didn't want me to talk to him."

Gatlin looked at Broussard, who had been listening quietly beside him, a lemon drop in one cheek. "What's on *your* mind?"

"When the divers were puttin' the body on the stretcher, some foam came out of his nostrils. That's a pretty good sign he was alive when he went into the water. I want to know his blood-alcohol level and the chloride content of the blood in his left and right ventricles. I also want to look at his brain macroscopically and microscopically."

"Blood alcohol, I get," Gatlin said. "What's this chloride stuff?"

"When somebody drowns, they usually take water into their lungs. Since seawater has a higher chloride concentration than blood, the chloride will enter the blood and be carried from the lungs to the left ventricle. Death occurs before this high-chloride blood can be distributed through the body. Hence a chloride difference on the right and left."

"You just said you already know he drowned," Gatlin said. "Why bother with all that?"

"I said he was alive when he went into the water, but I didn't say he was alive when he went into the shark tank. He could have been drowned in one of the freshwater tanks and then been dumped in the shark tank."

"He likely to have enough blood left for you to test?"

"I think so."

"You also said something about looking at his brain."

"If the evidence indicates he was alive when he went in with the sharks, the question is, was it an accident, suicide, murder, or did he have a stroke and fall in? A look at the brain will tells us about the latter."

"Lot of other choices," Gatlin said.

"That's where you come in."

Kit leaned forward and grabbed the front seat with both hands. "I don't see but one choice. Weren't you listening to what I said?"

"I was listening," Gatlin replied. "What I heard was that your caller never gave you his name. You don't even know that Jarrell was who you were going to meet."

"If it *wasn't* him, where was the one who agreed to meet me?"

"You were late. He might have gotten cold feet and left, or just got tired of waiting and left, or he was watching from a distance to see if you'd come alone and he saw you get out of the patrol car at the Hilton."

"That last one seems pretty farfetched," Kit said disgustedly. "But forget all that. What are the chances that Jarrell's death and my flat tire were simply coincidence?"

"Look it up," Gatlin said. "A coincidence is the occurrence of events that happen at the same time by *accident* but *seem* to have some connection. If it never happened, we wouldn't need a word for it."

Kit flounced back in her seat and folded her arms. "You are wrong."

"I'm not wrong, because I haven't decided anything yet. We're merely discussing the possibilities. But I'll tell you what...why don't you do a little background check on Jarrell. Then we'll compare your findings with Andy's and see where we are. Don't worry about Bobby Poag. I'm going to run him down tonight and see what he knows. As for Jarrell's wife, I'll inform her of her husband's death and leave it at that. You can follow up with her tomorrow."

TWELVE

THE NEXT MORNING instead of changing the tire herself, Kit called the gas station where she usually did business and they sent a man over who put on the miniature spare. She then drove to the station and sat by the candy machine in an old black chair whose stuffing showed through three splits in the vinyl, reminding her of the gill slits on a shark.

Ordinarily, she would have been vexed at the wait, but the two things she wanted to do today both required that she not begin too early. The lab would need some time to get the chloride and alcohol results Broussard had mentioned and she wanted to give Mrs. Jarrell a little time to herself before questioning her.

She got out of the gas station at 9:45 and dropped by a different vet to see whether they had the kind of heart-worm pills Lucky liked. Thankfully, they did. When she arrived at the hospital, she went directly to Broussard's office, where she also found Charlie Franks.

"I can come back," she said apologetically.

Broussard waved her in. "No need. Charlie was just tellin' me a Babe Ruth story. Go ahead, Charlie."

"Well," Franks began, "you know how Ruth was not very adept socially...."

Broussard nodded.

"He and the team owner were invited to dinner at the home of an influential couple the owner wanted to impress. So he gave Ruth specific instructions to behave himself and act like a gentleman—to say *thank you* and *please* and simply be polite. Everything went fine. The server would offer Ruth something and he'd take a modest portion... and he'd say thank you and he didn't talk too loud or tell any risqué stories, really trying to fit in. Then the server offered Ruth some asparagus. Ruth looked at what it was and said, 'No thank you,' then, turning to the hostess, he explained, 'Asparagus makes my urine smell.' "

Franks grinned mischievously, showing his widely spaced teeth.

"Inspirational story, Charlie," Broussard said earnestly. "Believe I'll have that quote embroidered on a pillow."

On his way out, Franks looked at Kit and winked happily.

Broussard shifted the lemon drop in his mouth to the other cheek, leaned back in his chair, and folded his hands over his belly. "Chloride levels say he was alive when he went into the shark tank. His blood alcohol was point o four. Even allowin' for the fact there might have been time for some concentration of his blood from water movin' toward the seawater in his lungs, before the sharks got him, that level makes it possible he was enough under the influence to have simply lost his balance and fallen into the tank. Grossly, the brain looked normal. Won't have the sections until late today. Highly unlikely, though, that anything there'll support your view."

"If you had to put money on it, which would you back, coincidence or murder?"

"At this point, I might just try to protect myself and bet both possibilities."

"Didn't you once tell me that where there's smoke, there's fire?"

"I'll admit to the sentiment, but not the cliché."

"So there you are."

"Except that the physical evidence gives no appearance of murder, no evidence of trauma to suggest he was physically forced into the tank, no—"

"But it's not as though you had all of him to study. Suppose someone shot him in the stomach and carried him to the shark tank."

"Where are the bloodstains on the floor? Why didn't the security guard hear a shot?"

"A silencer on the gun...he didn't bleed much—I don't know. Maybe he was pushed into the tank by someone he trusted. That wouldn't leave any evidence on the body."

"That's true."

"So why are you fighting me?"

Broussard chuckled. "Because that's what we do here. We argue...and try to punch holes in other people's positions. And if we do it well enough, the truth will eventually emerge. Remember, I said I'd put half my money on your theory. Now go out and prove it. Only..."

"Only what?"

"Don't put yourself at risk anymore, like you did last night."

Kit was surprised. Though he had often shown fatherly concern for her welfare by his actions, he had never before expressed it in words. "I'm touched," she said, unable to pass up the opportunity to see how far he'd go.

Broussard dropped his eyes and reached for some reports on his desk. "You wouldn't be if you knew how much paperwork it'd take to replace you. Go on now, and prove your point."

His forehead and the part of his cheeks she could see above his beard were tinged with pink. As she turned to go, he added, "Dinner tonight is at seven. Come about six forty-five so everybody can meet you."

"How should I dress?"

"We'll all be in tuxes. It's in the bylaws."

THE JARRELLS LIVED in a zero lot-line yellow brick two-story. The woman Kit had seen in a picture on Jarrell's desk at the aquarium was washing a car in the driveway. Even when Kit approached, the woman didn't look up.

"Mrs. Jarrell, I'm Kit Franklyn. We spoke a few minutes ago."

"Paula—call me Paula," the woman said, pushing and pulling a soapy sponge over the trunk with both hands, still not looking at Kit. She paused briefly to wipe the sweat from her forehead with her arm and went back to work. She was a blonde, not so overweight as to be plump but enough that it showed, especially in her face. Wisely, she wore her hair in a poodle cut. She was dressed in cutoff jeans and a short-sleeved red knit blouse with a white collar. Both were splotched with soapy water. Her feet were bare.

"Paul says that the similarity of our names shows how right we are for each other," Paula said. "We even have matching jackets, but Paul won't wear his if I wear mine."

Kit noticed that Paula was still referring to her husband in the present tense. Not good. But then, she hadn't had much time to get used to the idea that he was gone. "Paula...we don't exactly know what happened to Paul...."

"That's what the detective said last night."

With a sinking feeling, Kit realized that Gatlin had probably not mentioned the sharks. Knowing she was being a real coward, she decided that it probably wouldn't come up in this conversation, either.

"Paula, would you say Paul was a happy man?"

Still not looking at her, Paula picked up the hose and rinsed the soap off the trunk. Some of the spray drifted over Kit. "I asked him that once," Paula said. "After thinking about it for a few seconds, he said *happiness* was too strong a word. He said he was content, and that was better than being happy, because happiness is an acute emotion. Contentment, he said, was chronic."

"Was he moody?"

"Like everybody, he has periods when he needs to be left alone." She dipped the sponge in the bucket and went at the trunk again even though it was perfectly clean.

"When was the last time he had one of those moods?"

"Few days ago."

"When exactly?"

"I dunno.... Started Thursday, I guess. Usually, I just act like nothing is wrong and eventually he comes around."

"Did he drink?"

"Not even wine with dinner. Alcohol always gives him indigestion."

Kit did not know which was worse, talking to a widow who was so weepy that she could barely express herself or someone like Paula, who was cruising on automatic. "Could you give me the name of some of Paul's friends?" Kit opened her spiral pad.

Paula dropped the sponge into the bucket and picked up the hose. "He doesn't have many friends. Just the people he works with, and none of them are close. Paul says that friends are a liability."

"What did he mean by that?"

Paula shrugged, reached for the sponge, and started again on the trunk. Kit wanted to stop her but was afraid to.

Instead, she asked another question. "When did you and Paul meet?"

"Nineteen seventy-five. He was teaching biology at Dillard and I was running the bookstore. He came in one day to order a copy of *Fishes of the World*." The sponge came to a stop. Paula looked off in the distance. "I remember wondering why it was called *Fishes* and not *Fish of the World*. Odd how things come back to you when—" Abruptly, she went back to work, with even more vigor than before.

"How was Paul's health?"

Paula did not answer and, in fact, seemed not to have heard the question. Kit repeated it.

"His health?" Paula said blankly. "His health...it's good. But sometimes he throws his knee out and needs to take it easy for a day or two. Banged it on a cement block when he was a kid. You can still see the scar."

Not even Broussard could see *that* scar, Kit thought. She had no more questions but was concerned about leaving Paula by herself. "Paula, do you have any family here?"

"Not right here. My parents live in Morgan City."

"Would you like for me to call them?"

For the first time, Paula looked directly into Kit's eyes. "Call them? No need. I did that already. They should be here soon. And if there's one thing Daddy insists on, it's a clean car. Won't ride in a dirty one. So I have work to do...lots of work to do."

While Paula turned her attention back to the trunk, Kit quietly withdrew. She drove downtown and parked in a lot at the foot of Canal. It was a short walk to the aquarium, which was doing a brisk business.

Receiving more than one hostile look from those waiting to get in, Kit went to the head of the line and spoke to the young woman taking tickets. "Hi, I'm with the medical examiner's office, here to do a follow-up on the problem from last night, and I need to see Mr. Thomas."

"You should go to the administrative entrance," the girl said.

"Where's that?"

"Toward the French Quarter, about forty yards."

"Hey, lady." A balding guy wearing a gold chain around his neck leaned in so that his face was between Kit and the girl. "Hows about you two havin' this tête-à-tête on your own time. I gotta be back in Scranton week from today, and at this rate, I ain't gonna make it."

A cutting reply came to Kit's mind, but she saw his point and let it go. On the way to the administrative entrance, she wondered why she hadn't realized the night before that it was there, deciding finally that she had missed it because it was so far down and had been in the shadows of the building's portico.

From a staff member at the administrative entrance, she learned that the director and everyone else of any authority were in an important meeting and would not be out for some time, nor could they be disturbed. She left without accomplishing her main objective, which was to explore Paul Jarrell's office. However, she did learn something of interest. There was a desk at the administrative entrance where anyone entering at night had to sign in. And the person manning that desk had no view of the main entrance. The mystery caller had said he didn't want to be seen with her. *That's* why she had been instructed to come to the main entrance and not to the one with the check-in.

It would have been a convenient time for lunch, but she was not particularly hungry. Then, too, there was that affair at Broussard's tonight where the food would probably be very rich and bad for the hips. Better to skip lunch.

She returned to her office and spent the afternoon writing her report for Gatlin, including the impressions of her conversation with Paula Jarrell, a conversation that in so many ways supported her belief that he had been murdered.

THE SLIDES on the Jarrell case came up from the lab around three o'clock. As Broussard looked at how few there were on the tray, he briefly wished he had the rest of Jarrell's organs. Still, what would that accomplish? Suppose he had found that Jarrell had cancer of the prostate or the pancreas? Such a finding would figure into the case only if Jarrell *knew* about it. And he could have known about it only through a doctor. Kit would turn up any evidence like that.

Reassured that he had in his possession all he needed, he took two lemon balls from the bowl on his desk, popped them into his mouth, and turned on the stereo. With the familiar strains of *Swan Lake* filling the room, he seated himself at his microscope and removed his glasses, the tether around his neck keeping them within easy reach against his chest.

He had taken samples from a variety of locations in Jarrell's brain, which on gross examination had looked normal in all respects, as it did now under the $40 \times x$ objective of his Nikon. He moved quickly from slide to slide, needing only a few seconds on each field.

The most prominent cells in the cerebral cortex are the pyramidal cells, all arranged with their pointed ends facing the same way. As they slipped by in unending ranks, vitally connected to their neighbors, Broussard thought of ballerinas, linked hand to hand, their movements precise and delicate yet no more so than the neural choreography that made it all possible.

One by one, the slides passed in review, the pyramidal cells dancing by in time to the music, each of them structurally impeccable. Then a dancer stumbled. Broussard adjusted the condenser and touched up the focus.

Peculiar. Very peculiar.

He jotted down the stage coordinates so that he could return to the area if necessary and continued to sweep the section.

There it was again—and another.

He lowered the stage and put a drop of immersion oil on the slide. He rotated the 100 ×x objective into place and raised the stage until the oil made contact with the nose of the objective. The increased magnification, though, added nothing to what he had already seen. Scattered among the many normal pyramidal cells were a few whose nucleus contained a dumbbell-shaped pink inclusion.

This was something new, something he had never seen before—or was it? He had the vague feeling that he *had* seen it before or had read about it. But where? He sat for a moment with his eyes closed, his finger stroking the bristly hairs on his nose, shutting out the music, retreating from the present, shuffling through his years of experience. But if it was in there, it was well covered with thousands of other facts and observations.

Maybe Charlie could help. He put on his glasses, took the slide from the microscope, and walked down the hall to see Charlie Franks.

Before he could tell Franks what he wanted, Franks said, "I've got one for you; the body has two entrance holes, but only one projectile on a radiograph that looks like this." He held up a journal so that his hand blocked the left panel of a two-part photograph whose right panel showed a circular white object with a dark round center. "What are we dealing with?" Franks said.

"PMC ultramag cookie-cutter slug," Broussard said without hesitating. "Second hole was caused by the Teflon wad, which, of course, is radiolucent."

Franks lowered the journal, his face sagging with disappointment. "Damn. How'd you know that? I've been watching your mailbox. Your copy didn't get here yet."

"The truly gifted travel a higher road," Broussard said, thinking that if Franks had dusted the journal for fingerprints, he wouldn't be so shocked. Normally, he might have confessed, but he figured this evened the score for Charlie's asparagus story.

"Now you get a chance to impress me," Broussard said. "See what you make of these pyramidal cells."

Franks took the slide and put it on his microscope. While waiting for him to get it in focus, Broussard watched the screen-saver program displayed on Franks's computer. Franks had many such programs, but his favorite was flying toasters, a loop that showed a field of electronic toasters with flapping wings. A control panel allowed him to vary the number of toasters in the field and the color of the toast. Yesterday, the toast had been light brown. Today, it was nearly burned.

"This from that shark case?" Franks asked, his eyes fixed to his microscope eyepieces.

"Yeah."

"I guess we're talking about these nuclear inclusions?"

"I have the feelin' I've seen somethin' like that before, but I can't remember where."

Franks looked at Broussard. "If you've seen it before, you're one up on me." He dropped back to $40 \times x$ and scanned other areas. "Everything looks clean...no lymphocytic infiltration. So whatever it is, doesn't seem to have done any damage. Think it's viral?"

"Maybe. I'll have the lab run some EM sections and we'll see if there're any virions in it."

"Where's it from?"

"Rostral poles of the frontal lobes."

"Prefrontal cortex...any other areas have them?"

"No."

"Even here, there aren't many inclusion-positive cells. Probably nothing of any consequence."

"Probably not. You're on call tonight, right? 'Cause I'm gonna be tied up."

"It's covered."

GATLIN CALLED AT FOUR o'clock wanting a meeting with Kit and Broussard. Thirty minutes later, they were all gathered in Broussard's office, Gatlin sharing the green vinyl sofa with a stack of journals, Kit in one of the chairs in front of Broussard's desk. Broussard was behind the desk, rocked back in his chair, hands folded over his belly, saying, "And that's all I have."

Gatlin lapsed into thought, his index finger working at the corner of Kit's report, which lay unread in his lap. He motioned at Kit with his chin. "What'd you get from Jarrell's wife?"

"A lot," Kit said. "First, he was in good health, so we can rule out suicide over a health problem. But he *was* moody. His wife said one of his moods began last Thursday, which is when we ran the picture of Francie O'Connor in the paper. And he didn't drink—not even wine at dinner. So something very significant must have caused him to drink those two bottles of scotch you found in his office. Obviously, he was fortifying himself for our meeting.

"Also, his wife said he didn't have any close friends—that he'd once told her friends are a liability. That could go back to the O'Connor murder if he felt he had been drawn into it by some friends. He certainly was the right age to have been there. I had hoped his wife might have known him at the time of the murder, but they didn't meet until much later, so I couldn't get any more from her. I called the phone company to see if they had any record of a call coming to my phone from the aquarium, but they don't keep track of local calls.... I guess you knew that."

Gatlin sucked at his teeth and picked at the file folder with his finger.

"What do you think?" Kit prodded.

"Pretty weak case for a murder."

"Weak?" Kit said. "With all that I just told you? And what about Bobby Poag, that guy who was working with Jarrell? Why do you suppose Jarrell sent him home early? I'll tell you why...so he wouldn't be around when I showed up."

"I dunno," Gatlin said.

"Did you find Poag?" Kit asked.

"He doesn't know anything."

With her experience at the aquarium that morning fresh in her mind, Kit brought up a point not mentioned previously. "What about the main entrance to the aquarium being open when I got there? Doesn't that show it was Jarrell who called me?"

Gatlin sucked his teeth in thought, then said, "I guess you're interested in pursuing this...."

"Definitely."

"All right. Stay after it then. But I want a *daily* report."

After Gatlin and Kit left, Broussard tried again to think where he had run across dumbbell-shaped nuclear inclusions before. As Franks had said, it probably wasn't important, but it *was* something he didn't understand, and that made him uneasy.

THIRTEEN

KIT LOOKED AT HERSELF in the mirror. Having decided on her black silk suit with the full-length sleeves and fitted waist, the question now was how much décolleté to show. She unfastened the top button and bent over. Thinking that the sight might be too stimulating for the other guests, who, from Broussard's comment about being in tuxedos, would all be male, she redid the button. Besides, that would make the back all the more surprising. She turned and looked at herself over her shoulder, gauging the effect of the suit's lattice panel, which showed a great deal of her fine back. Pleased with her appearance, she added a single gold chain at her neck and a pair of oval gold-caged citrine earrings.

She arrived at Broussard's, to find seven cars already in the drive. The house was even more completely invested with vines and foliage than she had remembered, making the sprawling one-story structure look as though it had been there forever. From clefts in the greenery, light spilled welcomingly from the tall windows.

She went up the black stone steps and entered the familiar high-ceilinged alcove of white brick. From inside came the murmur of conversation mingled with the sounds of a string quartet playing a piece that for some reason made her think of canned ham.

The bell was answered by a houseboy in a starched white jacket. He bowed slightly. "Good evening, miss. Please come in."

The French front doors opened into a large room brightly lit by a huge crystal chandelier. The immense scale of the room and its appointments—the mammoth fresh floral arrangement on the grand piano, the delicate French tables, the upholstered French chairs and overstuffed sofas whose fabrics subtly plucked colors from the Isphahan carpets— were not at all compromised by the formal dress of the six men by the fireplace, who all turned in her direction. Broussard came toward her, one arm extended.

"Hello, Kit. Come and meet the others."

He took her to the five men waiting and said, "Gentlemen, our guest, Kit Franklyn."

They all raised their glasses and uttered a mixture of welcomes. Broussard gave her their names, beginning with the man to her left. "Kurt Halliday, Arthur Jordan, Haley Dagget, Clay Peyton, and Walter Browning."

"My pleasure, gentlemen. Thank you for inviting me."

Broussard leveled his finger at her. "Rum and Coke?"

"If you have it."

"We do. Be right back."

The five men he'd left her with were all in their late forties to middle fifties. The one on her right was probably too big to have ever been a jockey, but he wouldn't have missed the cut by much. His curly brown hair and gray mustache, though, gave him a tweedy look that seemed to call for leather elbow patches rather than racing silks. "It's always hard meeting so many new people all at once," he said. "So don't feel embarrassed if you get us mixed up at first. We won't mind."

Kit replied by pointing at the man to his right. "Clay Peyton," she said. Her finger jumped to the man at her far left. "Kurt Halliday." She pointed at the man in the middle. "Haley Dagget." Then shifted one to the left. "Arthur Jordan." Finishing with the one who'd tried to be so helpful, "And you're Walter Browning." Sure, doing it at random like that was a bit pretentious, but she figured as the guest of honor, she owed them something.

Browning applauded against the mantel with his free hand. "Well done, Kit. Well done."

"Since you had to vote on me, I assume you know what I do," she said. "What keeps you all occupied?"

"I own Browning Medical. We manufacture surgical instruments," Browning said. He deferred to the man beside him.

Clay Peyton was heavyset, with coarse features and thick lips, the sort of fellow who would likely even have hair on his back. "I'm an ear, nose, and throat man," Peyton said. He looked at Haley Dagget, who was by far the tallest of the five and appeared to have the lean muscularity of an athlete. Dagget was almost entirely bald, but it went so well with his cool gray eyes that Kit felt herself respond to him.

"I'm a neurologist and a neurosurgeon," Dagget said. "Probably the best in the state."

The others hooted. "Why so modest, Haley?" Peyton said. "You're among friends."

"All right," Dagget said. "Best in the South."

Broussard appeared at Kit's elbow with her drink. "I miss something?"

"Just Haley showing us how he's a legend in his own mind," Peyton said.

"Come on, Clay, let Art tell what he does," Browning said.

Arthur Jordan was short and quite overweight. He was bald only on top and his sandy hair was swept up on each side as though he had just pulled a sweater over his head. He was clean-shaven, with cherubic features. "Family practice," Jordan said.

He was exactly what Kit imagined a family practitioner *should* look like.

"Come on, Kurt, speak up," Peyton said. "I just remembered something I wanted to tell Art."

Kurt Halliday had large deep-set brown eyes and a thin face with a wide, expressive mouth. He looked like a man who took everything seriously. "Cardiologist," he said.

"Okay now, Art, I heard one you're going to appreciate," Peyton said. "There's this family, see, and they have two kids, a little boy and a little girl. The wife is a family practitioner and the husband is an ENT man, who can't understand why his wife has chosen the most poorly paid branch of medicine. One night, the wife is telling the kids the story of Adam and Eve and when she finishes, she says, 'Now children, who were Adam and Eve?'

"The husband comes in the door in time to hear the question. 'Who were Adam and Eve?' he says. 'Let's look at the facts. They had no clothes, no car, no place to live...they must have been family practitioners.'"

Peyton laughed heartily at his own joke. The others merely smiled, except for Arthur Jordan, whose face reddened. "Is it my fault that the federal government pays less for *thinking* about a patient's problem than *doing* something to him?" Jordan said. He looked at Kit. "Check the reimbursement schedule for Medicaid and Medicare, see how much they pay for a thirty-minute visit by a physician trying to treat the whole person versus what they pay for putting a drainage tube in their ears, something any baboon could do in five minutes."

Following this tirade, there was shocked silence. Even Peyton seemed taken aback.

Kurt Halliday stepped into the void and changed the subject. "Kit, tell us what it feels like to find a skeleton in your backyard."

Happy to help defuse things, Kit said, "It certainly changes the way you think of your home. I've only owned it for a few months and I was beginning to feel comfortable and secure there. But now, knowing what happened in it, I don't sleep as well. And I don't know if I ever will. Maybe after it's all resolved ..."

"What do you mean, resolved?" Halliday asked. "The victim identified?"

"We've already done that," Kit said.

Arthur Jordan's eyes widened with interest. "Who was she?"

"Her name's not important. But it does help us understand what probably happened."

"So there's a chance you'll be able to discover who did it?" Dagget asked.

"We have some leads."

"I guess if you knew *when* she died, you could figure out who lived in your house at the time. Wouldn't that be a good way to go?" Clay Peyton asked.

"That's a possibility," Kit said noncommittally.

"What about this fellow Paul Jarrell, the one they found in the shark tank at the aquarium last night?" Halliday said. "I heard on the news that you were there, too. Any connection?"

Since Kit had discovered Jarrell's body too late to make it into the morning paper, no one else seemed to have heard about it. In response to the clamor for details, Halliday recounted what he'd heard and then looked at Kit.

"So far, there's no evidence of a connection," Kit said.

"Then why were *you* there?" Peyton said.

"I was meeting someone."

"Pretty big coincidence," Peyton said. "What are the chances of the same person finding two bodies under unrelated circumstances in the same week?"

"If coincidences didn't happen, we wouldn't have a word for it," Kit said, glancing at Broussard.

From the moment the members had picked Kit as their guest of honor, Broussard had been concerned that she might talk too openly of her ongoing investigation. Now, seeing how well she was doing, he relaxed.

"Nice try," Peyton said. "But I can't buy your coincidence story."

"That, of course, is your prerogative," Kit replied, beginning to feel a trace of irritation at Peyton's abrasive manner.

Trying to head off trouble, Browning said, "Kit, give us some insight into your job as a suicide investigator. What's the most difficult part of it?"

"Determining intent," Kit said. "For it to be suicide, the deceased must have intended to die."

"Don't they leave notes?" Browning said.

"Sometimes, usually not. And that's where it can get tough."

"For example?"

Kit thought a moment and said, "Say that Clay is a CIA operative and he's captured by enemy agents who want information from him. Clay knows that to get this information, they will torture him mercilessly until he dies. Afraid of the pain, Clay takes cyanide. Suicide?"

"Of course," Browning said.

"Why am *I* the hypothetical example?" Peyton said.

"She's planting a seed and hoping it'll grow," Dagget replied.

"Go on, Kit," Browning urged.

"But suppose that Clay submits to the torture without talking and after three painful days, he dies?"

"How about using somebody else as an example," Peyton said.

"Why are you complaining, Clay?" Dagget said. "You just became a hero. I think it was worth it."

"So, is the second case suicide?" Kit asked.

"No," Browning replied. "It's murder."

"But Clay knew he would die," Kit said, "and yet he wouldn't talk. Didn't he have a hand in his own death? Wasn't it within his power to prevent it?"

"I see what you're getting at," Dagget said. "In the first example, he *intended* to die, knowing that dead, his secrets were safe. In the second example, death was a *by-product* of his decision not to talk. It was not his intent to die. It was his intent merely to protect his secrets."

"Very good, Haley," Kit said. "You have an excellent grasp of the nuances involved."

Dagget beamed at her praise.

"I don't see how those two examples create any problem for a suicide investigator," Peyton said.

"Let's take it a bit further," Kit said. "Ted is in great pain from a terminal disease. He obtains a lethal amount of a painkilling drug and takes it all at once, saying, 'I can't stand this pain, I want to die.'"

"Suicide, plain and simple," Peyton said in a bored tone.

"But suppose before taking the drug, he had said, 'I don't want to die, but I must have some respite from this pain'?"

"Same answer, suicide," Peyton said.

"Not according to the experts," Kit said.

"Then the experts are wrong," Peyton said. "Experts usually think too hard about things."

"I'm not surprised you think so," Arthur Jordan said. "I see what she means."

Peyton raised his thick eyebrows. "But then, you're more perceptive than we mere mechanics."

The houseboy appeared in the doorway to the hall. "Gentlemen and guest, dinner is served."

Kit had not yet made her final point, but the way Peyton and Jordan were sniping at each other, she was glad for the interruption.

Broussard gave her his arm and escorted her down the hall. The dining room was quite large and was lit by another crystal chandelier, but turned down low, so that the seven ivory candles in individual brass candlesticks on the table cast a flickering warm glow over the nut-colored oak wainscoting and made intriguing shadows on the red and blue Indian paisley print above it. In normal light, Broussard's collection of nineteenth-century paintings featuring sheep were quite lovely, but in candlelight they were even more impressive, shining like jewels in their simple gilded frames.

The table was covered with linen the same color as the candles and was set with china bearing a busy Oriental pattern of garlands and medallions that picked up the colors of the wallpaper. The water glasses were blue crystal inset with a clear filigree, the wineglasses clear crystal with faceted stems. As a centerpiece, there were two creeping figs in a pair of planters decoupaged with playing cards, a surprisingly effective idea.

As Kit bent to read one of the lettered place cards, Broussard pulled out the chair at the head of the table, saying, "Kit, this is yours."

Everyone took their seats but Walter Browning, who remained standing at the foot of the table. He folded his hands in front of him and said, "As current president, it falls to me to explain to Kit our rules. Once the menu is presented, no one is allowed to speak until the meal is finished. This ensures that each member may concentrate fully on the food and not have his attention diverted. It is also my role to propose the opening toast." He nodded to the houseboy, who had been waiting in the doorway with a bottle of wine.

When everyone had been served, Browning raised his glass and said, "First, I toast Andy Broussard for the generous use of his home."

"Here here," they all said, lifting their glasses.

"Second, I toast whoever it was that accidentally dropped the first brontosaurus steak in the fire and ate it, anyway."

"Here here."

"And lastly, I toast our guest, Kit Franklyn, and the missing fabric in her suit."

The "here here's" were the loudest yet and Kit felt her cheeks redden. Browning sat down and the houseboy placed an ivory card on each plate. Kit eagerly picked hers up and read the menu.

POACHED QUAIL EGG, GEORGIA CAVIAR, AND MARY-
LAND
CRAB CAKE
ON TOASTED BRIOCHE

* * *

FRESH SEA URCHIN CONSOMMÉ WITH SEA URCHIN FLAN
AND MULTICOLORED NOODLES

* * *

SEAWEED SALAD MACERATED IN GINGER WITH
CROUSTILLANT OF
SEA SCALLOPS AND GINGER EMULSION

* * *

ROCKFISH SAUTÉ, CRISPY SKIN; *TOMBÉE* OF TOMA-
TOES,
OLIVE, AND
BASIL; JULIENNE OF DRIED SHAD ROE AND LEMON·
CONFIT

* * *

FILET MIGNON OF MILK-FED LAMB WITH SPICES,
CHEESE GNOCCHIS,
AND SOUTH CAROLINA GRITS

*   *   *

CROUSTILLANT OF PINEAPPLE AND NECTARINE CONFIT
IN
HONEY-ALMOND
ICE CREAM WITH PEACH COULIS

Instead of the busy china already on the table, each
course was served on a simple white plate with a blue stripe
around the outer edge, giving the chef a blank canvas on
which to place his creations, which he did so artfully that
with each course, Kit's first approach with knife or fork
made her feel like a Visigoth about to pillage the Louvre.

This guilt was quickly forgotten with the first bite and she
lapsed into the same silent reverence that Broussard and
three of her other dinner companions were also experienc-
ing. Arthur Jordan and Kurt Halliday, though, seemed to
be eating mechanically, with no real appreciation for the
meal. Occasionally, they glanced meaningfully at each
other across the table.

When the meal was over, Browning left the room and
returned with a slim fellow with long blond hair and gold
wire-rimmed glasses. He was wearing a white smock that
buttoned far to one side. "Members and guest," Browning said, "I give you our chef, Molinar."

The others rose and began to applaud. Kit followed suit,
wondering whether Molinar was his first, last, or only
name. The chef bowed and the applause continued. He
bowed again and withdrew. They all returned to the great
room for brandy and more conversation, everyone mel-
lower now and less inclined to controversy. In all, it was an

extremely pleasant evening and everyone parted on good terms.

The chef and his assistant left an hour after the guests and Broussard slipped into bed around 1:00 A. M. By 1:15, he was sleeping soundly. At two, he began to dream. It was a simple dream. There was an explosion and then the image of a long black metal bar sailing upward, like a rocket, against a cloudless blue sky. When he woke the next morning, he remembered the dream vividly but gave it little thought.

WHILE WORKING on her report for Gatlin the afternoon before the Gourmet Society meeting, Kit had called Lester Thomas at the aquarium to arrange to see Paul Jarrell's office. Not fully understanding her relationship with the police, he had been uncooperative at first, but after checking with Gatlin, he had agreed to let her in the next morning at 8:30, before they opened to the public. He was waiting for her at the administrative entrance.

"What exactly are you looking for?" he asked as they walked to Jarrell's office.

"To be honest, I don't really know."

"Does your appearance here mean that Paul's death was not accidental?"

"We're not sure yet what happened."

Gatlin had sealed Jarrell's office with yellow POLICE LINE, DO NOT CROSS tape. Thomas unlocked the door, then stood aside. "Maybe you should be the one to break the seal."

Kit peeled the tape back and went in, Thomas following. She looked back at him. "I'd prefer to do this alone."

"All right. When you're ready to leave, pick up the phone there and dial five three seven. I'll come and show you out."

Jarrell's tiny office had no windows and was spare and functional. Straight ahead, occupying nearly the entire wall, was a metal desk. On the left wall was a short bookcase filled with books that appeared to have been well used. A similar bookcase against the opposite wall held a variety of seashells. On the top were two plastic-embedded fish skeletons sitting on wooden stands.

She began by studying the entries on Jarrell's calendar; "staff mtg., call the Shed Aq., pick up Af. cich., order meth. blue...." Finding none of this useful, she opened the middle drawer of his desk and surveyed the contents: a roll of peel-off red dots, a small pair of needle-nose pliers, an orange Hi-Liter, an AA battery, half a roll of Life Savers, a spoon wrapped in brown paper, a small tube of silicone adhesive, a pebbled rubber thumb cover, and lots of paper clips. But no clues.

What appeared to be three drawers on the right side of the desk was actually a file drawer. She scanned the file indexes: Outstanding purchase orders, Old purchase orders, Suppliers, several marked References, Correspondence.... She removed the correspondence file and went through it, replacing it a few minutes later, unenlightened. She closed the file drawer and turned to the top drawer on the other side of the desk. There, she found Paul Jarrell's checkbook.

Flipping through the check register, she came to one bearing a familiar name. On the first of May, Jarrell had written a check for $350 to Clay Peyton. It seemed a peculiar thing to find—since Paula Jarrell had said that Paul's health was fine. And there was something else. She thought back to the previous night's conversation, to when Kurt Halliday had brought up Jarrell's death. She distinctly remembered him calling Jarrell by name. Then, Clay Peyton had joined in, pressing her hard about the circumstances that had brought her to the aquarium, not once letting on that he had known Jarrell.

Very interesting.

She put the checkbook back where she had found it and made a quick inspection of the remaining drawers, which contained nothing of interest. What she wanted now was a talk with Clay Peyton.

FOURTEEN

KIT LOOKED UP Peyton's office number in the Yellow Pages and called from Jarrell's phone. She got a woman who said that Peyton did not see patients on Tuesdays. When asked for Peyton's home phone number, she refused to give it, a futile gesture, since Kit found it easily in the White Pages. Peyton told her to come on over and didn't even ask what she wanted.

Peyton lived in a large beige stucco two-story with a clay tile roof and an oval-topped, columned portico. The house was set well back from the road and had a nice lawn. The area next to the house was landscaped with palmetto and yucca. Her ring was answered by a tall redhead wearing a pale green Scheherazade outfit with a halter that crisscrossed over her chest, leaving the lower third of her ample breasts exposed.

Kit introduced herself. Getting no reaction of recognition, she added, "Dr. Peyton is expecting me."

"Oh yeah," the woman said, her good looks ruined by a whiny voice. "He's inna back, with his latest toy."

"May I see him?"

"Inna back, I said. Follow the walk." She shut the door.

Kit stepped off the porch and followed the sidewalk to a small structure of similar architecture as the house. She knocked and went in without waiting for anyone to answer.

Clay Peyton was standing on a large patch of fake grass, a golf club in his hand. On each side, he was enclosed by netting that ran from floor to ceiling. Ahead was the image of a fairway rear-projected onto a giant movie screen.

"Ever see anything like this?" Peyton said. "Watch."

He teed up a ball and made a few practice approaches with his club before taking a hefty swing. The ball squibbed off the club head and smacked into the upper-right corner of the screen. The real ball fell onto the fake grass, but its image appeared on the screen exactly where the real one had hit. With the projected scene following, the imaged ball flew through the air and angled into some weeds bordering the fairway.

"I did that to show you how the system deals with hooks and slices," Peyton said.

From the vessel pulsing at his temple, Kit did not believe that he had bungled the shot on purpose. Peyton leaned down and pulled at the fake grass with his fingers, coming away with a piece about a foot square. He replaced it with a square of material that looked like a shag carpet. "Simulated rough," Peyton said. "Held in place with Velcro."

He retrieved the ball, set it on the simulated rough, and whacked at it with a mashie or a niblik or whatever they call those clubs with the tilted metal heads. The ball hopped feebly and barely touched the screen, which shifted to show the ball still in the weeds.

"Anyway, you get the idea," Peyton said, the vein pulsing again.

There were a couple of aluminum lawn chairs nearby, but Peyton did not invite her to sit. "Why did you want to see me?"

"I just came from Paul Jarrell's office, where I found that last month he wrote you a check for three hundred and fifty dollars."

"Who's Paul Jarrell?"

"The man who died at the aquarium late Sunday night. Are you saying you didn't know him?"

"First time I ever heard the name."

"Kurt Halliday mentioned it last night when he was telling us all how he'd heard the story on the news."

"I wasn't paying that much attention to catch the name."

"Why then do you suppose Jarrell wrote you a check?"

"How the hell do I know?" The vein at his temple was throbbing furiously. "I don't think I like the direction you're going with this. Are you trying to implicate me in some way with this case?"

"Not at all. I'm just trying to find out about that check."

"Sure, in the same way that you were just *coincidentally* at the aquarium Sunday night. I gotta tell you, if this is any indication of your abilities as an investigator, you're in the wrong line of work. If you're looking for suspicious circumstances, ask Kurt Halliday how he happened to remember the name of the guy that died after hearing it the one time on the news. Who's able to do that? And how about the way Jordan and Halliday were looking at each other across the table at dinner. What was *that* all about? You want more... I'll give you more. Ask Haley Dagget where *he* was Sunday night. Now, if you'll excuse me, I've got things to do."

When the door had closed behind Kit, Peyton reset his ball on the simulated rough. With his hands gripping the club too tightly, he chopped at the ball and missed. Growling, he threw down his club, snatched up the square of simulated rough, and threw it against the door.

On the way to her car, Kit congratulated herself for a very promising interview.

THROUGH HIS RECEPTIONIST, Haley Dagget agreed to squeeze Kit in for a few minutes between appointments. Arriving at his office, she found it packed with patients engaging in the usual waiting-room rituals of staring at the wallpaper and thumbing through magazines they'd never read at home. Apart from a woman whose mouth drooped noticeably on one side, they did not look like a collection of people with defective nervous systems. Their numbers seemed to back up Dagget's boast at the gourmet dinner that he was an exceptional doctor.

She identified herself to the nurse behind the check-in counter and was shown into Dagget's office, with the assurance that he would be with her shortly.

Dagget breezed in a few minutes later, equally as interesting-looking in a white coat as he had been in a tux. He extended his hand. "Hello, Kit, this is a surprise."

They shook hands and he went behind his desk. He sat down and folded his hands on the glass covering the desktop. "What can I do for you?"

Knowing how her question was going to sound, Kit tried to soften the impact by setting it up with a disclaimer. "I want to ask you a question, but before I do, you should understand that I'm merely gathering background material. I'm not trying to suggest anything."

Dagget leaned back in his chair and folded his arms in front of him, a subconscious gesture of protection. He adopted a wary expression. "I'm listening."

Reluctantly, Kit pulled the pin. "Could you tell me where you were between twelve and one Sunday night?"

Frost settled in Dagget's cool gray eyes. "Why ever would you want to know that?"

Realizing that she couldn't expect anyone to answer such a question without knowing why it was being asked, Kit said, "Someone has mentioned your name in connection with the death of that fellow at the aquarium."

Dagget rocked forward in his chair, looking genuinely shocked. "That is absolutely ridiculous. *Who* mentioned my name?"

"I can't tell you. You should know that at this point it's a totally unsubstantiated offhand comment. But I do have to check it out. I hope you understand."

Dagget seemed to relax a little. "All right...since you put it that way, but I'd still like to know who mentioned me."

"Sorry." She waited for him to answer the question.

"Sunday night...between midnight and one, you say?" His brows knitted in thought. "I was at Parkside Hospital checking on two patients I operated on earlier that day. Ordinarily, I wouldn't be at the hospital that late, especially after a day of surgery, but these were difficult cases and I was concerned about them, especially in their first few hours after coming off the table."

"Do you often operate on Sunday?"

"Rarely, but these folks couldn't wait until Monday."

"Would it take an hour to examine two patients?"

"Parkside is about twenty minutes from my home. I was including the drive over and the drive back."

"Parkside is in Kenner, isn't it?"

"Yes."

"And you live in . . ."

"Harahan."

"I see by your ring that you're married."

"What does that—"

"Your wife . . . she could verify the time you left and the time you returned?"

"When I left, yes, but she was asleep when I got back. Listen, I don't want you bothering . . ."

Kit waved her hand in dismissal of his concern. "There's no need for me to see her. You've told me what I need to know. Harahan and Kenner are a *long* way from the aquarium. You're covered, just as I knew you would be." She stood up. "Sorry to have bothered you, especially with so many patients waiting."

Dagget stood as well. "Don't mention it, I'm glad to have things straightened out."

PARKSIDE HOSPITAL had recently fertilized all their flower beds, and the halls on the ground floor smelled of cow manure. Kit stepped up to the admissions and information window. "Could you tell me where the rooms for Dr. Dagget's patients would be?"

"What's his specialty?" the clerk asked.

"Neurosurgery."

"Fifth floor. The elevators are down there."

Kit followed a middle-aged woman carrying a potted plant onto the elevator and they rode in silence to the second floor, where they had to make room for two hundred pounds of registered nurse and a gurney carrying a toothless old woman hooked up to an IV bottle. Kit often rode with similar cargo at Charity Hospital but had never grown comfortable with being this close to a flickering life. She dealt with it now as she always did, by keeping her eyes and her mind elsewhere. On three, she and the woman with the plant had to move farther to the rear to let on two young men in incredibly wrinkled green scrubs.

The nurse's station on five was right in front of the elevator. Kit stepped to the counter and the young nurse behind it looked up. She was Asian and basically pretty, but with an asymmetric pout on her upper lip that gave her a permanent sneer. It seemed like something that could be

fixed, but surely she would have done it if that was true.
"May I speak to the head floor nurse, please," Kit said.

The girl picked up a microphone. "Gwen Nix, please
come to the nurse's station. Gwen Nix to the nurse's station."

Kit was surprised at her perfect diction.

A short, stocky woman in white came out of a room
down the hall, steamed toward them, and presented herself at the nurse's station. Expecting from her walk that Nix
would be a cold woman who believed that a little pain never
hurt anybody, Kit found herself looking into a friendly face
with warm hazel eyes.

Kit introduced herself and said, "I'm investigating a case
for the New Orleans police. Is there a place where we can
talk?"

"Down here," Nix said. She led Kit to an examining
room behind the nurse's station. Kit went in first and Nix
followed, closing the door behind her and leaning against
it, hands in the pockets of her lab coat.

"When a doctor visits a patient on this floor," Kit began, "does he sign in or anything?"

"No. They come and go with no restrictions."

"If a doctor was on the floor, would you know about
it?"

"Not necessarily. They could come in while I'm busy in
one of the rooms and leave without my ever having seen
them. Who are we talking about?"

"Before I mention any names, you should understand
that this is just a background check. He's not being charged
with anything and, in fact, probably has nothing whatever
to do with the case I'm investigating."

"Understood," Nix said crisply.

"It's Haley Dagget. He told me that he was here Sunday night between twelve and one checking on two patients he operated on earlier in the day."

"The part about him having two fresh cases on the floor that night is certainly true. They're still here and doing fine. He's a good surgeon."

"Could we ask them if he was here Sunday night?"

"First, you'd have to okay it with the chief administrator. We always try to protect our patients' privacy. But in this case, I wouldn't bother. They wouldn't have been in any shape to know when or even if their doctor visited them. There may be another way, though. Wait here."

Nix left the room and returned shortly with two metal clipboards thick with papers. She laid one on the examining table and flipped through the sheets on the other. She studied one of the pages for a few seconds and shook her head. "No record here of a visit from Dr. Dagget." She laid that board down and picked up the other. Finding the sheet she wanted in that one, she ran her finger down it. "Nothing here, either." She showed Kit the page. "This is the progress chart of one of Dr. Dagget's patients. Here you can see an entry by one of the nurses made at eleven o'clock. Here"—she slid her finger down two lines—"is another entry at one o'clock, by the same nurse. No entry by Dr. Dagget. It's the same on the other chart."

"Could he have visited and not made an entry?"

"Dr. Dagget is not one to make rounds at night. In fact, I've never known him to do it. He lets the nursing staff and the resident on call handle the routine things, figuring that if he's needed, we'll call him. Besides, a doctor can charge Medicaid and Medicare for every visit he makes to a patient. But he'd better be sure he can document the visit. They all know that, so an attending always writes something on the chart, even if it's nothing more than 'vital signs stable.'"

"*Always* writes something?"

"Oh I suppose once in a blue moon he might forget. But we're talking about someone who came in at a very inconvenient time. If it was me, I'd sure want credit for the visit."

"But it *could* have happened."

"It's possible...." Then Nix added, "You ever respond to the Publisher's Sweepstakes letter?"

"No."

"Me, neither."

WHEN EVEN A FRESH CORPSE is opened, it exudes a sweet sickly smell that today remained in Broussard's nostrils far longer than it should have, probably because the body he'd just left was that of an infant, dead because of a simple throat infection, neglected until the tissues had become so swollen, they had obstructed her throat, suffocating her. Now, his arm seemed almost too heavy to lift as he punched the elevator for the floor where the fine-structure lab was located.

The electron microscopes were under the supervision of Jan Dietz, a naturalized Ph.D. from Austria. Dietz's operation was so good that you could give him a section already prepared for light microscopy and he could reclaim it from the slide, re-embed it, and slice it further into impossibly thin wafers so that its secrets could be probed by electron beams. Broussard found Dietz bent over a set of micrographs, looking at them through a pair of lenses on short legs.

Dietz looked up. "Ah, Andy. You haf come as though reading my mind. Your pictures are on the dryer." He stepped so close his face occupied the zone where Broussard's glasses couldn't focus an image. "And how is your day?"

Broussard stepped back. "It'll have to improve a lot just to be lousy."

"Perhaps you will find happiness in my pictures."

Broussard followed Dietz to a piece of equipment that dried pictures on a hot silver drum. Dietz gathered up a handful of eight-by-tens from where they had fallen into a plastic tray and handed them to Broussard with a slight bow. A snapping sound came from the cooling dryer and for a moment Broussard thought Dietz had clicked his heels together. "When you need us again, we are here," Dietz said.

Broussard took the pictures to his office, where he fished two lemon balls from the glass bowl on his desk, slipped them into his mouth, and sat down to study the pictures of Paul Jarrell's pyramidal cells. Dietz had done his usual stellar job, recording in crisp detail the ultrastructure of the nuclear inclusions that Broussard had thought might be viral.

Generally, viral particles are circular or polygonal, the latter often in crystalline arrays that make them quite distinctive. The inclusions in Jarrell's cells, however, were composed of amorphous material that gave Broussard no hints as to their origin.

He slapped the photographs onto his desk in frustration. What the devil *were* those things? He got up, went to the Mr. Coffee, and poured some Gevalia into his big cup decorated with dancing crayfish. He put the cup to his lips and drank, expertly holding a lemon ball in each cheek so he wouldn't swallow them.

Dumbbell-shaped nuclear inclusions.

Dumbbell-shaped nuclear...

He leaned his rump against the desk and stroked the hairs on the end of his nose. That phrase...*Dumbbell-shaped*— His thoughts were shattered by the sound of the telephone.

There followed a brief conversation so unsettling, it temporarily drove everything else from his mind.

WHILE BROUSSARD had been picking up Jarrell's pictures from Dietz, Kit had returned to her office and found someone knocking on the door.

"Looking for me?" she said.

The man turned. It was Walter Browning.

"Yes I was," Browning said. "Do you have a few minutes?"

When they were both comfortably seated in Kit's office and had exchanged some meaningless small talk, Browning crossed his legs and said, "I talked to Clay Peyton a little while ago and he said that you came to see him early this morning."

"That's right."

"He also said he muffed a couple of golf shots and got so mad, he said some things he shouldn't have, things that really had no bearing on the subject you were discussing. He wouldn't tell me what those things were but said you should disregard them, because it was just his anger talking. And he said to tell you he'd try to find out about that check and get back to you."

"I don't understand where you come in. Why didn't he call me himself?"

"Two reasons. One, he just felt like such an idiot afterward, he didn't have the nerve, and two, he didn't think you'd believe him. I'm here as sort of a bad-character reference. If you'd ever played golf with him like I have, you'd know how irrational he can be if he's having a bad day.

He's a fine man in most respects, but golf brings out the worst in him. He bought that computer simulator so that he could throw his tantrums in private."

"And you made a special trip over here to tell me this?"

"No. I probably wouldn't have done it if I wasn't going to be in the vicinity, anyway. I've got a lunch date with the Tulane chairman of orthopedics to discuss production of a new fixation nail he's developed. And now that I've delivered my message, I'd better get over there."

They shook hands, Kit thanked him for coming, and he left. As the door shut behind him, Kit pulled out the phone book and looked up the number of the Tulane department of orthopedics.

She punched in the number and, when they answered, said, "This is Walter Browning's secretary. Has Mr. Browning arrived yet?"

"Who is Mr. Browning?" the voice said.

"I believe he has a lunch appointment with the chairman," Kit said. "But maybe I'm mistaken. Could you check, please?"

"I'm looking at the appointment book," the voice said. "And I have nothing for Mr. Browning."

"Could the chairman have made the appointment himself and forgotten to inform you?"

"He never makes his own appointments. Everything gets referred to me."

Kit mumbled something and hung up, her head buzzing with the morning's events. A shadow appeared on the frosted glass panel of her door, followed by a couple of knocks.

It was Broussard.

"Hope you haven't made any plans for tonight," he said.

"Why?"

"'Cause I just got an odd call from Arthur Jordan, who said he wanted to talk to both of us at his hotel at eight o'clock. I told him we'd come.''

"He say what he wanted to talk about?''

"The body we found in your backyard.''

FIFTEEN

SINCE IT WAS NEARLY NOON, Kit and Broussard headed for Grandma O's for lunch.

"What do you think Jordan's going to tell us?" Kit asked, trying to talk over the sound of the traffic on Tulane Avenue.

"He sounded pretty nervous," Broussard replied. "I'm afraid to say what I think."

"Because you believe he was involved in the murder?"

Broussard pressed his lips together and nodded.

"Maybe he simply overheard someone talking about it."

"Maybe."

Unsure of what significance to attach to her encounters with Peyton, Dagget, and Browning and thinking that Jordan might clear all of that up, Kit decided not to mention these matters to Broussard just yet.

After lunch, to get her thoughts in order and to satisfy Gatlin, Kit returned to her office and wrote up everything she had learned that morning, as well as her subjective impressions of each of the three men. Generally, she was pretty adept at spotting a liar, but the only one of the three who she had thought from his manner might not be telling the truth was Haley Dagget. Her failure to find any evidence he had been at Parkside Hospital Sunday night confirmed that impression.

And what of Walter Browning? From his behavior in her office, he had appeared to be telling the truth, but he had definitely lied—at least about meeting the orthopedics chairman for lunch. And if he'd lied about that, could she believe anything he said? Without much effort, Kit could see Peyton nervously making a phone call to Browning after she'd left ... could almost hear Peyton saying how he'd blurted out some things he shouldn't. Could hear Browning curse and tell Peyton to keep his mouth shut and that he would try to repair the damage.

So where did Dagget come in? Maybe Browning and Peyton weren't involved at all. Maybe it was Dagget ... and Arthur Jordan. But then why did Browning lie about his appointment for lunch? And wasn't it Peyton who had put her on to Dagget in the first place?

God.

Maybe it was *all* of them, all except Kurt Halliday. She thought about what Peyton had said about Halliday remembering Paul Jarrell's name from the news. Was that really so unusual? She had a talent for remembering names herself. But then there were those odd visual exchanges between Jordan and Halliday at dinner.... And, of course, Paul Jarrell had to be worked in....

Jesus. If she kept going like this, they'd need the Superdome to hold all the suspects. Her head began to feel like an overinflated tire and she stood up and paced the office, rubbing her neck. The pressure of her hand felt good, but not as nice as when Teddy used to do it for her. She suddenly had a need to hear Teddy's voice.

She went to the phone, picked it up, and hesitated, her fingers poised over the first digit for the alligator farm in Bayou Coteau. But what would that accomplish? She hadn't reached any decision. It would only complicate things.

Instead of calling Teddy, she entered her own number, hoping that there might be a message from Teddy on her answering machine, an illogical hope, since he had her office number and would probably have called her there if he wanted to talk.

There was only one message.

"Kit, this is John Tully. Gimme a call when you can."

Not yet ready to reimmerse herself in the confusing facts before her, she delayed their further consideration by calling Tully.

"Kit Franklyn?" Tully said. "Yeah. Hullo, Kit. Good of you to call so soon. Listen, a couple more of my new crosses came into flower and they're good ones. Maybe better than the one you picked the other day. But maybe not. Think you could stop over sometime today and lemme know what you think?"

"I could drop by later. How about five o'clock?"

"Say, that'd be good. And maybe you'd ah . . . you'd let me show my appreciation by stayin' for dinner."

"John, that's not really necessary."

"Didn't offer because it was necessary. Did it because I wanted to. What do you say? I'm old, but I don't have any eatin' habits that'd make you sorry you stayed. Still got my own teeth, so there'd be none of that clackin' you get with phony choppers."

Thinking how lonely life appeared to be for Tully, Kit decided it wouldn't kill her to give him a little company. "All right, John, I accept."

"Hey, that's good. I'll expect you at five."

Immediately after she hung up, the reality of what had just taken place sank in. Picturing the two of them eating next to a pile of potting soil, she mumbled, "What *have* I done?"

Her fears about dinner proved to be unfounded. When she arrived, she found Tully's kitchen spotless. The kitchen table was covered with a clean tablecloth and was set with matching dishes. In the center of the table were three large red roses floating in a crystal bowl. Tully himself looked different and it was several minutes before she realized it was because his hair was wet-combed and parted.

Dinner was a fresh garden salad sprinkled with rose petals, and chicken fettucini with French bread. The entrée was no surprise, for Kit had seen the Budget Gourmet boxes in the wastebasket. There was no wine, because as Tully said, "I want to be awake the whole time you're here."

During dinner, Tully spoke interestingly and surprisingly eloquently of growing up in Atlanta and being in the crowd at the premiere of *Gone with the Wind*. Of how Vivian Leigh had looked right at him and smiled, and how for the next month, he had spent every spare cent at the theater, seeing the film a dozen times. He told of his years as a gold miner in Honduras and how frightened he had been as an infantryman at Normandy.

After dinner, Tully brought out four small rose plants and Kit gave him her opinion, picking one of the new ones over her previous favorite. Driving home, she did not feel as though she had done anything noble by visiting the lonely old man but, rather, had simply spent a pleasant hour or so with someone she liked.

Though not much of a TV fan, Kit remained in front of the set after the news to watch a self-defense program for women on a local cable channel she usually ignored. Could she push a Bic into someone's throat and gleefully watch them drown in their own blood as the instructor advised? She doubted it.

Broussard arrived at 7:40, driving his yellow T-bird. She had never before seen him in any color shirt but white. Tonight, it was pale yellow, with a yellow bow tie. She dropped into the seat next to him and shut the door. "Your shirt matches the car," she observed.

"Nothin' intentional," he said, backing into the street. "Phillip gave it to me for my birthday and has been askin' if I've ever worn it. Now I have."

They circled the block in silence, turned onto St. Charles, and headed for downtown. A kid in a pickup with fancy mud flaps and rubber webbing stretched across the back instead of a tailgate sped past, rap music blaring from his open windows.

"So," Broussard said, "do you think youngsters really like rap or is it just a stick in the eye to the rest of us?"

"Still worried about what Jordan will say?"

"Been tryin' not to think about it. Guess you didn't notice."

"I noticed. But we'll be there in a few minutes. How about filling me in on a little background before we see him. Like where you two met."

"One of the members of our Gourmet Society moved out of state and Walter Browning brought us Arthur."

"Now *that*'s interesting."

"How so?"

"I mean in a general way."

"No. You mean in a specific way. What's up?"

"I'd rather not say right now."

"Why?"

"I may be wrong."

"No shame in that."

"Try it sometime, especially with an audience, and let me know how *you* like it."

"You're too sensitive."

"I'm just allergic to Babe Ruth stories."

Despite his concern for Jordan, Broussard let loose with a rumbling chuckle.

"What is it about Jordan that makes you like him so much?"

"I've always admired the fact that he'll treat folks who he knows will probably never be able to pay him."

"I noticed that he wears a wedding ring. His wife going to be in on this?"

"I heard they're separated. She's in their house and he's temporarily livin' in a suite at the Winchester."

"Kids?"

"No."

"Wonder what brought on the split?"

"Not my area of expertise."

"He seems like too good a man to be a murderer. I'm betting he was an unwilling witness."

"We'll soon find out. There's the hotel."

The Winchester was thirty stories of black glass and glistening ceramic block that had gone up so quickly and looked so darkly efficient that it seemed to Kit like a great carrion feeder that had arrived one night on silent wings. To hear that it now had in its belly half the remains of Jordan's dying marriage did nothing to dim the analogy.

They parked in the first floor of the hotel garage and went in the front entrance, preceded by a fiftyish woman in spike heels, pink slacks, and a pink blouse. She was accompanied by a snuffling bulldog wearing a pink jacket and a pink baseball cap held on with an elastic band under his chin. The dog was on a choke chain but still managed a quick exploration of the doorman's leg with his muzzle on the way inside, leaving dark wet marks on what was a spotless tan uniform.

Inside, the hotel was cool but not comfortable, the transient, unsettled lives of its inhabitants hanging stiffly in the air. Surely Jordan had done himself no favor by coming here, Kit thought.

They had entered a narrow paneled corridor that stretched away before them with no obvious bank of elevators. The woman with the dog picked him up in her arms and stepped onto the escalator to their left, which went up to the mezzanine and, most likely, the lobby. Without checking to see what Broussard wanted to do, Kit followed the woman onto the escalator.

From his elevated vantage point, the dog watched Kit with doleful eyes, his tongue dripping saliva on his master's arm. Behind Broussard, Kit heard two women gossiping openly about an acquaintance and she glanced over her shoulder to see what people who did such things with witnesses present looked like. She found them normal in appearance and well dressed in tailored suits, each wearing a HELLO MY NAME IS . . . sticker on her lapel.

The next few seconds were a blur. A scream from the top of the escalator jerked Kit's head around. On the mezzanine, a woman was staring at a point high above the escalator, her hand covering her mouth. Kit looked up and saw a dark shape wrapped in vines and green leaves hurtling toward her. Instinctively, she shied from the object and stumbled down one step, losing her balance and falling against Broussard. The moving stairs carried her back to nearly the same spot and the object plummeted by, whipping her with a strand of foliage. It slammed onto the escalator with a sickening jolt.

Frightened, the dog lurched from his master's arms and scrambled up the escalator to the mezzanine, where he dashed for safety, his chain bouncing behind him. For a fleeting instant, Kit was in shock. A heartbeat later, she realized that the object at her feet was a man lying chest-down but with one leg bent at an impossible angle, his head twisted backward so that his scalp rubbed against the side of the escalator. Through the tortured expression on his fact, Kit recognized Arthur Jordan.

BROUSSARD MET GATLIN at the Winchester's front entrance. Gatlin looked at the old pathologist with an appraising eye and said, "Good-looking shirt. What have we got and how's it happen you're here before me?"

Broussard pointed at the top of the escalator, both sides of which had been shut off by the maintenance crew. "He's up there."

Ignoring the cop who was making sure that civilians took a different route to the mezzanine, Gatlin started up what was normally the down escalator, closely followed by Broussard, who gave him a quick overview of the situation.

Jordan lay about where he had been deposited by the escalator. He had been moved only as much as was necessary for Broussard to determine that he was dead. He was covered by a sheet, brought by a maid at the request of the shaken hotel manager. Two uniformed cops kept away the crowd that had gathered.

Broussard lifted the sheet and Gatlin bent over to look at the body, which had a vine clutched tightly in one hand.

"He was alive when he went over the sixth-floor railing," Broussard said.

Gatlin looked up. Above a short wall topped by a wood and brass railing, each floor opened onto the thirty-story atrium like a balcony. Set into the wall below the railings were narrow planters whose contents cascaded in leafy tendrils down the sides of the atrium.

"Damned goofy way to build a hotel, if you ask me," Gatlin growled. He looked at Broussard. "Why'd you say he was alive when he took the spill? It's what I'd expect."

"We expected to meet him in his rooms."

Gatlin pawed the air with one hand. "All right. I get the point."

"His neck has a circular bruise around it that wasn't caused by his fall. Looks like someone tried to strangle him in his room and left him for dead. He recovered, staggered into the hall, and tried to get help by signalin' from the balcony, but he leaned out too far."

Gatlin's surprise showed on his face. "Where'd you get all that?"

"The part about him leanin' out too far and signalin' for help, from that lady over there...." He pointed to two armchairs across the lobby where Kit was holding an old lady's hand in her own. "She saw him immediately before he fell."

"She see anyone with him?"

"No. I took a look in his room and found a piece of cord that had been cut from the telephone lyin' on the floor. Not much doubt about its purpose. Most likely, it was his short neck that saved him."

"Could have used a pair of wings to go with it. You didn't move anything, I hope."

Broussard's bushy brows crept together in reproach.

"All right, all right. Cut me some slack. I'm not used to having a pro first on the scene. Usually, it's some gomer in size-fifteen Keds kicking shell casings into the sewer grate. Can I assume there's a uniform preserving the integrity of the scene upstairs?"

"You may."

Gatlin whistled at Kit and crooked his finger at her. When she reached him, he said, "Doc, as of now, you're off the case."

"Why?" Kit asked, perplexed. "Have I done something wrong?"

"Not at all. Things have just gotten too hot for you. It's one thing to put an untrained person on a case with cobwebs all over it, and it's another when a body almost falls on you. You turned up anything lately I should know about?''

"It's all typed up and sitting on my desk.''

"See what you can do about getting it on *my* desk.''

SIXTEEN

To say that Kit was unhappy at being taken off the Francie O'Connor case would be like saying that killer hurricanes usually bring bad weather. Sure, now that there had been one probable and one certain new murder, it was reasonable that Gatlin would have to take a more active role. But to dismiss her entirely as if she were a child, incapable of contributing anything now that things had heated up, was intolerable. Anyone well acquainted with Kit knew that when she was angry, her ears became flushed and hot. Right now, they were the color of well-ripened cayenne peppers. This was what was on her mind as the office phone rang.

"Would you please hold for Mr. Isom?" a female voice said.

Isom? The name was vaguely familiar.

"Ms. Franklyn, this is Harry Isom. I have a message that you called."

Kit's mind grappled with the name, then she remembered. "Mr. Isom, I'm with the medical examiner's office and the New Orleans Police Department and we're trying to locate Shirley Elizabeth Guillot. We hoped that since you once handled a real estate transaction for her, you might be able to give us some information on her whereabouts."

"That's possible," Isom said. "But first you have to come to my office and show me your credentials. I'm not in the habit of discussing my clients with anyone. But if this is police business, that's a different matter."

Isom reminded her of his office location and agreed to see her today if she could get there within the hour. After hanging up, she grabbed a spiral pad and headed for the door, then paused, remembering that Gatlin had taken her off the case.

She had no delusions as to the most appropriate action—tell Gatlin about Isom's call and stay out of the way. But it was so unfair after all the work she had already done. And there was her promise to Leslie. To let Gatlin handle this by himself would be like abandoning her again. She decided to forge ahead and let Gatlin respond as he saw fit. Since office sanction of any activities related to this case had been withdrawn, there was something she felt obliged to do before going out.

THE AUTOPSY on Arthur Jordan had been done early that morning and it confirmed Broussard's impressions of what had taken place at the scene. Still perplexed about the dumbbell-shaped inclusions in Paul Jarrell's pyramidal cells, and too curious to wait for time-consuming paraffin processing, Broussard had sent some small pieces of Arthur Jordan's brain to the lab for frozen sections. Now, as he studied them through his microscope, he was disappointed but not surprised. Jordan's pyramidal cells were entirely normal.

There was a knock on the door. He called out a welcome and reached for his glasses. Kit entered, closed the door behind her, and remained close to it, her manner uncharacteristically timid.

"I need some personal time this morning," she said.

"Anything you need help with?"

"No, I can handle it. It's no big deal."

"Take whatever time is necessary."

"Thanks. I'll probably be back in an hour or so."

Reflecting on her behavior after she was gone, Broussard hoped that she wasn't doing what he thought she was doing.

Isom shared a renovated redbrick Victorian town house with a Realtor and a beauty shop. Below his name on the door to his suite was the ghost of a second set of lettering that had been scraped off but had left enough glue behind to still spell Loscovitz. His secretary, a dewlap-cursed lady wearing so much pancake makeup that it could have been tilled and planted, presented Kit to Isom without even checking to see whether he was ready. They found him looking for a book among the ponderous volumes on the shelves behind his desk.

Of average height, Isom had more hair than many men his age and wore a small mustache. He was not more than a few pounds overweight and had good color—except for the bags under his sunken eyes, which almost looked as if they had been blackened with charcoal.

"You planning on standing the entire time?" Isom said.

As Kit sat in one of the chairs that formed a semicircle in front of Isom's desk, a voice from behind her said, "Siddown."

She looked over her shoulder and saw a mynah in a domed black cage.

"Siddown," the bird repeated, then added, "Objection.... You're in contempt.... All rise.... Siddown.... Bailiff, take him away."

"That's Litigious," Isom said, putting himself in his desk chair. "He always gets mouthy when someone new is around. Ignore him. He'll calm down."

"So you're a bird lover," Kit said.

"Lover? I hate him. He belonged to my partner, Sid Loscovitz. Sid died in January. Take my advice, never go to the bedside of a dying friend, at least not one who still has enough strength left to recognize you. Sid's eyes fluttered open, he touched my hand, and pleaded for me to take care of his bird when he passed. What could I do? So there he sits, a bigger pain even than Sid was. You wouldn't happen to know the life span of a bird like that, would you?"

Kit shook her head. "Sorry."

"Siddown.... All rise...."

"Shaddup over there," Isom said. He looked at Kit. "You were going to show me some identification?"

When he was satisfied that Kit had proper credentials, Isom said, "Shirley Guillot is dead, too. Died about seven years ago."

Kit moved to the front of her chair. "Why on earth did you bring me over here and demand my ID just to tell me that?"

"Because I do not believe that my obligation to a client ends when they die. In fact, if anything, death strengthens it, because they are then in no position to defend themselves against slander."

"Slander and libel," Litigous said. "All rise...."

"How well did you know Shirley Guillot?"

"Enough to know that she was a good woman, hardworking, sensible, knew the value of money."

"Was she married?"

"Widow ... husband died in an industrial accident a few years after they were married. She earned her living by buying houses and operating them as rental property. I handled the paperwork for all her real estate transactions."

"If I gave you an address, could you tell me if it was one of her rental properties, as opposed to a house that she personally lived in?"

"It wouldn't surprise me."

Kit recited her own address and Isom opened a file folder in front of him and began going through it. In a minute or so, he looked up. "Rental... from the time she bought it until she sold it to get enough cash to leverage a deal on a small apartment building."

"Did you handle her operation on a day-to-day basis?"

"Just acquisition and disposition. She liked to do all the other herself, and rightly so."

"Do you have any idea what happened to her possessions after she died?"

"Could be. Sid was the one who drew up her will and acted as executor." He left his chair and went to a bank of file cabinets against the wall. After a short search, he pulled out a file and opened it on top of the cabinets. A few seconds later, he said, "Everything went to her sister, Eugenie Sonnier."

"Do you have her address?"

Isom scanned the file some more and gave her an address in Lafitte, a tiny community about twenty-five miles south, then said, "Sid made a note here that she has no telephone."

"But that was seven years ago."

"If you like, I'll have my secretary check the book for you."

"I'd appreciate it. Does the file mention her husband's name?"

Isom checked the file again and said, "No, but how many Sonniers can there be in such a small place?"

Actually, his secretary found none. So if Eugenie was still there, she hadn't used her inheritance to join the twentieth century.

Kit stood up and expressed her thanks. Isom said something appropriate and Litigious said, "Siddown." As Kit left, Litigious added, "You're in contempt." Over the sound of the closing door, she heard Isom say, "Shad-dup."

From the telephone in Isom's outer office, Kit called Broussard to say that she would be gone for another few hours. Informed by Broussard's secretary that both he and Charlie Franks had gone to a scene, she was unable to deliver the message personally. Though her thoughts were primarily on Eugenie Sonnier, she did wonder what kind of case would require two pathologists.

IN A FASHIONABLE SECTION of the city near Lake Pontchartrain, Broussard was in a bookcase-lined study, standing next to a tufted leather chair containing a body slumped over a large mahogany partner desk. The corpse lay facedown on the desk's tan leather writing surface, its right arm in its lap, the left dangling so that the fingers pointed at a disposable syringe lying on the plastic floor mat under the chair. On the desk, a few inches from the top of the corpse's head, was an open screw-top bottle half full of a clear liquid.

Broussard was reading a typed letter lying beside the corpse's right ear.

To Whom It May Concern,

I have taken my life because it has become of no further value to me. Years ago, when Arthur Jordan and I roomed together as students, we picked up a girl in the French Quarter and took her back to our rooms, where something terrible occurred. We were both so drunk that neither of us knew exactly what happened, but we woke and found the girl strangled. Afraid to let this be known, we buried her in the backyard and said nothing. For more than twenty years, we have lived with the fear that one day the body would be found.

Then it was found, by Kit Franklyn. After meeting with Franklyn at the Gourmet Society dinner, Jordan lost his nerve and wanted to confess. But I disagreed.

Eventually, Jordan's persistence wore me down and we agreed to reveal to Franklyn and Andy Broussard what had taken place. Jordan arranged a meeting at his apartment for eight o'clock this evening (Tue.). I arrived shortly after seven fully expecting to do what I had agreed to do. But I suddenly saw what confession would mean. The humiliation...prison...or worse.

I had always believed the events of that awful night so long ago were an aberration, that I was incapable of such a heinous act as murder and that it must have been Jordan who did it. I know now I was wrong, because a few minutes after my arrival I panicked and when Jordan went into the bathroom, I cut a section from the telephone cord and waited for him to come out. When he did, I strangled him. After using a towel to wipe everything I might have touched, I left by the stairs.

Driving home, the realization of what I had done...of what I really am hit me. This is knowledge I cannot live with. I am truly sorry for everything and hope that the good I have done as a physician somehow mitigates the other....

Kurt Halliday.

Broussard stepped back to give Charlie Franks a look at the letter.

"What do you think?" Gatlin said to Broussard. "Everything look right?"

"Too soon to tell," Broussard replied. "But he's in full rigor, so that fits."

"What do you think's in the bottle?"

"We'll need the lab for that. The poolin' of blood in his fingers and his face, except where his forehead and nose are touchin' the desk, indicate he died where he sits. We'll know more about that when we get his clothes off. Who found him?"

"The uniforms outside. When he didn't show at eight o'clock this morning for rounds, somebody got worried and started looking for him. When they couldn't turn him up, they asked the department to send a car over here. They saw him through the window."

"He live alone?" Franks asked.

Gatlin nodded.

The room was flooded with light from Ray Jamison's Polaroid as he took an orienting shot from across the room. Behind Broussard, Louie Bordelon, a blond fellow with a complexion the color and texture of a newborn mouse, pulled Halliday's computer keyboard to the end of the table beside the desk and began dusting it for prints.

Broussard made a hitchhiking gesture at Bordelon and said to Gatlin, "Since you brought Louie out, I guess it's occurred to you that this is a mighty convenient death."

"The thought crossed my mind," Gatlin replied.

Satisfied that his last picture was a keeper, Jamison slipped it into his shoulder bag and stepped up to the desk. He took an angled overhead shot and said, "That's everything, if you want to move him. I'd give you a hand, but I pulled a muscle last week trying to lift the kid's swing set."

"I didn't know they let people with your genes reproduce," Franks said, grinning. He motioned at Gatlin. "Come on, I'll help."

Gatlin took up a position on the other side of the body. "Let's just leave him in his chair."

They slid the chair well away from the desk and hovered close by to see whether Halliday was going to stay put without help. When it became clear that he would not topple, Gatlin said, "Louie, you got anything there?"

"About what I expected," Bordelon said. "Nothin' but smears."

Gatlin looked at Franks. "Can you get that printer to do something? I want to compare its typeface with the letter."

"If Louie hasn't gummed up the keyboard, I can."

Bordelon wiped the fingerprint powder off the keyboard and slid the board over to Franks, who positioned it in front of him and turned on the printer and the computer. A message in a flashing box appeared on the monitor: *PROGRAM CRASH. DO YOU WISH TO RESURRECT?*

Franks's fingers darted over the keyboard. The screen changed and he gloated. "Ha. Halliday must have simply shut the computer off after printing the file. There it is, back in its entirety. You still want a copy?"

"Forget it. That answers my question."

Franks's fingers jigged again over the keyboard and he beamed. "Care to know when the letter was written?"

"No, I've suddenly gone brain-dead and lost interest," Gatlin growled.

Ignoring Gatlin's sarcasm, Franks said, "Nine o'clock last night."

"An hour after Jordan did his swan dive. Okay, thanks." Gatlin opened his little black book and scribbled himself a note.

"Is that it for me?" Jamison asked.

"Yeah, you can take off," Gatlin said, still writing. When he finished, he looked at Bordelon and pointed at the syringe. "Louie, see if you can get anything off that"—he shifted his finger to the bottle on the desk—"and that. And cap the bottle before doing anything. We don't want to lose the contents."

A faint hint of annoyance passed across Bordelon's face at what he apparently considered unnecessary instructions.

Gatlin turned to speak to Broussard and found him with his rubber-gloved hand in the corpse's left pocket. He came out with a pocketknife. "I was wonderin' what he might have used to cut Jordan's phone wire," he said, carrying the knife to the desk.

"Don't know why," Gatlin said. "There was a set of steak knives in Jordan's little kitchen."

"True," Broussard said. "But it's comfortin' to know that somethin' in his pocket supports what he wrote in his letter."

Gatlin looked at Bordelon. "Do the knife, too, will you?"

"Charlie, I'm curious," Broussard said. "You bothered by the fact that Halliday just cut the computer off after he was through rather than shuttin' down in a more conventional manner?"

Franks shrugged. "A little. But for a guy that's about to kill himself, the conventional behavior train has already departed."

"I'm not crazy about typed suicide notes," Gatlin said, "but at least he signed it. I'm sure we'll be able to find some sample of his signature for the document section to compare with the one on the note. You'll take responsibility for the bottle and syringe?"

"We'll send 'em to the lab soon as we get back," Broussard said. "Should have somethin' this afternoon."

"When can you do him?"

"We already got a customer from Woodsy New-some.... Charlie, can you take that one?"

Franks nodded.

"Check with me about two-thirty."

Gatlin looked at Bordelon. "Anything?"

"A good one from the bottle, but other than that, nothing to write home about." Bordelon lifted the print from the bottle with a piece of adhesive tape, then proceeded to print the corpse.

"You know whose fault all this is, don't you?" Gatlin said to Broussard.

Knowing Phillip almost better than Gatlin knew himself, Broussard said, "Kit Franklyn?"

Gatlin pointed his finger at Broussard like a gun and fired it with his thumb.

SEVENTEEN

BARATARIA BOULEVARD begins at the West Bank Expressway as a major city artery. A few miles south of its origin, where the new section is not yet open, the road narrows. A couple of miles farther it enters Jean Lafitte National Park and there is a distinct increase in the number of furry or armored carcasses flattened on the pavement. When it emerges from the park, the road joins Bayou Barataria and, from that point on, the bayou is its constant companion. With each succeeding mile, the houses seem increasingly to belong to people who work the bayou and who advertise the yield of their labors in hand-lettered yard signs:

CRAWFISH . . . SHRIMP . . . TRAWLS DIPPED.

Kit shook her head, totally puzzled at that last one. According to the number on the mailbox she had just passed, she was only a few minutes from the home of Eugenie Sonnier. After such a long trip, she fervently hoped that it wasn't all going to be a waste of time. She briefly considered what it would take for it to be otherwise: Eugenie must still live at the address in Isom's files, she must be home, and she must have saved what would seem like a lot of worthless papers from her sister's estate, not to mention the fact that her sister must have kept those same papers long after they had become dated. She saw now with greater clarity than she had at any point so far how tenuously she had hung her hopes. Had she not been so close to her destination, she might have turned around and gone home.

On her right, the masts and rigging of two battered veterans of many shrimping seasons sat bobbing on the waves created by a passing motorized skiff, the rubber tires across their sterns and along their sides keeping them from scraping the dock. A little farther on, she had to cross into the oncoming lane and slow to a crawl to pass safely a small knot of nearly naked children gathered around a tanned young man holding an alligator snapping turtle by the tail.

Then, she was there.

The original part of the Sonnier house was a low rectangle with its narrow dimension facing the street. Considering how tiny the original house was, the shedlike addition halfway back on the right must have been a godsend. The house was covered with a film of apple green paint so thin that the almond-shaped plugs in the plywood sheathing were visible even from Kit's car. Like all homes in the area, it was built on cement blocks to keep it a safe distance from bayou floodwaters. They were well out of the running for "yard for the month," for there was litter everywhere: a pile of sand, a wooden stepladder, old timbers arranged like a tepee, buckets and wire, a folding lawn chair, a lawn mower, a bicycle with no wheels, two huge spools from some electrical cable, and a sign offering HARD-SHELL CRABS 4 SALE, painted on the hull of an aluminum boat upside down on three fifty-five-gallon drums. Beside the house, weeds grew around a dozen rusting vehicles. Kit found all this heartening, for it suggested that the Sonniers were savers.

To the left of the house, beyond the display of dead rolling stock, was Gautreaux's Grocery, clothed in unpainted board and batten. On the store's front porch, two hulking men wearing canvas hats and dirty T-shirts sat on an old car seat, their sneaker-clad feet sprawled out in front of them, each with one big hand wrapped around a beer bottle.

To the right of the house, there was a tall metal building with a sign over the wide door opening: S AND S BOAT RE-

PAAR. FIBERGLASS OUR SPECIALTY. So what if they couldn't spell, Kit thought. If you needed your boat repaired, you'd know where to come.

Resting on oversized sawhorses in front of the metal building was a large boat with a deck cabin. Beside the boat, a woman wearing goggles, jeans, and a sweat-stained blue T-shirt that profiled breasts whose dimensions could best be expressed in length rather than cup size was working an electric sander over a patch below the boat's waterline.

Kit's attention returned to the Sonnier house, which did not possess a driveway but, instead, had a swath of oyster shells spread across the front so that there was room for five or six vehicles to park nose-in. Since there was a station wagon and two pickups in front of the house, Kit figured that somebody had to be home.

She pulled in beside the station wagon and got out, the humidity making it feel as if there was almost as much water in the air as in the bayou. Already sweating, she crunched across the shifting oyster shells and followed a sandy path to the house. Through the aluminum storm door, she saw a long-handled scrub brush hanging on the front door. Puzzled, she wondered whether this was some sort of seasonal decoration, like a Christmas wreath. But what season would be celebrated by a scrub brush? Something to do with fish, maybe. She opened the storm door and pressed the doorbell.

"It don't work," a voice said from close behind her.

Startled, she turned and saw the two men from the grocery.

"That's why this is here," the closest one said, reaching past her, so that his armpit came within an inch of her nose. She recoiled from the smell, a combination of sweat and shrimp. He picked the brush off its nail and banged on the door with the back of it, then looked at her with a beery grin that showed more tongue than teeth.

"I don't think anybody's in there, Floyd," the other one said with sly insincerity. He was just a few inches shorter than Floyd, but his mouth was bigger and gaping, like the beaky jaws of the snapping turtle she had seen earlier. Both of them had tiny porcine eyes and bad skin that made a clean shave an impossible dream. It suddenly dawned on Kit that they were related, probably brothers.

The one with the brush banged on the door again, then cocked his head to listen. "I believe you're right, Boyd. They ain't nobody home."

"There are three vehicles out front," Kit said. "So they have to be somewhere close. Do you have any idea where?"

Floyd rehung the brush and scratched his neck. "I think I know where one of 'em is."

She waited for his answer, but he obviously wanted to be coaxed. "Where?"

"Right there." He pointed to Boyd, who pointed back and said, "If I ain't mistaken, there's another one."

"Them's our trucks," Floyd said. He laughed, looking at the ground and shaking his head as though he'd pulled off one of the world's great gags. Laughing, too, Boyd hit Floyd lightly on the shoulder with his fist.

"Then you two would probably know where I can find Eugenie Sonnier," Kit said.

Floyd got control of himself first and pointed next door at the woman with the sander. "That's Ma over there."

"Thanks." Kit pushed past the two lummoxes and made her way next door, Floyd and Boyd following.

Eugenie was covered with a film of gray dust and her sweat made muddy trails as it meandered down her cheeks. The sander was making so much noise that Kit could not get Eugenie's attention. Holding her breath, Kit stepped into the dust and touched the woman's back. Eugenie looked up and cut off the sander. She pulled her mask down around her neck, the relatively clean skin beneath it making the rest of her look even dustier.

"Mrs. Sonnier, my name is Kit Franklyn. I work with the police in New Orleans and we're conducting a murder investigation that could be helped by your sister Shirley's old business records. I'm here to determine if you have any of those records and, if so, to ask if I might examine them."

Without replying, Eugenie pulled the mask up, turned on the sander, and went back to work. Puzzled, Kit moved away from the dust and the noise to where Floyd and Boyd were waiting. Seeing them a few feet away instead of in her face, she noticed that both had guts so big that their navels sucked at their shirts like open mouths.

"Coulda told you she wouldn't talk to you," Floyd said.

"Why's that?"

"Last two years, she ain't spoke to nobody that can't talk French...less it was me or Boyd, 'cause we don't, or somebody wantin' their boat worked on."

"She makes a exception for biness," Boyd said. "On accounta when she didn't, there wasn't hardly no work."

"Why aren't you two helping her?"

"She fired us this mornin'," Floyd said.

"But she'll put us back on tomorrow," Boyd added. "It's her way."

"Did you hear what I told her?" Kit asked.

"Sure, we ain't deaf," Floyd said. "You a cop?"

"No, but I work with the police. Since you heard what I said, maybe you could tell me if your mother has any of her sister's papers."

"We got some stuff used to belong to her," Floyd said. "Dunno why we're savin' it."

"It's Ma's way," Boyd explained.

"Papers . . . that sort of thing?"

"Mostly papers," Floyd said.

"And some furniture," Boyd added.

"Do you think you could talk to your mother for me and ask her if I could see those papers?"

Floyd pulled his little eyes back in his head until they were almost covered by the fatty folds above them. "Might be we could work out somethin'. . . ." He glanced at Boyd, who casually began to edge around behind Kit. Before she could react to these danger signals, Floyd grabbed her at the elbows. Quickly, she brought her forearms up inside his, came over the top and down, breaking his hold. Reversing the motion of her arms, she brought them up in a sweeping arc and clapped him on the ears with her open palms. She bolted for the car, surprised that the moves she saw on TV actually worked. When she sped by, foot hard on the accelerator, Floyd was still bent over, holding his head. Boyd simply looked bewildered.

KIT PULLED INTO Grandma O's parking lot shortly before noon, intending to get more than lunch. Grandma O met her at the door.

"Doc Franklyn, how you doin'? City boy got here a few minutes ago. What you gonna have?"

"What's the special?"

"Half a ham and cheese po' boy and a bowl of duck gumbo."

"Sounds good."

"An' a glass of iced tea?"

"Yeah, and maybe a favor if you could manage it."

"Depends on what it is and how fast you can talk. Ah gotta lotta hungry folks waitin'."

Kit explained what she wanted and warned her about Floyd and Boyd. Apparently unafraid, Grandma O agreed to help, providing that they made their little expedition the next day after she had seen the kitchen off to the right start for the evening meal. She said that 3:30 sounded about right, then went off to get Kit's food.

Hoping that Broussard wouldn't quiz her about where she'd been, Kit threaded her way between the rapidly filling tables to where he was having two specials and two lemonades.

"I see you ordered for both of us," she teased.

"Man does not live by half a po' boy alone," Broussard said, "least I can't. Sit down, I've got some news."

He proceeded to tell her about Kurt Halliday. When he finished, she said, "Have you done the autopsy yet?"

"First thing after lunch," he said, taking a bite of his sandwich.

"You said his letter mentioned Arthur Jordan. Anybody else?"

His mouth full, Broussard shook his head.

"The signature on the letter, has it been verified?"

Broussard took a drink of lemonade. "Phillip called just before I left to come over here and said that Doyle Fleming, their document examiner, swears it's genuine."

Kit shook her head. "Not only is this too convenient but it leaves too many—"

Grandma O arrived with Kit's food and put it in front of her. "Doc, you need anything else, jus' holler. City boy, you still content over dere?"

"I'm fine."

Grandma O left and Kit continued her thought. "It leaves too many loose ends."

"For instance?"

"Paul Jarrell, for one. The letter didn't mention him."

"There's still no proof that he was ever part of it."

"Are you still clinging to that fantasy?"

"So there *is* proof? Somethin' I haven't heard about? Somethin' more than a hunch?"

She shook her finger at him. "You watch. When this is all over, you'll see that I'm right."

"You said loose *ends*. What else?"

"You wouldn't like those any better than Paul Jarrell, maybe less."

"Try me."

She told him about Clay Peyton, Walter Browning, and Haley Dagget.

"Interestin', I'll give you that," he admitted. "You've told Phillip all this?"

"In the greatest detail. By the way, who was it that first mentioned me as a guest for the gourmet dinner?"

"Arthur Jordan."

From over Kit's shoulder, Grandma O said, "Doc Franklyn, somethin' wrong with your food?"

"No, it's great." Under Grandma O's stern look, Kit tried the duck gumbo and made appreciative noises, which wasn't hard, because it was sensational. Satisfied, Grandma O cruised off to check for other slackers.

"Are you taking Halliday's suicide at face value?" Kit said.

"I'm not givin' it any value until all the data are in."

"When will that be?"

"Phillip is comin' over at three."

"Mind if I eavesdrop?"

"Not at all. I'd appreciate your views." He took a long pull on his lemonade and looked at her innocently. "Knowin' how you like to get after a problem, it must be hard sittin' on the sidelines."

Their eyes met briefly and she saw in his that he knew what she was doing with her personal time. This was a relief, for the thought that she was doing things behind his back caused her considerable anguish. She wanted now to discuss it openly with him but realized that to do so would be to put him in an awkward position with his friend Gatlin. To get their relationship back on an honest footing without compromising him, she said pointedly, "Well, one does what's necessary."

To show that he understood, he said, "Will you be needing any *more* personal time?"

"Matter of fact, yes. I need to go somewhere tomorrow at three-thirty."

He nodded and sipped some more lemonade. "You know best. 'Least I hope so."

"Don't worry, I won't be going alone."

For the next few minutes, they concentrated on their food, then Broussard said, "By the way, when you get back to the office, you'll find a note I left on your door. This mornin', a patrol car answered a call about a man with a gun terrorizin' the customers in a K Mart. When the cops confronted him, he raised the gun as though he was gonna use it and they killed him. Come to find out, the gunman was only sixteen and the gun wasn't real. Case like this, there's gonna be a lot of different versions of what happened and those cops'll take a lot of heat. How about seein' what you can turn up on the victim."

"I'll get right on it."

Upon returning to her office, Kit found not one note on the door but two, the extra one being a message to call Adrian Iverson. After calling around and getting the information she needed to begin her investigation of the police shooting, she called Iverson, who, like Tully the day before, wanted her opinion on some hybrids that had recently bloomed. Though she was growing a bit weary of making these visits to the two men and she had a great deal to do with this new case, it was only fair that what she had done for Tully, she should do for Iverson. Therefore, she agreed to stop by around five o'clock, hoping that she could tie that visit in with one related to the new case.

EIGHTEEN

BROUSSARD SHIFTED the lemon ball in his mouth to the other cheek. "Lab report says the bottle on Halliday's desk contained a saturated solution of potassium chloride."

From the green vinyl sofa, Gatlin said, "What exactly *is* that?"

"A simple salt. Harmless if taken orally, but injected into the blood, it disrupts the membrane potential of cardiac muscle so that the heart stops."

"Is it quick?"

"Very."

"So that's why the syringe was on the floor. He died so quickly that there wasn't even time to pull the needle from his arm. The arm dropped; the syringe fell out. This salt, is it hard to get?"

"Be a rare research laboratory that didn't have some sittin' on a shelf."

"The bottle is common, too," Gatlin said. "It's what they call a scintillation vial. It's used to hold radioactive liquids when they're being analyzed in a counter."

"Didn't know you were so science-oriented."

"You ask questions, you learn. I stopped by Halliday's lab and talked to his technicians. Apparently in addition to being a good surgeon, he had a busy research operation going. They also showed me a drawerful of the same kind of syringe he used." Gatlin shook his head. "Funny, a man dies and all the people who work for him think about is if they're going to lose their job." He sucked his teeth in thought. "Nice logical choice of a way to go, don't you think? Cardiac surgeon uses something that he knows works on the heart . . . fast and—was it painless?"

"Probably."

"Hey, how about a little skepticism here," Kit said from one of the chairs in front of Broussard's desk. "You two aren't exactly setting new standards for piercing analysis."

"Okay, paint us a different picture," Broussard said.

"Suppose Halliday was forced to write the note and sign it by a gunman who also made him inject himself."

"Kurt Halliday was not a passive man," Broussard said. "He was quick to anger and a fighter. I don't believe he would have cooperated to the point of injectin' himself."

"All right, then . . . a gunman and an accomplice. Halliday types the note and signs it; one of them holds the gun on him while the other restrains him so he can be injected."

"Simply holdin' his arms wouldn't be enough. He'd have to be held more securely than that, and there was no evidence of restraints on the body."

"Drugged, then."

"Other than a lethal concentration of potassium, the lab found nothin' unusual in his blood, and they looked hard." Since he was playing devil's advocate, Broussard waited for Kit to mention that an unusual drug could be missed if you didn't know what you were looking for. Getting no rebuttal, he said, "I should amend my comment about Halliday not injectin' himself. I don't believe he would have even signed the note under those circumstances."

Kit threw up her hand. "Wait a minute. Haven't we taken a wrong turn here. The discussion started out with facts and now we're into guessing how someone might have behaved in a particular situation."

"Kind of like what we do when we take your psychological profiles into consideration in a case," Broussard said.

"That's particularly appropriate if you've known the person for a long time as Andy has known Halliday," Gatlin said. "But even without that, I'm leaning toward suicide."

"Why?"

"Because of all those facts you mentioned, not one of them contradicts that conclusion." He began to enumerate on his fingers. "The signature on the letter is genuine; the letter was written long enough after Jordan was strangled to allow Halliday to drive to his lab, make up the potassium solution, pick up a syringe, and go home; the position of the body was exactly right for the quick death that Andy says most likely occurred; and we found a good print from Halliday's left ring finger on the bottle containing the lethal solution. There's just nothing out of line."

"Except enough loose ends to weave a rug," Kit said.

"Paul Jarrell?" Gatlin said.

"And the things that I put in my last report. Have you followed those up?"

"Not yet, but I will."

Nothing Kit had just heard made her sorry she had gone to see Isom instead of passing that information along to Gatlin. Nor did she feel any remorse about the trip she had planned for tomorrow. *Somebody* was going to have to show these two how wrong they were.

After the meeting, Kit left to talk to some people who knew the young man shot by the police. Gatlin did not say where *he* was going. For a few minutes after the meeting, Broussard mused about the object he had found earlier in Halliday's hair and how interesting coincidences really do happen.

Earlier, when Broussard had sent them the pieces of Halliday's brain for frozen sectioning along with a rush request, the histo lab was having some sort of minor crisis.

The sections arrived in Broussard's office with a note of apology fifteen minutes after Kit and Gatlin had left.

He began with the sections from specimen number four, a small segment of Halliday's prefrontal cortex. A moment later, he pushed his chair back and shot to his feet.

They were there. Halliday's pyramidal cells had even more dumbbell-shaped inclusions in them than Paul Jarrell's did.

He began to pace the room. When he had found those odd structures in Jarrell's brain it had been merely interesting. Now it was much more. Now he *must* remember where he had previously encountered them.

He stopped pacing and leaned his rump against his desk. Mentally clearing away all extraneous thoughts, he marshaled his resources into a search for that scrap of information that had so far eluded him. His finger crept to his nose and he began to stroke the stiff hairs on the tip.

At such times, he imagined himself a visitor in his own mind, transported to the dark pool where old memories hide. He waded in and began to work the bottom, dragging his feet, examining pieces of the past as they broke loose and bobbed to the surface. It was an inefficient method of searching and much remained hidden. Finally, tiring of the effort and realizing that the pool often gives up what you seek after you walk away, he went into the forensic office and informed Margaret that he was going out for about an hour.

He took the elevator to street level and stepped into the afternoon sun. Unlike Kit and Charlie, he did not mind the heat, partly because air conditioning made his joints a little stiff.

He walked the two blocks to Canal Street and turned toward the river. The trip was a diversion to keep his mind free from heavy matters that might interfere with the process he had set in motion. His destination was the Demouchet Art Gallery on Royal, where a few days earlier he had seen an excellent sheep painting whose price he found excessive, considering the work was unsigned and Demouchet could say only that it was by the "Scottish School.'"

Most of Broussard's paintings were from Epstein Imports, because Joe Epstein wasn't afraid to discount and would do so while Broussard was still in the shop. Chet Demouchet was a harder nut and it usually took several days and a return visit before he would come down.

Broussard reached Royal some minutes later and experienced the usual sense of anticipation at the grand clutter of antique shops that stretched in front of him for many blocks. The long walk and the hot sidewalks made him glad he would soon be inside again.

A block from the art gallery, he passed under a sign for the Express Y'urself T-Shirt shop and remembered how years ago the location had been an excellent little bookshop specializing in old volumes with leather bindings and decorative endpapers. It had been run by a man named . . . Nathanial Lancon.

Broussard grinned. It's working, he thought. It had been at least ten years since Nat Lancon had passed on, and he had called up the name without effort.

Chet Demouchet was sitting at the bureau plat that he used for a desk. He appeared to be writing out a receipt. Seeing Broussard, he stood up and raised his hands in front of him in a pleading gesture. "Doc, you blew it. You can't always expect that something will wait until you can make up your mind. There *are* other customers in the world." He came from behind the desk.

Broussard could not help but notice Demouchet's flowered tie before all else, for it was loud and long—a good two inches below his belt. The rest of his clothes were in the same vein, pleated olive pants with almost a clownish bagginess and a long-sleeved white shirt with padded shoulders and western stitching. Not yet in his forties, his hair had already retreated a considerable distance from his forehead, which had recently received too much sun. He was clean-shaven and his face had a softness about it that suggested he would behave badly in a crisis.

"I take it from what you said that the paintin' I was interested in has been sold," Broussard said.

"Not two minutes ago . . . to that lady back there."

Broussard had been aware of another customer in the gallery. Now, he looked directly at her. Hearing herself being discussed, she turned and came toward them.

She was tall and carried herself proudly. There was pride also in the fact that she did nothing to hide the gray in her dark hair, which she wore swept back and tucked cleverly into itself above the nape of her graceful neck. Her features were good and her makeup so delicately applied that there was some question in Broussard's mind as to where it had been used.

She was dressed simply but well, yellow heels, yellow linen dress and a yellow scarf at her throat, pearls at her ears. Looking at all that yellow, Broussard found himself thinking of lemon sorbet.

"I couldn't help but overhear," she said. "Have I just purchased a painting that had also taken your interest?" Her voice was like a soft southern breeze pushing the wind chimes on a long veranda.

"Looks that way," Broussard said. "But you mustn't give it a second thought. I had my opportunity and didn't exercise it."

"Well, I do apologize. And I'm so sorry to have practically snatched it from your fingers. It makes me feel awful. . . ."

"So awful you'd be willin' to let me have it?"

"Nothing would give me greater pleasure, but you see, I've already planned where it will hang, and you know how empty a spot looks once you've gotten used to seeing a painting there. And I *have* grown accustomed to the idea."

Broussard chuckled to himself. His suggestion had been a test to see whether she was the real article, for no true southern lady would give up so easily something she coveted.

"Do you have many paintings?" she asked.

"I wouldn't say many. It's a relatively recent interest."

"I'm afraid that paintings are my weakness. Ordinarily, I wouldn't purchase an unsigned work, but I'm particularly fond of scenes with sheep in them, and this one is so well done."

"Sheep are also *my* interest."

She smiled and Broussard felt a long-dead part of him stir. The dark pool gave up another memory: Long blond hair...eyes he could drown in...a mind that saw through the tiniest flaw in an argument...residency matching time...him to remain here in forensic pathology, her to anesthesiology in New York...many letters at first, visits when possible...then letters less frequently, heavy work load, too tired to write...finally, the letter that had crushed him...pain...and later, as he recovered, numbness that had never left. This was what made probing the dark pool dangerous. You could not control what came to the surface. Faintly, he heard the woman across from him identify herself.

"Elizabeth Louvier."

He banished the thoughts she had started and took her offered hand. "I'm Andy Broussard."

"Dr. Broussard's the Orleans Parish medical examiner," Demouchet said. Broussard had almost forgotten that Demouchet was still standing there.

"Would that be of the Baton Rouge Broussards?" Louvier asked.

"No, the New Orleans Broussards, except for a brief hiatus when my parents lived in Bayou Coteau." From the look in her eyes, Broussard saw that it was better not to be a Baton Rouge Broussard.

"I'm a great admirer of residential stability," Louvier said. "But I'll not hold a brief hiatus against you. In fact, I'd like to hear more about your family, your work, and, of course, your paintings, but I really must run." She reached in her bag and came out with a card that she gave to Broussard. "Call me and we'll talk sheep." From the sparkle in her eyes, it was obvious the pun was intended. "And I *am* sorry about the painting...."

Broussard dismissed her concern with a wave of his hand. She looked at Demouchet. "May I expect delivery tomorrow?"

"Without fail," he said. "Let me get your receipt."

And then she was gone, leaving the gallery, Broussard thought, cheerless and empty. He looked at her card. Her address was in the best section of St. Charles Avenue.

"Hey, Doc, you better make your move on that one," Demouchet said. "She's between husbands and she's loaded. You could merge collections...or anything else that occurs to you."

Demouchet's suggestion was not only crude but also ridiculous. Wishing to hear no more about it, he put Louvier's card in his shirt pocket and told Demouchet to give him a call if any more sheep paintings came in. He left and headed back to the office, trying to clear his head of Elizabeth Louvier, but she was as unwilling to leave his thoughts as she was to give up the painting. The chord she had struck in him went beyond her pleasing appearance, her good mind, and their mutual interest in art. He saw in her, the Old South, the south that he had known as a boy and liked far better than what it was now becoming.

At Canal and Basin Street, something bobbed to the surface of the dark pool: the dumbbell-shaped inclusions. *He remembered.*

BROUSSARD WAS a meticulous filer of the records and slides from his own cases, but nothing else that came into his office ever went into a file cabinet, ending up instead in one of the many piles of journals, letters, and papers that sat about the room like African termite mounds. Many who had seen his office concluded from this that he was hopelessly disorganized. They were wrong. Once he knew what he wanted, he could find it in those piles as quickly as though it had been filed.

Heart thudding, he went to a mound rising from the floor beside his vinyl sofa and set the upper two-thirds of the stack aside. From the top of what was left, he picked up a fifteen-year-old letter and refreshed his memory.

Dear Dr. Broussard:

We would like to obtain a second opinion as to the cause of a death that has recently occurred at our facility. Enclosed is the medical history of the deceased, the autopsy and lab reports, and slides of all the organs.

I realize that this is an imposition on your busy schedule and want to thank you in advance for helping. There will, of course, be an honorarium provided for your services. When you have finished reviewing the enclosed material, please return to:

The Cotswald Institute
1 Institute Drive
Sheridan, Wyoming 82801

Respectfully,
Bradly Kinard, M.D.
Asst. Director

Attached to the letter was Broussard's reply:

Dear Dr. Kinard:

After examining the material you recently sent, I find that I concur with the conclusion reached by the pathologist who performed the autopsy; namely, that death was most likely caused by cardiac arrhythmia secondary to coronary atherosclerosis.

Sincerely,
Andy Broussard, M.D.
Chief Medical Examiner for Orleans Parish,
Louisiana

Also attached to Kinard's letter were some notes Broussard had made to himself, one of which said, "Peculiar dumbbell-shaped inclusions in samples from the rostral poles of the cerebral cortex. Significance???"

Broussard took the letters to his desk and set about trying to get in touch with Bradly Kinard.

From whoever it was that answered the phone at the Cotswald Institute, he learned that Kinard had retired. Believing that what he sought was more likely in the institute's files than in Kinard's possession, he explained what he wanted from Kinard and was placed on hold.

While waiting, he got a lemon ball from the bowl on his desk and put it in his cheek. Had he ever personally known anyone from Wyoming? He didn't think so. Was that because people from Wyoming never leave or was it because its small population reduced the odds? What would it be like living in a place where the eyes of the cattle freeze shut in winter? Probably if you were the ME there, you'd need a four-wheel-drive Jeep. A T-bird wouldn't cut it. And you'd probably have to cover—

"Hello, Dr. Broussard. Sorry to keep you waiting. This is Dr. Rutland. What can I do for you?"

Broussard recited his story one more time and was again placed on hold.

Wyoming...pretty scenery...probably not enough murders though, to keep a man busy... What would he do to keep his mind sharp—work crossword puzzles? Lot of good trout streams in that part of the country. And they say trout are clever. Could you get crawfish up there? No way he'd want to live there if you—

"Dr. Broussard...Dr. Rutland again. You are probably unaware of the fact that much of the work at our institute is done under contract to various federal agencies. This greatly restricts the openness with which we can discuss our activities. Having said that, I am happy to add that most of what you want to know has recently been declassified. I think the best course would be for me to send you a letter and some other material. Then if you still have questions, you can give me a call."

"This is pretty important."

"I'll get it out today, with overnight delivery."

KIT DID NOT MAKE much headway that afternoon in her investigation of the police shooting. Following her visit to Iverson, she got to thinking about Floyd and Boyd. This sent her to a hardware store, where she bought a small canister of tear gas made to resemble a lipstick. After a quick dinner at a West Bank Arby's, she went home, glad that she was heading into the city rather than being part of the traffic flowing out of it in a maddeningly slow exodus.

There was so much churning in her head that when she was walking Lucky, she wandered into the range of an oscillating sprinkler whose spray wrecked her hair and allowed her skimpy bra to show through her blouse. Later, half-watching the news with her legs thrown over the side of her armchair, she tried to see Gatlin's and Broussard's point of view. But however she looked at it, Halliday's suicide came up about as palatable as yellow snow.

Near the end of the news, she developed a headache that began behind her eyes and quickly diffused into an ache of uncertain location. She clicked off the TV, went into the bathroom, and took two aspirin. Going to the bedroom, she lay down for a few minutes that lasted until sunup.

ON THE WAY HOME, Broussard picked up two large redfish fillets at a market that bought directly from local fishermen and boasted, "Our fish are so fresh, it's like they were faxed to us."

To the sounds of Stravinsky's *Petrouchka* played by the Boston Symphony, he turned the fillets into redfish meunière with a pecan-butter sauce, surrounded by new potatoes and slices of glazed carrots and cucumbers. Since he had exhibited some restraint by preparing only two fillets, he had ample room for a generous helping of the bread pudding with lemon sauce and Chantilly cream he had made the night before.

After dinner, he brought Princess, his Abyssinian cat, in from the garage and she sat in his lap purring while he read several articles in the *Journal of Forensic Sciences*. In an article discussing the proper design of an autopsy room's ventilation system that would make it safe to work on cyanide victims, whose stomachs routinely liberate dangerous amounts of hydrogen cyanide when they are opened, he noticed an error in the author's calculations of air turnover. Unable to let such an error go uncorrected, he put the cat down and went to his desk, where he drafted a polite letter alerting the journal to the problem.

With that finished, he went back to his recliner and picked up a limp paperback that was part of his continuing quest to read every novel written by Louis L'Amour. This one, *Son of a Wanted Man*, a copy he'd found in The Book Mart on Calhoun, would make—what was it? He opened the folded list he was using for a bookmark and checked...number forty-two. Only forty-four to go. Reading them was the easy part. Finding them was what slowed him down. But that was also much of the fun.

He put the bookmark on the table next to the chair and sat with the book in his lap, reflecting on how nice it was to have Charlie on call. Broussard loved his work, but being on call did get under your skin, part of you always waiting for the phone to ring, your pulse racing when it did. It was good to be able to relax fully occasionally.

He began to read, but every few minutes he would detect in L'Amour's starry western sky heavenly bodies shaped like pyramidal cells and would see dumbbell shapes among the sagebrush.

He finished his book around 10:30 and rose to get ready for bed. Before throwing his shirt in the dirty-clothes hamper, he checked the pockets and found Elizabeth Louvier's card. He looked at it for a lingering moment. Deciding that he was too old for such foolishness, he walked to the bathroom wastebasket and dropped the card into it, a gesture of questionable sincerity, since he had memorized her number.

Later, between the sheets, he dreamed, not of Elizabeth Louvier but of a train. He was standing on the track, his eyes fixed on the faraway point where the tracks seemed to merge. At first, he could see only faint puffs of steam. Then, through his feet, he could feel the vibrations of wheels. The train itself came into view, menacingly black, looming large by the second, the thunder of metal on metal hammering in his head, coming closer. He tried to jump aside, but his feet were fused to the cross ties. It was upon him and there was an explosion that sent a black bar hurtling into a cloudless blue sky. Abruptly, the dream ended and he slept peacefully the rest of the night.

NINETEEN

ON HER WAY to pick up Grandma O, Kit mulled over the critical piece of information she had just obtained in her investigation of the police shooting. The clerk at the toy store where the victim had bought the gun remembered him saying, "I bet if you pointed this at a cop, he'd shit." The comment was too cryptic to determine whether the victim had wanted to die or was just pulling a stupid prank. In any even, it corroborated the cop's story about thinking he was in danger, and it would likely clear him.

Her rear tires were barely into the restaurant parking lot when she saw Grandma O coming toward the car. With her was Bubba.

"You a little late, Doc," Grandma O said.

In a world filled with uncertainty and change, Oustellette fashion was a constant. Grandma O was dressed as always, in so much black taffeta that Kit wondered whether her little car was big enough to hold the woman. As for Bubba, Kit imagined his closet: a row of green baseball caps on the shelf, the bills all pointing forward; next to them, a stack of navy blue T-shirts; under the shelf, a dozen pairs of navy coveralls.

"Guess Ah'm a surprise," Bubba said.

"When Ah tol' Bubba 'bout dem two men, he insisted on comin' along to see dat we don' get in trouble," Grandma O explained. "Hope you don't mind."

"Absolutely not. I welcome the help."

To one not acquainted with Bubba, Kit's comment might have seemed patronizing, since outwardly he was physically no match for Floyd and Boyd. But Kit knew from past experience that there was more to Bubba than was obvious. As for Grandma O needing Bubba to protect her, things would have to get pretty ugly before they exceeded her ability, for Kit had once seen her tear a bottle cap in half with her bare fingers, then cackle happily.

With the passenger seat pushed back as far as it would go, Grandma O managed to get herself and all of her dress inside the car, but she did not look very comfortable. They were barely under way when Grandma O said, "So, Doc Franklyn, how you an' dat alligator farmer gettin' along? You close to haulin' him in? Ah know dat's a nosy question, but Ah'm a nosy ol' lady."

"We're sort of at an impasse."

"Who made it, you or him?"

"Little of both, I think."

"A woman needs a man," Grandma O said. "In fac', Ah been thinkin' of gettin' married again mahself, but Ah can't fin' none anywhere near da man mah husban' was. So if you got a good one, you need to hang on to him, an' when you get him..." She looked at Bubba in the backseat. "Bubba, put your hands over your ears."

Bubba did as she asked and she said to him, "Can you hear me?"

Bubba shook his head.

"Den how come you know what Ah jus' said. Tighter now...." Satisfied that he couldn't hear, she leaned toward Kit and screened her mouth from Bubba with her left hand. "Dere's a sayin' aroun' Houma dat when you take a Houma girl to bed, you better wear a thick shirt."

"I don't—" Kit began.

She lowered her voice. "Dat means you likely to get scratched if you don'. A man never divorces a Houma girl."

She patted Kit's arm. "So if you get dat alligator farmer, dat's how to keep him." She looked at Bubba and nodded.

He took his hands from his ears and said, "Doc, can we stop at dat McDonald's?"

"You can't be hungry, all Ah fed you before we left," Grandma O said.

"It's not dat."

"What den?"

In the mirror, Kit saw Bubba blush.

"Speak up, boy," Grandma O urged. "Ain't no mind readers here."

"Ah have to..." Bubba searched for a way to express what he wanted. Then his face brightened. "Ah have to take a Macwhiz."

ARRIVING AT THE SONNIER house thirty minutes later, Kit drew a sharp breath. There was nothing left of its roof but blackened timbers that arched starkly against the sky like charred fish bones. The glass in the storm door was broken out and the inner door gaped open. Floyd and Boyd were poking around in the carbonized remains of a sofa in the yard but looked up at the sound of Kit's car on the oyster shells out front.

As Kit and her passengers got out of the car, their nostrils were filled with the sour smell of the family's burned possessions. Floyd and Boyd came toward them, anger written on their faces and in their fists.

Floyd bellied up to Kit and leaned into her face. "Ain't you done enough?"

Kit stepped back. "What do you mean? I had nothing to do with this."

"Ain't no way we're gonna believe that. You come nosin' around, askin' questions. Then that same night, we get burned out. You brought this on us all right and we figure we owe you.''

He rocked back on his heels to throw a punch, but Grandma O put her foot in his belly and pushed him off balance. Cursing, his brother aimed a fist at Grandma O, but she stepped aside and he stumbled past her, his momentum carrying him into the front of Kit's car, where his head made a dent in the grill. He slid to the ground and rolled onto his back, moaning and holding his head. Floyd came at Kit again. She reached for her tear gas lipstick but discovered that her bag was in the car. Bubba moved between them.

"Step back," Bubba ordered.

Floyd grabbed Bubba and lifted him like a child, his hands in Bubba's armpits. "Or what, shorty?" Floyd said, holding Bubba's face level with his own.

"Or dis," Bubba said, pulling a large pistol from the pocket of his coveralls and putting the barrel against Floyd's left ear. "Sometimes Ah can make da bullet come right out da opposite ear," Bubba said, "but usually it don't."

"I'm puttin' you down," Floyd said.

"Dat's what got you in dis mess in da first place," Bubba said.

"What do you want, then?"

"Go ahead...but take it slow."

Floyd gently put Bubba on the ground and Bubba took the gun from Floyd's ear. "Now help dat fellow up and both of you sit on da groun' over dere."

When the two brothers were rump to the grass, Bubba looked at Kit. "Ah think dey ready to behave now."

Kit moved closer. "What happened here?"

Floyd shaded his eyes with his hand and looked up. "While me and Boyd were out havin' a few beers and Ma was visitin' with old lady Hebert, somebody set us afire, as if you didn't know.''

"What makes you think it wasn't an accident?''

"'Cause the firemen that put it out said it wasn't.''

"You said your mother was visiting a friend. She wasn't hurt, then?''

"Nahh. She's okay. There she is now.''

Kit looked behind her and saw Eugenie Sonnier coming across the road from the small run-down white house whose yard contained a painted statue of the Virgin Mary in a shrine made from a half-buried bathtub. Where yesterday, Eugenie's face had been streaked with sanding dust, it now bore the strain of losing her home.

Kit figured that if Eugenie blamed her for the fire, she might be angry enough to speak English, especially since Bubba was holding her sons at gunpoint. But before Kit could find out, Grandma O spoke to Eugenie in French, pointing first at Bubba, then to Floyd and Boyd. The conversation went back and forth for several minutes, Eugenie's responses seeming to grow less hostile with each exchange. Eventually, she pointed at her burned-out house, then at the house across the street, then down the road, apparently recounting in detail what had taken place.

Finally, Grandma O looked at Kit. "What you want to ask her?''

With the house and its contents burned, it all seemed quite hopeless, but Kit said directly to Eugenie, "Did any of your sister's papers survive the fire?''

Eugenie might have lost her home but she still had her principles, for she pretended not to hear the question. Grandma O restated it in French and then Eugenie answered, gesturing as she did to the rusting vehicles in the side yard.

Grandma O turned to Kit. "She say dey weren' in da house. Dey're in dat panel truck."

Though truly sorry for Eugenie's losses, Kit's outlook brightened. "Ask her if I can look at them."

Eugenie agreed but said that the keys had been lost in the fire.

"We don' need keys," Bubba said, his free hand digging in his pocket for his Swiss army knife. He jerked his head at Floyd and Boyd. "Dose two gonna be any more trouble?"

Grandma O said something to Eugenie, who went to her sons and slapped each of them on the head. Leaning ominously over them, her finger pointing to the grocery next door, she then said the only English word that Kit ever heard from her—"Git."

Floyd and Boyd got off the ground and went back to the car seat on the grocery's front porch, where Kit had first seen them. Eugenie returned to the air-conditioned house across the road.

Bubba pocketed the pistol and headed for the panel truck, Kit and Grandma O following through calf-high weeds. Reaching the truck, Bubba began to work on the rear door lock with a pick he had previously made from one of the blades on his knife.

It had been unbearably hot standing in the yard, but here, surrounded by metal that radiated the sun's heat, it was much worse. Sweat beaded up on Kit's upper lip and forehead and trickled down her back. Grandma O fanned herself with her hand. Sweat soaked through the back of Bubba's coveralls as he poked his probe delicately into the lock.

Bubba worked at the lock for only a few minutes. Because of the heat, the two women were convinced it was much longer. He stood up and tried the door, but it did not open.

"Mus' be rusted shut," he said.

"Lemme try," Grandma O said. She took hold of the handle, put her foot on the bumper, and tore the door open, its rusty hinges screaming in protest. Heat poured from the van in shimmering waves that backed them all away.

"We gonna need some ventilation in dere," Bubba said. He went to the truck and climbed in. A few seconds later, the door on the driver's side squealed open. Crossing to the other side, he kicked the passenger door open, then climbed out and came back to where Kit and Grandma O waited, his face flushed from the heat.

Kit stepped up to the truck and looked in. It was filled with cardboard file boxes and bundles of newspapers. On some of the boxes, she could see dates scrawled in black.

"If you want, Ah can hand dem boxes out one at a time an' you can look through 'em in da car, where it's cool," Bubba suggested.

"We won't need all of them," Kit said, "only the ones for 1962, '63, '64, and '65."

"Ah'll get 'em," Bubba said, climbing in.

Kit offered her car keys to Grandma O. "How about getting the air conditioning going for us?"

"You ain't takin' pity on a ol' woman 'cause of da heat, are you?"

"Grandma O, there's nothing about you that evokes pity."

"Jus' checkin'," she said, taking the keys.

Bubba appeared in the truck's door opening with a box. "Nineteen sixty-four," he said.

Kit took the box from him and put it on the ground, sweat pearling from every pore.

Another box: "1962."

She set that one on the first. Sixty-three went on top of that, and '65 on top of that.

Bubba jumped from the truck. "Which one you want first?"

"Doesn't matter... the one on top."

Bubba carried the paper record of Shirley Guillot's life for 1965 to the car. Kit got into the back and Bubba put the box on the seat beside her. Then he got in the front seat and shut the door.

"You two look so hot, you makin' me feel guilty," Grandma O said, remarkably freshened compared to her appearance five minutes earlier.

For a while, Kit and Bubba simply sat and enjoyed the wonderful sensation of cool air blowing across their steaming bodies. Then Kit took the top off the box and began going through the contents.

The box was only about three-quarters full, but the files in it were held upright by an adjustable crossbar. All the files were labeled in a neat hand.

In back was a thick file containing the year's "Dear Abby" articles from the newspaper. In front of that, another contained Ann Landers's columns from the same period. The rest of the box was devoted to business papers arranged so that the records for each of her properties occupied a different section. Within a section, there was a folder for repairs/maintenance—general, several for repairs/maintenance of specific apartments, as well as folders for property taxes, insurance, utilities (general), or utilities for specific apartments. And most importantly, each section had a file for leases.

She flipped through the box until she found the section devoted to her own house, then searched for the lease file, her pulse quickening as she realized how close she was to a potentially significant discovery.

There it was.

She pulled the lease from the file and unfolded it. Her eyes went to the bottom, looking for signatures. There were four of them: Shirley Guillot and . . . three other names she didn't recognize. She let her hands drop to her lap.

"Didn' find what you were lookin' for?' Grandma O asked.

"No."

"Dere's more boxes out dere," Bubba said. "You want another one?"

"If you wouldn't mind."

The next box covered 1963. Three tenants had also signed that lease, none of them repeats from 1965, none of them people Kit knew.

"Agin?" Bubba said, seeing the look on her face. She nodded and he gamely got out of the car, wrestled the box from the backseat, and went for the next one.

The lease signed in 1962 contained two of the same names as in 1963 and a new one, also unfamiliar to Kit.

"When you lookin' for somethin', you oughta look in da las' place first," Bubba said, getting out of the car, "'cause dat's always where it is."

"You ever think about what you say before sayin' it?" Grandma O asked.

Bubba looked at her in surprise. "Person did dat, dey wouldn' ever say anything." As Bubba brought the box for 1964, Kit noticed water stains on the bottom that extended up the sides for three or four inches. With a sinking feeling, she searched for the lease, hoping that it wasn't... She found the file and removed the lease, the water stains that had crept into it from its lower-left edge crushing her spirit.

She unfolded the document and her eyes edged slowly down the page. The *k* and *u* were blurred by water, but "rt Halliday" was clearly readable. The entire first name and part of the last were missing in the signature below Halliday's but "ordan" was still there—*Arthur Jordan*. Below Jordan's name, there had been a third signature, but it was unreadable.

How could this be? She thought of all the things that had conspired to keep the identity of the third person from her: four boxes; three perfectly sound, the one she needed, water-damaged; three signatures, the two she already knew, on the top, farthest from the water's effects, the last one, obliterated. And weren't most modern inks indelible? Jesus. It was as if she wasn't meant to solve this thing.

Remembering how Sid Loscovitz's name had left a remnant of itself on Harry Isom's door, Kit held the last signature up to the light, tilted the paper, and looked hard.

Nothing.

"You actin' like you foun' somethin'," Grandma O said.

"Almost," Kit said. "But the important part was washed away when the box got wet." Then she had a thought. Doyle Fleming, the forensic document examiner. Gatlin had always said that he was a magician. She'd take it to him and see whether he could make out the name.

But suppose he could and suppose the name he found was Paul Jarrell? That would pretty much be the end of the line for her part in the investigation even though there would still be questions. Deciding that she was being too pessimistic, she dismissed this concern and said to Grandma O, "Would you take this document to Mrs. Sonnier and ask her if I can borrow it for a few days? Tell her it's important. Be persuasive."

"Ah'll do what Ah can."

From the rear window, Kit watched Grandma O cross the road and knock on the door of the house with the bathtub shrine. A woman Kit had not seen before answered and went for Eugenie. When she appeared, there was a short conversation and Grandma O came back to the car. She opened the door and held out the lease. "She say keep it long as you want."

Bubba took the last box back to where they had found it and closed the truck. Kit put the lease in her handbag. Remembering how the bag had not been on her shoulder when she had reached for her tear gas, she made a mental note to do a better job of keeping it with her.

Once they were all back in the same seats as on the trip out, Grandma O said, "Doc Franklyn, she also say if you was to take a few French lessons, she'd let you date Floyd."

Kit looked at Grandma O in disbelief. Playful sparks sizzled in the old woman's black eyes and she broke into a gleeful cackle.

TWENTY

BROUSSARD HAD BEEN watching all day for the material from the Cotswald Institute, but it had not arrived. He looked at his watch—nearly five o'clock. But in Sheridan, Wyoming, it was an hour earlier. He reached for the phone, hoping that he could get Rutland and find out what had gone wrong. Before his hand touched the receiver, his secretary came in with an overnight mail envelope.

With a casual air that belied his excitement, he opened the envelope and quickly read the cover letter. By the time he had finished, he understood the dream he'd been having and a lot more. Included with the letter were half a dozen photocopied pages of a scientific report with sections blacked out so they couldn't be read, obviously portions that were still classified. He skimmed the pages. When he reached the last line, he was reasonably sure that he knew it all. He picked up the phone and punched in Gatlin's number.

KIT DROPPED Grandma O and Bubba at the restaurant, thanking them for all they had done. On her way out of the parking lot, she checked her watch—5:10. No point in taking the lease over to Doyle Fleming now. He had probably already left for the day.

She arrived home ten minutes later and was reminded of why people have dogs as Lucky danced happily around her legs. She picked him up, scratched him under the chin, and carried him to her answering machine, where there was a message to call Adrian Iverson.

He answered promptly. "Adrian, this is Kit."

"Hello, Kit. I know you must be getting awfully tired of this, but I had two new plants bloom today and I think they may be the best of the lot. I was hoping their buds would open yesterday so you could rank them with the others, but they didn't cooperate. Do you suppose... Goodness, this is difficult. Could you possibly come out tonight and give me your opinion? I hate to spring this on such short notice, but I'm leaving on a trip early in the morning and will simply not enjoy myself if I have to leave without hearing your opinion. Please come. I have a little something I was going to send you for the patience and kindness you've shown me, but I'd much rather give it to you in person. So what do you say?"

It had been a hot, tiring day and Kit was looking forward to a cool shower and her silk robe. But Iverson was such a gentleman and so appreciative of her efforts that she was unable to refuse. Then, too, he needed some new specimens, for she believed that right now, Tully's best had him beat. "Sure, I'd be glad to come. I can be there"—she paused to consider when the rush-hour traffic would clear—"at six-thirty."

"Wonderful."

A few minutes later, she got another call.

"Dr. Franklyn, this is Haley Dagget. I understand that you've been asking questions about me at the hospital and I think you and I should talk again."

"All right. Go ahead."

"This is not something I want to discuss over the telephone. Could you come to my office? I've really gotten backed up today, but I should be clear in an hour or so. To be on the safe side, let's say seven-fifteen."

Picturing how empty Dagget's office might be then, Kit said, "The time is fine, but not in your office. Someplace more public."

"I don't want our conversation overheard."

"You can whisper."

"Very well. There's a restaurant called the Olive Tree across the street from my office. Is that acceptable?"

"Yes."

"I'll see you then."

Iverson at 6:30, Dagget at 7:15. That meant she couldn't give Iverson more than fifteen minutes, which should be more than sufficient.

"TOOK YOU LONG enough to get here," Broussard said.

Gatlin cocked his head and squinted at Broussard. "Remember when that chemical plant mistakenly discharged pesticide into the river... all those fish belly-up?"

"I remember."

"Those fish had a better day than I had today. What's so urgent?"

As Broussard talked, Gatlin seemed less and less tired. When Broussard was finished, Gatlin said, "Want to take a little ride?"

"Suppose he's not there?"

"Where's your phone book?"

Gatlin looked up the number he wanted and jabbed it into the face of the phone with his finger. A few seconds later, he hung up without saying anything into the receiver. "He's there."

KIT PROCEEDED ONTO the Huey P. Long Bridge with no misgivings about crossing it. She did not have the same confidence about meeting Haley Dagget. To her mind, there was a distinct difference between following up the

Sonnier lead that Isom had given her and meeting Dagget.
The first had developed entirely *after* Gatlin had ordered
her off the case. The second was a continuation of something she had started *before*.

Hmmmm.

What had seemed like a sharp difference when she began this train of thought had suddenly evaporated and she
saw that she was way over the line in both circumstances.
But it was like the Huey P. Bridge—once you entered the
approach, you had to cross.

Iverson met her at the door in tan pants and a knit shirt
with tan and white ancient Egyptian designs on a black
ground. It was the kind of outfit Teddy would never wear
but would look good in.

"Come in. Come in," Iverson said heartily. "The test
blooms are all ready, along with a little surprise."

"A good surprise, I hope."

"I think so."

As she followed him to the back, the clock with the
Westminster chimes struck the half hour. Upon reaching
the study, Iverson said, "You go ahead and get comfortable and I'll get the surprise."

In the few seconds that she had before Iverson returned,
Kit's thoughts drifted back to the gourmet dinner and she
tried to picture Arthur Jordan and Walter Browning together. Was Browning tall enough to have strangled Jordan? She thought he was. But Haley Dagget would have
had a far easier time of it....

"Here we are," Iverson said. He was carrying a magnif-
icent orchid bearing many huge flowers.

He put the plant on the floor beside her chair. "I've
taped instructions for its care on the pot. And when your
rose garden is ready for planting, you let me know. Don't
you dare *buy* any roses."

"I'm overwhelmed," Kit said.

"It's the least I could do, considering what you've done for me. Now, let's see what you think of my new babies."

Not wanting to lose track of the time, Kit checked her watch while Iverson went to get the flowers—6:34....

Iverson returned with the usual silver tray and four clam-shell containers. She went quickly through the ritual and, to Iverson's pleasure, picked one of the new flowers as the best of the lot. Without having Tully's best in front of her, comparison was difficult, but she thought that Iverson now just might have the edge.

Iverson turned to put the silver tray on the table next to his chair and Kit checked the time again—6:45.

No. That was impossible. There was no way that it had taken eleven minutes to rank the roses. Something had to be wrong with her watch. Just then, Iverson's Westminster chimes struck the three-quarter hour. She glanced at Iverson and saw a peculiar look on his face.

Her brain struggled to understand, tried to bring order where there was only disorder. Events of the past ten days whirled by, hopelessly mingled. Then a single powerful beacon sliced through the confusion. Her headaches. Each of her recent headaches had occurred a few hours after visiting Iverson.

She tore at her handbag and checked the compartment where she had put the lease. It was empty. She looked back at Iverson, who now wore a sad expression. Her gaze dropped to his right hand and her throat closed. He was holding a pistol.

"Stupid of me not to think of the clock," he said. "But the way things have been going, they were bound to get worse. I have the papers you're looking for. I'm sorry for the headaches . . . and for everything else."

"The roses..." Kit said, nearly choking on the words. "You've been doping the roses."

"Only the final one in each series. That's why the last one always had a forgettable fragrance. It's a drug called Mepridil. You won't find it in the *PDR*."

"What does it do?"

Keeping the gun trained on her, Iverson carefully sat down. "It makes the subject freely responsive to questioning and fosters a childlike trust toward others. The subject will do essentially everything they are instructed to do except harm themselves. The effect is quite short-lived after a single exposure, on the order of five to seven minutes. After recovering, the subject remembers nothing that happened during the time he was drugged. When the subject is under the drug's influence, the pupils dilate. Upon recovery, they return to normal. I've always believed the dilation is what leads to the headaches."

Iverson's voice reverberated in Kit's head: "freely responsive to questioning." Oh God. She had visited Iverson the day she was to meet Paul Jarrell. Is that how Iverson knew of the meeting? *Had she told him?* "My flat tire the night Paul Jarrell...died. Was that you?"

"It was the only way I could think of to delay you."

Guilt for Jarrell's death settled over her like a suffocating blanket.

"In case you're blaming yourself for Jarrell's death, you really shouldn't," Iverson said. "You had no choice."

Her thoughts ratcheted from Paul Jarrell to Arthur Jordan. Had she been responsible for that, as well? She was so confused now that she couldn't remember the sequence of events. Had she visited Iverson after Broussard had told her about Jordan's call? "How did you know about our meeting with Jordan?" she asked.

"I was the one who suggested it to him. After meeting you at the Gourmet Society dinner, both he and Halliday became very rocky and I was afraid they were going to talk. I told Jordan that I thought Halliday was going to make a deal by sacrificing us and that we ought to beat him to it. Jordan thought I came to his apartment so we could tell our story to you and Broussard together. I told Halliday the same thing about Jordan and set up a meeting at his home later that night to discuss what we should do. I thought with all three of them gone, that would be the end of it, but you wouldn't stop."

"The fire last night in Lafitte . . . ?"

"When you said they might be in possession of records that would implicate me, I had to do something. Apparently, I was unsuccessful."

When you said . . . Floyd Sonnier had been right. She *had* been responsible for getting them burned out. "What happened that night?" she asked.

"What night?"

"Years ago . . . the girl who was killed."

Iverson's expression saddened. "Pretty much what I put in Halliday's suicide letter. . . ."

"You typed it?"

"He couldn't. His pupils were too dilated. It was about all he could do to sign it. What I put in there was mostly true except"—he paused and his face grew sadder still—"except that I killed the girl. We'd all been drinking heavily and the others had passed out. After it happened, I was shaking and began to drink again. Looking back, I still can't believe it, but I fell asleep and I wasn't the first to wake up. So I pretended that I had been as drunk as the rest of them and was as ignorant of what had happened as they were."

"The rest of them being Halliday, Jordan, and Jarrell?"

"Yes. Jarrell didn't live in the house. He was a friend of Halliday's and was around a great deal."

"Why didn't you mention Jarrell in Halliday's suicide letter?"

"You had told me Gatlin and Broussard were not convinced that Jarrell was involved. I thought if I included him, it would increase the chances they would find some discrepancy in the story I put in the letter." He shook his head and his gaze shifted inward. "It all got so complex."

His attention returned to Kit. "When we picked her up, I never intended to kill her. It just happened. There was so much stress in medical school that we were all nearly to the breaking point. You can't know what it's like if you've never experienced it. That kind of stress makes you do things…act in ways you never thought you could. You have to find a way to release it or go mad.

"I'm not an evil man. You must see that. I did a lot of good. There are hundreds of people making a difference in this world because of my skills as a surgeon. I didn't operate on just anyone. I reviewed the cases carefully, weighing the contributions they were capable of making against the cost. And I did try to keep the cost low." Iverson's eyes glistened with tears. "I'm not an evil man. The balance sheet will show that."

He seemed on the verge of cracking and Kit thought she would try to help him along. "You're deluding yourself," she said. "Kurt Halliday and Arthur Jordan could have treated thousands more patients. But you murdered them. Who knows how much good might have been done by people who will die because Arthur Jordan and Kurt Halliday will not be there for them?"

"I don't want to hear this."

"You're retired. You don't even practice anymore. If all that's important is the balance sheet, Jordan's and Halliday's lives far outweighed yours. Face it, you killed them to save your own skin. There was no other reason. Admit it. You were no longer productive, they were. Your actions have been totally self-serving."

Iverson's face hardened and she knew she had failed.

"Am I to be dealt with as they were?" Kit asked.

"I can't let you live. I wish I could, but it's impossible. There will be a gunshot, a terrible accident, a loaded gun going off as I was showing it to you. I'm sorry."

Kit had allowed her hand to remain in her bag since seeing that Iverson was holding a gun. She slowly removed it and stood up. "If there's going to be an inquiry, you had better hide this," she said, moving toward him. She pressed the button on her tear gas lipstick, simultaneously pushing off on her left foot.

She was too far away for it to be fully effective, but some of the tear gas reached Iverson's eyes. He roared in pain and flinched. Gunfire echoed in Kit's ears and a bullet skimmed across her left forearm, making a raw trail in her flesh that screamed as the air hit it.

She dashed through the curtains and out the French doors to the rose garden. Heart hammering in her wound, she ran for the perennial garden and angled across it, trampling the false indigo, crushing the Jupiter's beard. On to the sidewalk that led to the green houses. Was Iverson close behind? She didn't dare look. She bolted for her car but saw the bridge across the bayou begin to close.

Trapped. She was trapped.

She veered to the right and headed for the greenhouses, hoping she could reach them before Iverson saw where she had gone.

The tropical greenhouse... lots of foliage... hard to see through it. She ran down the narrow walkway, leaves slapping her face, whipping her bleeding arm. Where to go... where to hide?

The plants were on low cement tables that ran the entire length of the greenhouse, one in the middle, one on each side. She looked under the center table. Thank God. Lots of pots and other stored material that would prevent a clear view from one end to the other. She dropped to her stomach and slithered under the table, hating the idea almost as soon as she had done it.

The door she had come in opened. *Iverson.*

Her lungs were starved for air, yet she was afraid to breathe, fearing that he would hear her gasping. Her wound was lying in the dirt, but there was nothing she could do about it. She felt nearly ripped in two by indecision—run now or stay hidden. Her face burned from the effort of running and she was wrapped in wet heat.

A sound beside her: the potbellied pig... the damn pig... snorting... giving her away. She pushed its inquisitive snout away from her face. It squealed in protest. She had to move. But where was Iverson?

The pots that kept him from seeing her also kept her from knowing his position. She squirmed around to where she could peek down the way she had come. There he was, standing a few feet from the door, apparently trying to locate the pig over the sound of the twittering birds.

She wiggled to the opposite side and became entangled in some wire. An idea pushed through her terror. She freed herself from the wire and slid her head and shoulders from under the table. The exhaust fans at her end of the greenhouse. Yes... the protective screens still had not been installed. Grabbing the wire, she rolled onto the walkway and crawled toward the fan, ignoring the pain of the rough concrete on her knees. She stopped at the last metal leg that supported the table and wrapped the wire around it. She pulled the wire tight and secured the other end around the leg on the opposite table.

Rising into a crouch, she crept back along the center table, looking for the right plant. There... Shielded by so much foliage that Iverson could not see her, she climbed onto the table and pushed the big plant into the right aisle, blocking it. She jumped down, ran to the end of the table, and crouched down to wait.

Iverson's feet appeared on the left walkway, her view of the rest of him blocked by overhanging foliage. He advanced slowly, placing his feet carefully. When he was as close as she could stand for him to get, she opened the greenhouse door and rattled it so he would get the message. She scuttled to the outside and headed toward the house.

Iverson broke into a run. The wire caught his left ankle and he stumbled forward, arms windmilling, eyes wide with horror as the whirling blades of the exhaust fan waited.

His right arm caught the edge of the frame that held the fan, keeping him from falling into it. His left hand hit the motor housing and skidded forward, two fingers sliding into the spoked pulley for the fan belt, where they were instantly mangled.

He screamed and cradled his mutilated fingers in his gun hand. Dazed by the pain and angry now for what Kit had done to him, he lurched from the greenhouse and saw her running toward the perennial garden. With no thought of how he would explain her being shot from behind, he raised the gun and fired twice.

Kit heard the shots and the sound of the bullets slamming into the brick wall ahead of her at almost the same moment. *The wire had not worked.* She had come this way vaguely intending to get to the telephone, but Iverson was too close for that.

Desperately needing to get out of his line of fire, she continued into the walled perennial garden, crossed it, and entered the rose garden, her thoughts fragmented.... The front door... could go out the front... locked... it could be locked...or he...suppose he went around...was waiting there...

Her eyes darted over the rose garden, looking for a way out. They came to rest on a tall wooden door in the back wall. She ran to it, praying that it wasn't locked.

The door operated by a latch that gave her no trouble. She slipped out and closed the door behind her. Across the rose garden, Iverson believed that things had finally started to turn his way.

Kit plunged into the dense forest on the other side of the garden wall, failing to notice the two galvanized tubs by the door and the marks on the bare ground around them. Tree roots seemed to lift out of the spongy ground and grab at her feet. Stiff palmetto fronds lashed at her arms and her eyes burned from the sweat that ran into them. On a tree to her right, too high for her to notice and facing the other direction, was a white sign with red letters: TRESPASSERS BEWARE.

She ran blindly, changing direction constantly, clusters of skinny Spanish moss-laden trees always in her way, one part of the forest looking like another. Her hair lay against her face like wet draperies. Her clothing stuck to her skin. The wound on her arm burned and she had an ache in her side. Unable to go on, she stopped and sucked at the thick air that was able to nurture the rootless Spanish moss yet gave her no sustenance.

What was that?

She turned her head and listened—nothing. But there had been something....

The forest was so dense that a man standing fifteen feet away might never be seen. On his knees, he could get much closer, for palmetto and ferns formed a visually impenetrable ground cover higher than her waist. She forced herself to move on. Whatever was there followed.

Unable to keep the same course for more than a foot or two at a time, she picked her way through the forest, which now seemed even more intent on holding her back. Abruptly, the trees and undergrowth thinned and she dashed across a small clearing. As the foliage on the far side engulfed her, she looked back and all hope fled. Pursuing her was a black humpbacked horror too ugly to exist—a Russian boar, bigger than any she had seen at the zoo, with tusks that made her frighteningly aware of how utterly defenseless she was.

"THIS IS WHAT I meant when I said you might not be able totally to surprise him," Broussard said, gesturing at the open bridge. "We'll have to call on that phone and see if he'll open up. How 'bout I not mention that you're with me?"

"You're getting to be a deceitful old codger," Gatlin said.

KIT LOOKED FOR A TREE to climb, but there were few large enough to support her, and those that were had no limbs she could reach. The forest thinned again—the bayou.... She ran to the edge and was about to jump in but heard the bellow of a bull alligator close by. Thinking of it waiting for her, she froze. Then thirty yards to her right, across the bayou, she saw Broussard. She cupped her hands to her mouth and screamed for help. Behind her, the boar burst from the undergrowth.

She turned. Pig sweat glistened on the boar's snout and its steely little eyes bored holes in her heart. An erect ridge of stiff black hairs bristled along its back and it began to make guttural huffing noises. Kit's eyes fixed on its two sets of hideous yellow tusks: the shorter, a pair of Arabian daggers curling upward from each side of its snout, frightening enough by themselves but accompanied by a pair of splayed ivory broadswords that jutted skyward from its lower jaw. Faintly, she heard Teddy's voice: "... they had to put a stop on the lance to keep the boar from running up the lance and gutting the horse."

The boar's mouth never stopped moving, opening and closing, churning its saliva into ropy strands that dangled from its lower jaw, the motion stropping the two pairs of tusks together in a bony clatter. Frantically, Kit looked back at the bayou, where something moved below the duckweed. The boar darted forward in short choppy steps and hesitated. She slowly edged sideways and her foot hit a piece of water-soaked wood. Slowly, she dipped her knees and picked it up, not liking its punky feel.

On the other side of the bayou, Broussard ran along the bank. Puzzled, Gatlin got out of the car and followed. Broussard drew even with her and saw the boar. He shouted for her to get in the water.

The boar took a few more short steps and huffed menacingly. Then it charged. Kit stepped to the side and hit it across the forehead with her club. The partially rotted wood crumbled away from a solid core, which cracked as it broke on the boar's hard skull.

The animal stumbled and dropped to its knees. Too rattled to think clearly, Kit plunged back into the forest. The boar struggled to its feet, teetered briefly on its spindly legs, and went after her.

Kit was now far past any normal level of endurance but adrenaline powered her forward, dodging, stumbling. She was close enough now to the house to see the widow's walk and . . . Iverson standing on it with something in his hand. There was a shot and a bullet ripped through the palmetto a foot away.

Dimly, she saw how well things had played out for Iverson. He could kill her now and claim that he was shooting at the boar. She dodged a small tree and a bullet shredded its bark. There was another shot with a different sound and Kit heard tinkling glass. Iverson disappeared.

She came to another clearing and hesitated, afraid to cross it, fearing that Iverson was still up there with his rifle. She was struck in the legs by a heavy weight and went down. The boar continued past her into the clearing, where it turned and stared at her. It made a false charge and stopped, its hairy tail flicking, mouth moving, tusks clattering. Then it came for her. Instinctively, she drew her knees to her chest, put her forearms over her face, and braced for the hit.

From above her came the sound of gunfire. The boar squealed and half-turned, staggered a few feet to the left, and fell. It quivered briefly, then lay still.

The foliage parted and she looked up—into the face of Phil Gatlin, whose clothes were wet and covered with gray slime and duckweed. "You all right, Doc?"

"I think so," Kit said, breathing so heavily, she could barely talk.

He knelt beside her. "You could have made things a lot easier if you hadn't gone back into the woods at the bayou."

"I wasn't exactly"—her chest heaved and she felt light-headed—"in full control of the situation. How'd you...find me in here?"

"Sort of guessed your location by the angle of Iverson's rifle."

"Was it you that chased him off the widow's walk?"

"I didn't know what was happening for sure, but I couldn't take the chance that he was shooting at you, so I made him quit."

"Where..."

"Hold on. Let's make sure that thing is dead. I don't want it getting up after we've turned our backs."

Gatlin crept slowly across the clearing, his gun aimed at the boar, which showed no movement. He approached it warily and kicked it in the rump. It still did not move. He circled around to the head, pointed the gun, and said, "Just to be sure."

Kit winced as he fired.

"Jesus, look at those tusks," Gatlin said. "Maybe I should— "

A blur came out of the undergrowth behind Gatlin and hit him in the back of the legs. As he went down on top of the dead boar, the gun flew from his hand.

Gatlin rolled off the first boar, and the second, which was a twin of the first, charged again. One of its tusks went into Gatlin's pant leg and ripped it open, getting some of his flesh, as well. Tacking to the right, it ran across Gatlin's chest, one sharp hoof kicking him in the mouth. Blood welled from the fallen detective's split lip.

Kit struggled to her feet and ran to where she thought the gun had hit the ground. Dropping to her knees, she wiped at the weeds in a wide arc with her arm. Where the hell was it?

The boar shifted its attention to Kit. It circled to her left, huffing in anger, its mouth churning out saliva. Then it came, full speed, its sharp hooves pummeling the grass. Kit scrambled up and pushed herself, stumbling, toward the forest, but she quickly lost her footing and pitched to the ground again on all fours. The boar, now only a few feet away, turned its head, intending to hook her in the belly and open her up.

A shot rang out. The boar squealed and went down. It struggled to rise, but another shot thudded into its ugly hide, finishing it. Still on her knees, Kit turned and looked with disbelief at the dead boar. Confused, she glanced at Gatlin, who still lay where the boar had left him. He pointed upward—toward the roof of Iverson's house, where on the widow's walk she saw a familiar shape holding a rifle: Broussard.

TWENTY-ONE

"WELL, IT'S NOT AS BAD as it could be," Broussard said, gently cleaning the blood from the gash in Gatlin's leg.

"That supposed to make me feel better?" he said through his swollen and cut lip.

He and Kit were sitting at Iverson's kitchen table. "Where's Iverson?" Kit said, holding a towel soaked in cold water against her forehead.

"Shortly after all the gunfire started, I saw the bridge swing closed. Then Iverson came barrelin' down the drive. Nearly hit your car, Phillip. I called it in on the car radio and also asked for an ambulance. You two could use one."

"That was nice shooting," Gatlin said. "Where'd you learn to handle a rifle like that? Thought you didn't like guns."

"I'll tell you about it someday," Broussard said. "Lucky for you two that Iverson left his rifle and a box of shells on the roof."

They heard the sound of sirens and were soon joined by a couple of paramedics and two uniformed cops.

"What's the word on that suspect we called in?" Gatlin said to the cops.

The older one shook his head. "Hope you didn't have your heart set on talking to him, 'cause he pulled into the path of an eighteen-wheeler on U.S. Ninety. Trucker's okay, but your man is dog food."

KIT SHIFTED HER WEIGHT and the white paper on the examining table crinkled under her. Her arm hurt, but otherwise she was feeling well enough to think about all that had happened, including the things Iverson had said while holding the gun on her in his study—things she did not understand. What had he meant when he said he had tried to keep the cost low? And all that talk about operating only on people who could make a difference? She flashed on her conversation with Lily Lacaze, the part where they had been talking about Francie O'Connor disappearing and leaving her clothes behind, and Lacaze had said that wasn't so uncommon....

Roses planted in plastic containers...

No one else allowed...

Oh my God.

She got off the examining table and ran into the hall, where Broussard was waiting. "I think there's more," she said, "buried in his rose garden."

SINCE THE LIGHT was fading, the search of Iverson's rose garden had to be delayed until the following morning. After all she had suffered, Kit slept far later than she intended, so that when she arrived at Iverson's, there were already two patrol cars, Victoria French's van, Gatlin's Pontiac, Broussard's red T-bird, and some other cars she didn't recognize in the drive. Broussard and Gatlin were sitting in Gatlin's car. She walked over, opened the back door, and put her head in.

"Have they found anything?"

Broussard invited her in. "Won't know the final count for days," he said, "but it looks bad...real bad. Victoria's brought in some extra help and they've already gotten down to the first one. It's a young female. My guess is, they'll all be female."

"I think this is going to close a lot of missing persons files," Gatlin said through his still swollen lip. He looked at Kit. "What's your take on this? He say anything to help you understand it?"

"Nearly as I can figure, he'd been doing this for years. He talked a lot about stress, how it builds up, how you have to find an outlet. It's pretty clear now that killing young women was his outlet. He made a big point about how he operated only on people who could make a difference and how he tried to keep the cost low. I think that 'low cost' meant prostitutes. Francie O'Connor was just the beginning. And you know, I think that he really believed his position was morally defensible. The frightening thing is how this went on for so long without anyone knowing."

"All goes back to bodies, Doc," Gatlin said. "Without bodies, you don't know what's out there, plus hard-core hookers are so transient, they often don't have anybody who really cares about them. Wouldn't be surprised if he'd tricked the ones he picked up into giving him information about other potential targets."

"Tell us again how *you* happened to be over here yesterday," Broussard said. "And this time, give us a few more details."

Kit recounted what she had learned from Harry Isom and described how she had found the lease with Jordan and Halliday's name on it. She told how Iverson had been drugging her and had taken the lease from her bag.

While Kit talked, Gatlin made notes in his little black book. When she was finished, he said, "Probably isn't all that important now, but we'll take a look for that lease."

"I'd check the armchair on the bookcase side of the fireplace in the study," Kit said. "I think that's also where he got the gun . . . from under the cushion."

Gatlin scribbled again in his book and said, "As for you ignoring my orders—"

"I know I was wrong, but I was so personally involved in this, I couldn't stop." She went on to tell them about her part in Leslie Music's suicide, stressing how much Francie O'Connor resembled Leslie. It was a story that touched both men and she saw from the look on Gatlin's face that he was willing to forget what she had done. "What about you two?" Kit said. "How did you know it was Iverson?"

"Andy figured it out," Gatlin said. "Tell her."

"Maybe later," Broussard said.

"Not later, now," Kit insisted.

"Well, the first clue was some peculiar structures I found in the pyramidal cells of Paul Jarrell's prefrontal cortex. I had the feelin' I'd seen somethin' similar before but couldn't remember where. Arthur Jordan's brain didn't have them, so it seemed like maybe it wasn't significant. Then when I was doin' the autopsy on Kurt Halliday, I found a little praying mantis in his hair. Struck me as quite a coincidence that I'd picked one off you the day before."

"Iverson must have carried it to Halliday's house on his clothing," Kit said.

"Obvious now, but then, it didn't necessarily mean anything. Shortly after you two left the day we had our meetin', I discovered the same odd structures in Halliday's brain that I had found in Jarrell's. Figurin' it was time I remembered where I'd seen 'em, I did. Years ago, I consulted by mail on an autopsy of someone who died at a place called the Cotswald Institute. I had seen the same strange structures in slides from that brain, but it didn't have anything to do with the cause of death.

"Naturally, I called the institute to see what I could find out about the case and they sent me some material. Seems they were doin' research on drugs that could be used for interrogation purposes and that the case I consulted on was a volunteer who had died after bein' exposed to one of the drugs they were testin'. The package they sent me included a report written a few years before the death they'd contacted me about. That report described the effects of the drug on a dozen volunteers. It didn't take much gray matter to see how its effects could fit into the deaths of Jarrell and Halliday.''

He shook his head. "I should have come up with at least part of the answer a lot sooner. The night of the gourmet dinner, I had a dream that might have lasted all of five seconds, but it was a big clue; the sound of an explosion and the image of a black iron bar hurtling into the air. I just didn't know what it meant. The night after seein' the slides of Halliday's brain, I dreamt about the same thing, but this time there was a train in it. When I read the material the institute sent me, I realized those dreams were tryin' to remind me of Phineas Gauge.''

"Phineas Gauge..." Kit repeated the name slowly. "I've heard that name somewhere before."

"He was a nineteenth-century railroad worker who had an accident," Broussard said. "An explosion drove a three-foot iron bar into his cheek and out the top of his head, scrambling his left prefrontal cortex. Incredibly, he survived, but his whole personality was changed. Before his accident, he was steady and reliable. After he recovered, he was so irresponsible he lost his job."

"I remember," Kit said. "...he's generally considered to be the first recorded prefrontal lobotomy."

"Didn't they used to lobotomize mental cases?" Gatlin said.

"Certain kinds, yes." Broussard replied. "...in the forties and fifties."

"Not with an iron bar, I hope."

"Only slightly more refined," Broussard said. "Folks that were hearin' voices before the operation could still hear 'em afterward, but they no longer seemed to matter. It also became clear that many of the patients who had the operation came out of it shorn of the concepts of fear and caution. Sort of like they'd lost an internal governor. Such a person wouldn't think twice about goin' up on a catwalk over a shark tank with somebody he shouldn't trust...or signin' a suicide note somebody else wrote for him ... or ..."—he looked pointedly at Kit—"talkin' too much about a case they were workin' on...."

"We get the picture," Kit said.

"The drug the institute was usin' transiently affected some of the same cells whose output is prevented in a lobotomy and also blocked short-term memory circuits."

"But where does Iverson come in?" Kit said. "How did he know about the drug?"

"He was the author of the report from that institute," Broussard said. "Before he went into neurosurgery, he was a biochemical psychologist. I knew he had worked in industry for years before becomin' a neurosurgeon, but I didn't know where."

"That explains how he, Jordan, and Halliday came to be housemates as medical students even though he was a lot older," Kit said. "But if the drug leaves a marker in the affected cells, why did he use it? Surely he knew you'd find it."

"I don't believe he'd ever seen slides of a human brain that'd been exposed to the drug. He was long gone from the institute when that volunteer died. So he probably didn't know."

Kit sat back and thought about what Broussard had said. Suddenly, she remembered. "Wait a minute. What about Jarrell's check to Peyton, Browning lying when he came to see me, and Haley Dagget?... Good grief! I forgot...I had an appointment last night with Dagget."

Always looking as though he believed smiling was a felony, Gatlin's mouth drooped even more at the news that she had ignored his orders more thoroughly than he'd thought. But he said nothing.

"Anyway, what about Dagget not being at the hospital like he said he was, the night Paul Jarrell was killed?" Kit said. "Where does all that fit in?"

"It doesn't," Gatlin said. "The check from Jarrell to Peyton was for Jarrell's mother, who was a patient of Peyton's."

"Why didn't he tell me he had a woman patient named Jarrell?"

"Because he didn't have one. She had divorced Paul Jarrell's father and married again...not well, as it turned out, since he couldn't even pay her doctor bills. Walter Browning was telling you the truth about *why* he came to see you. He was simply mistaken when he said he was having lunch with the *chairman* of orthopedics. He was actually meeting the *deputy* chairman, who schedules his own appointments. As for Dagget, he's been bedding one of the medical students doing a clerkship with him. He was with her the night he told you he was at the hospital. He and Peyton are up for some piss-ant award from the local medical society and Peyton was just trying to stir up trouble for Dagget when he sent you after him."

"How could three men who seemed so involved in this case be so uninvolved?" Kit said. "How could I be so misled?"

"You know, something like this once happened to Babe Ruth," Broussard began. As Kit's face fell, he chuckled and said, "But maybe I'll tell you about that later. Actually, you were doin' fine. Given time, you'd have figured it out. Phillip's just had more experience."

"I'm so flattered," Gatlin said.

"I don't know, maybe you're right," Kit said. "Would you mind if I took some personal time this morning?"

"Seems to me, after yesterday, you ought to take at least the whole day."

"No, I want to get back to work, but I have to do something first."

"Will I see you at lunch?" Broussard asked. "I'm buyin'. Phillip's already agreed to come."

"Wouldn't miss it."

Kit returned to her car and drove home, where she changed into shorts, a tank top, and running shoes. On the way to get her straw hat out of the closet, she paused at the telephone, then picked up the receiver and pecked out a number. When her party answered, she said, "Teddy, this is Kit."

"Kit! God, it's good to hear your voice. Does this mean you've got everything figured out...about your life, I mean...what it is you want?"

"No, I don't have anything figured out, but I've realized that I've got plenty of time to work on it. Meanwhile, if you'd like to come over Saturday..."

"I would. I most definitely would."

"Then it's a date, and Teddy...bring a thick shirt."

That taken care of, she put on her straw hat and went into the backyard. The mounded earth was still soft and her shovel bit into it easily. Lifting as much dirt as she could manage, she thought briefly of two women who looked similar enough to be sisters, then began filling the pit.

Epilogue

Victoria French and her assistant recovered the remains of twenty-three young women from Iverson's rose garden. Upon receiving a letter from Phil Gatlin, the authorities in Sheridan, Wyoming, thoroughly searched the places where Iverson was known to have lived while working at the Cotswald Institute. They found nothing. The notice of Haley Dagget's divorce was in the paper a month after the case ended. Six months later, the Louisiana Rose Society awarded John Tully second prize for his hybrid Kit's Choice. This rose is currently under further development by Jackson and Perkins.

MUDLARK
SHEILA SIMONSON

A LARK DODGE MYSTERY

BEACH BODY

Former book dealer Lark Dodge and her husband, Jay, have traded California for the rustic beaches of Washington State's Shoalwater Peninsula. At first, life is no more complicated than house renovating and baby making. But a carpetbag of dead sea gulls and a corpse on the beach put things on a more adventurous path.

The victim is Cleo Hagen, an outspoken land-development advocate. She's also the ex-wife of Lark's neighbor, a writer whose house mysteriously burns down. And though circumstantial evidence makes him the prime suspect, Lark, with her knack for crime solving, believes there are motives that go much deeper. And what she discovers puts her life in jeopardy.

"An intriguing twist..."   —*Publishers Weekly*

Available in June at your favorite retail stores.

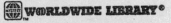

THE LAZARUS TREE
Robert Richardson
A Gus Maltravers Mystery

First Time In Paperback

A PRETTY PLACE FOR MURDER

In the picture-postcard English village of Medmelton, the air remains thick with enchantment of centuries past. Here, women have strange eyes—one brown, one green—and superstition and magic still rule.

When a famous London poet is murdered beneath the legendary Lazarus Tree, Medmelton is forced into the spotlight. Eventually the curiosity seekers drift away, but the mystery still lingers. And Gus Maltravers, at the request of a friend alarmed by the strange behavior of his stepdaughter, agrees to investigate.

"Richardson returns in top form..."
—*Kirkus Reviews*

Available in April at your favorite retail stores.

LAZARUS

FIRST WIFE, TWICE REMOVED
CLARE CURZON

A THAMES VALLEY MYSTERY

First Time In Paperback

TOXIC LOVE

Two disturbing deaths have Superintendent Mike Yeadings's team spread out from the Thames Valley to Amsterdam, looking for answers.

The first victim, Penny Winter, a divorced mother of two, dies as a result of food poisoning. Someone sent her tainted pâté with intent to kill. The second victim, Anneke Vroom, was a young Dutch national found crammed into an antique mahogany chest. She was shot full of heroin--and pregnant.

As the investigation of the separate incidents develops in sinister parallel, the men and women of the Thames Valley Police Force will confront more untimely deaths before tangled skeins come together to create a diabolical tapestry of murder.

"Clever misdirection."   *—Kirkus Reviews*

Available in May at your favorite retail stores.

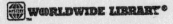

DEATH by DEGREES
Eric Wright

First Time in Paperback

An Inspector Charlie Salter Mystery

LITERALLY—AND FIGURATIVELY—DEAD

The politics and infighting to elect a new dean at Toronto's
Bathurst College turns to murder when the winner is
discovered dead.

Though the case appears open-and-shut—an interrupted
burglary and a suspect neatly arrested—Inspector
Charlie Salter believes otherwise when he begins
investigating anonymous notes warning that the killer
lurks in the groves of academe.

Scandal, blackmail and layers of deception line the corridors
at the college…all the way to the dark truth surrounding the
killer's identity.

"Excellent series…humor and insight."
—*New York Times Book Review*

Available in June at your favorite retail stores.

 **WORLDWIDE LIBRARY**®

DEGREES

DEADSTICK
Terence Faherty